TALES FOR A STORMY NIGHT
THE COLLECTED CRIME STORIES OF
DOROTHY SALISBURY DAVIS

Author of *A Pale Betrayer* and
Where the Dark Streets Go

"This collection is a landmark in contemporary crime fiction. Dorothy Salisbury Davis brings to her short stories the same combination of suspense and compassion that has long distinguished her novels. It is almost unique among modern mystery writers."
—Edward D. Hoch

"Mrs. Davis is one of the admired writers of American mystery fiction. . . . She has a cultured style, handles dialogue with a sure ear, and understands people better than most of her colleagues . . . She has few equals in setting up a standard type of puzzle, complete with misdirection and surprises. Her special strength lies in transcending the puzzle, using it as a vehicle to develop character."
—Newgate Callendar
The New York Times Book Review

"Mrs. Davis is one of the truly distinguished writers in the medium; what may be more important, she is one of the few who can build suspense to a sonic peak."
—Dorothy B. Hughes
Los Angeles Times

TALES FOR A STORMY NIGHT

THE COLLECTED CRIME STORIES OF

DOROTHY SALISBURY DAVIS

 AVON
PUBLISHERS OF BARD, CAMELOT, DISCUS AND FLARE BOOKS

All of these stories originally appeared in *Ellery Queen's Mystery Magazine* except for "The Muted Horn," which first appeared in *Fantastic Universe,* and "The Last Party," which was first published in *Who Done It?,* edited by Isaac Asimov and Alice Laurence.

AVON BOOKS
A division of
The Hearst Corporation
1790 Broadway
New York, New York 10019

The Countryman Press edition contains the following Library of Congress
Cataloging in Publication Data:

Davis, Dorothy Salisbury.
  Tales for a stormy night.
  1. Detective and mystery stories, American.
2. Crime and criminals—Fiction. I. Title.
PS3554.A9335A6 1984   813'.54   84-21425

First Avon Printing, November 1985

To the memory of Fred Dannay

Contents

Introduction

We have a rule in our house: we are not allowed to say "Always." We do say it of course, and mostly in the circumstance from which it was meant to be eliminated. "You always leave the light on in the basement." "You always forget to let the cat in"—as though any cat in our house would long tolerate our forgetfulness. Always, I suspect, is the signet of a long marriage. And a happy one. Otherwise, how would it have survived so many Alwayses?

I was about to say I always go to a rural setting for my short stories, and to the city for longer fiction, but always does not hold here either. "The Purple is Everything" could only have happened in a city like New York. This is so also of that wisp of a story of Irish perversity, "Sweet William," as well as the more recent romp, "The Devil and His Due." Best to say simply that I have been blessed with two backgrounds. I spent my childhood and adolescence on midwestern farms, my adulthood in or near the city. My friends have heard me quote ad nauseam, "Sweet are the uses of adversity," but I believe it is profoundly so for the writer. I don't think an artist ought to starve, but I think it helps to have known hunger. I grew up during the Great Depression. Nor was it over when I left the farm forever. Or when I left, only to take it with me. The soul is marked with childhood's wounds, and I am grateful for mine. As a writer, I don't know what I'd have done without them.

I am surprised on rereading these stories to find missing in them even a suggestion of a crisis in religious faith, a subject that hovers over so much of my longer fiction. I am amused to discover that in stories where religious affiliation is mentioned it is Protestant. My only rationale at this distance is that I must have assumed Protestantism to be a shortcut. Having said that I am tossed back in memory to the family dictum that it was an easy religion to live by but a hard one to die by. This implant in my youth may not have caused a wound, but obviously it left an irritation at which I am still scratching. And I find on further thought that in one of these stories the crisis had to be precipitated by religious justification.

"Born Killer" is set in rural northern Wisconsin, what my mother used to call the wilds of America, and I discovered long after writing it that it was her story. Her hatred for the farm and her longing for Ireland shadowed the lives of my father and me. She emigrated to America at the age of twenty-seven, certain she would never see home again. Nor did she, fearing the ocean more than the fires of hell. Flying was not a commonplace during her lifetime. But the Ireland she left was as vivid to me as to herself. Her tales were rich and macabre, as was her language: My heart's scalded with you . . . Happy as a goat a-hanging . . . It would melt the heart of a wheelbarrow. If you asked what was for supper: Sweep's heels and roasted snow. When I read Hans Christian Andersen's story of the chimney sweep I got the picture. And to What did you bring me from town, Mother? A bonny new nothing with a whistle on the end of it. But she always did bring something. And a final sampling, if someone were looking for something she did not think worth the effort: Looking for daylight up an entry. I didn't unriddle that one until a few years ago when I groped my way through the vestibule of a house in Belfast. She grew in melancholy with the years and would sometimes tell me of the blow on the head she received as a child and how she thought it had retarded her mind. I did not know when writing "Born Killer" that my mother was Elizabeth, I, George, and the righteous father my own. At this writing, it is my favorite of my stories. But then, my favorite cat is always the one in my lap. It is disconcerting to coddle a parcel of them at one sitting.

My father, despite that streak of righteousness—or possibly because of it—was a cheerful man. He was a Micawber, convinced that everything was going to turn out right. A few days after Black Friday in 1929 he bought the first new car of his life, a Marmon, and drove us happily to the East Coast where my mother had her first smell of the sea in over twenty years. He and I climbed every possible set of steps from the House of Seven Gables to Washington Monument. We shared a love of history—and of animals—and, in time, of politics. It seems curious to me that the story with which I associate him most strongly is "Lost Generation," which is a horror story. In its writing I may have tried to exorcise my memory of the blind horse that fell into the well. My father almost killed himself and the hired man in the attempt to save it. I may have tried, but I can still hear the scream of the animal and the gunshot and the stillness afterwards into which intruded my father's sobs.

The hardest thing for me to account for as a writer is why I am a crime writer. It does not hold to say I am giving vent to suppressed anger. I could kick the cats or pound bumps on Harry. I think it goes more to craft, to the nature of the mystery form itself; more bluntly, to the demands the medium relieves the writer of having to put on herself, both psychological and technical.

When I married I left the church—or again, left to take it with me, and one of the first things my husband gave me was the urge to write. I did not want, nor was I able, to write about myself. I got around that monumental problem by writing about something else of which I knew virtually nothing, murder. No matter where the writer starts in the murder mystery, the game is already afoot, and it concerns the ultimate in human misbehavior. Nothing a writer can say about the villain or the suspected villain, or even the unknowing villain, is too terrible. It is only unsuitable if it is unbelievable. And that is where craft enters and where, by the back door, this writer, almost unbeknownst to herself, began to probe the darker possibilities of her own nature. I don't think I have written a villain in whom I am not present.

This may well account for why I am fonder of my villains than of my heroes who, no matter how I try to make them stand tall, have a tendency to slouch into glory. And I don't think it would help them much if I were to sit at my desk mulling the contents of my wee box of good deeds. The plain fact is villainy is more interesting than virtue. The best I can do for them is to make them, too, fallible, potential villains perhaps, and then urge them to proceed upwards. I have often wondered why I was so inordinately pleased when someone said of one of my villains, "the poor bastard." I suppose I made him human, dangerously and recognizably so, and felt rewarded. Better, of course, than to have had it said of my hero. Many years ago I was preening myself on praise I received in a letter for the novel, *A Gentle Murderer,* until I came on the line: "Would God there were more Tim Brandons in this world." Tim Brandon was the murderer. In one of the stories in this collection, "A Matter of Public Notice," the detective identifies all too consummately with a killer.

Then there are the stories written strictly for fun—about the bizarre McCracken sisters, "By the Scruff of the Soul" and "Natural Causes." I have to trace the sisters back to my Aunt Mary, who was actually my mother's cousin, a larger than life character of Irish American lore. She came from the Protestant side of the family, but converted on marrying a young Chicago fireman. No one was ever more critical of the Catholic Church than my Aunt Mary, and no one ever turned on you more fiercely if you dared say a word against it.

Within months of marriage, the fireman was killed while volunteering on his day off. Aunt Mary never remarried, but she gave shelter to a sequence of younger men, over fifty years, of whom her only requirements, according to my mother, were that they be able to carry a tune and an occasional bucket of slops. Even I, with my convent education, knew they were useful in more areas than that. She could not carry a tune herself, but she carried a stick in the years I knew her with which she conducted the music and prodded all laggards into the dance. She bequeathed her property and life savings to the Chicago Fire Department.

Undoubtedly the most traumatic event of my younger life was the discovery when I was seventeen that I was an adopted child. I came on my baptismal certificate in the bank deposit box while doing an emergency chore for my father. A year passed before I told my adoptive parents that I knew. I told my father first—in the barn, and then at his suggestion went into the house alone and told my mother. It was the only time I remember seeing her cry. This is material I have not used, by my own reckoning, except in describing shock. That whole room tilted over on its side and then somehow fell back into place again. I put everything back the way I found it. Except me. Fifty years later I am at work on a novel the major detection in which goes to the pursuit of a parent vanished before memory.

I am indebted to two people for stories I would never have thought of on my own. To Harry, who is an actor, for "Backward, Turn Backward." He brought home a broadcast experience that almost panicked him, the appearance during the show of a character not in the script. And to my late dear friend, Margaret Manners, who gave up a story to me when she was unwise enough to tell me how a painting could be stolen. I fell in love with the idea on the spot. I even remember the spot, Sixth Avenue and Twenty-fourth Street, a few paces in those days, from Guffanti's Restaurant. The story: "The Purple is Every-

thing." Both stories were Edgar nominees, as was "Old
Friends."

But putting by consideration of roots and derivations,
my ultimate thanks must go to Ellery Queen, most particularly to Frederic Dannay, to whose memory this book
is dedicated. His interest was tireless, his provocation
constant and his encouragement unflagging. Except for
Fred, the stories, save one or two, might not have been
written; if it hadn't been for his perceptive criticism and
patient editing, I doubt that some of them would have
been publishable. And whatever would the writers and
readers of the mystery short story do without the *Ellery
Queen Mystery Magazine?*

Dorothy Salisbury Davis, 1984

Spring Fever

Sarah Shepherd watched her husband come down the stairs. He set his suitcase at the front door, checked his watch with the hall clock, and examined beneath his chin in the mirror. There was one spot he sometimes missed in shaving. He stepped back and examined himself full length, frowning a little. He was getting paunchy and not liking it. That critical of himself, how much more critical of her he might be. But he said nothing either in criticism or compliment, and she remembered, uncomfortably, doing all sorts of stunts to attract his eye: coy things—more becoming a girl than a woman of fifty-five. She did not feel her twelve years over Gerald . . . most of the time. Scarcely aware of the movement, she traced the shape of her stomach with her fingertips.

Gerald brought his sample spice kit into the living-room and opened it. The aroma would linger for some time after he was gone. "There's enough wood, dear, if it gets cold tonight," he said. "And I wish you wouldn't haul things from the village. That's what delivery trucks are for . . ." He numbered his solicitudes as he did the bottles in the sample case, and with the same noncommittal attention.

As he took the case from the table, she got up and went to the door with him. On the porch he hesitated a moment, flexing his shoulders and breathing deeply. "On a morning like this I almost wish I drove a car."

1

"You could learn, Gerald. You could reach your ac-
counts in half the time, and . . ."

"No, dear. I'm quite content with my paper in the bus,
and in a town a car's a nuisance." He stooped and
brushed her cheek with his lips. "Hello there!" he called
out as he straightened up.

Her eyes followed the direction in which he had called.
Their only close neighbor, a vegetable and flower
grower, was following a plow behind his horse, his head
as high as the horse's was low, the morning wind catching his thatch of gray hair and pointing it like a shock of
wheat.

"That old boy has the life," Gerald said. "When I'm
his age that's for me."

"He's not so old," she said.

"No. I guess he's not at that," he said. "Well, dear, I
must be off. Till tomorrow night, take care of yourself."

His step down the road was almost jaunty. It was
strange that he could not abide an automobile. But not
having one was rather in the pattern. A car would be a
tangible link between his life away and theirs at home.
Climbing into it of an evening, she would have a feeling
of his travels. The dust would rub off on her. As it was,
the most she had of him away was the lingering pungency
of a sample spice kit.

When he was out of sight she began her household
chores—the breakfast dishes, beds, dusting. She had
brought altogether too many things from the city. Her
mother had left seventy years accumulation in the old
house, and now it was impossible to lay a book on the
table without first moving a figurine, a vase, a piece of
delft. Really the place was a clutter of bric-a-brac. Small
wonder Gerald had changed toward her. It was not marriage that had changed him—it was this house, and herself settling in it like an old buddha with a bowl of
incense in his lap.

A queer thing that this should occur to her only now,
she thought. But it was not the first time. She was only

now finding a word for it. Nor had Gerald always been this remote. Separating a memory of a particular moment in their early days, she caught his eyes searching hers— not numbering her years, as she might think were he to do it now, but measuring his own worth in her esteem.

She lined up several ornaments that might be put away, or better, sold to a junkman. But from the lineup she drew out pieces of which she had grown especially fond. They had become like children to her, as Gerald made children of the books with which he spent his evenings home. Making a basket of her apron she swept the whole tableful of trinkets into it.

Without a downward glance, she hurried them to the ashbox in the backyard. Shed of them, she felt a good deal lighter, and with the May wind in her face and the sun gentle, like an arm across her shoulders, she felt very nearly capersome. Across the fence the jonquils were in bloom and the tulips, nodding like fat little boys. Mr. Joyce had unhitched the horse. He saw her then.

"Fine day this morning," he called. He gave the horse a slap on the rump that sent him into the pasture, and came to the fence.

"I'm admiring the flowers," she said.

"Lazy year for them. Two weeks late they are."

"Is that a fact?" Of course it's a fact, she thought. A silly remark, and another after it: "I've never seen them lovelier, though. What comes out next?"

"Snaps, I guess this year. Late roses, too. The iris don't sell much, so I'm letting 'em come or stay as they 'like."

"That should bring them out."

"Now isn't that the truth? You can coax and tickle all year and not get a bloom for thanks. Turn your back on 'em and they run you down."

Like love, she thought, and caught her tongue. But a splash of color took to her cheeks.

"Say, you're looking nice, Mrs. Shepherd, if you don't mind my saying it."

"Thank you. A touch of spring, I suppose."

"Don't it just send your blood racing? How would you like an armful of these?"

"I'd be very pleased, Mr. Joyce. But I'd like to pay you for them."

"Indeed not. I won't sell half of them—they come in a heap."

She watched his expert hand nip the blooms. He was already tanned, and he stooped and rose with a fine grace. In all the years he had lived next to them he had never been in the house, nor they in his except the day of his wife's funeral. He hadn't grieved much, she commented to Gerald at the time. And little wonder. The woman was pinched and whining, and there wasn't a sunny day she didn't expect a drizzle before nightfall. Now that Sarah thought of it, Joyce looked younger than he did when Mrs. Joyce was still alive.

"There. For goodness' sakes, Mr. Joyce. That's plenty."

"I'd give you the field of them this morning," he said, piling her arms with the flowers.

"I've got half of it now."

"And what a picture you are with them."

"Well, I must hurry them into water," she said. "Thank you."

She hastened toward the house, flying like a young flirt from her first conquest, and aware of the pleased eye following her. The whole morning glowed in the company she kept with the flowers. She snapped off the radio: no tears for Miss Julia today. At noon she heard Mr. Joyce's wagon roll out of the yard as he started to his highway stand. She watched at the window. He looked up and lifted his hat.

At odd moments during the day, she thought of him. He had given her a fine sense of herself and she was grateful. She began to wish that Gerald was returning that night. Take your time, Sarah, she told herself. You don't put away old habits and the years like bric-a-brac. She had softened up, no doubt of it. Not a fat woman, maybe, but plump. Plump. She repeated the word aloud. It had the sound of a potato falling into a tub of water.

But the afternoon sun was warm and the old laziness came over her. Only when Mr. Joyce came home, his voice in a song ahead of him, did she pull herself up. She hurried a chicken out of the refrigerator and then called to him from the porch.

"Mr. Joyce, would you like to have supper with me? Gerald won't be home, and I do hate cooking for just my-self."

"Oh, that'd be grand. I've nothing in the house but a shank of ham that a dog wouldn't bark for. What can I bring?"

"Just come along when you're ready."

Sarah, she told herself, setting the table, you're an old bat trying your wings in daylight. A half-hour later she glanced out of the window in time to see Mr. Joyce skipping over the fence like a stiff-legged colt. He was dressed in his Sunday suit and brandishing a bottle as he cleared the barbed wire. Sarah choked down a lump of apprehension. For all that she planned a little fun for her-self, she was not up to galloping through the house with an old Don Juan on her heels. Mr. Joyce, however, was a well-mannered guest. The bottle was May wine. He drank sparingly and was lavish in his praise of the dinner.

"You've no idea the way I envy you folks, Mrs. Shep-herd. Your husband especially. How can he bear the times he spends away?"

He bears it all too well, she thought. "It's his work. He's a salesman. He sells spices."

Mr. Joyce showed a fine set of teeth in his smile—his own teeth, she marveled, tracing her bridgework with the tip of her tongue while he spoke. "Then he's got sugar and spice and everything nice, as they say."

What a one he must have been with the girls, she thought, and to marry a quince as he had. It was done in a hurry no doubt, and maybe at the end of a big stick.

"It must be very lonesome for you since Mrs. Joyce passed away," she said more lugubriously than she intended. After all the woman was gone three years.

"No more than when she was with me." His voice matched hers in seriousness. "It's a hard thing to say of the dead, but if she hasn't improved her disposition since, we're all in for a damp eternity." He stuffed the bowl of his pipe. "Do you mind?"

"No, I like the smell of tobacco around the house."

"Does your husband smoke?"

"Yes," she said in some surprise at the question.

"He didn't look the kind to follow a pipe," he said, pulling noisily at his. "No, dear lady," he added when the smoke was shooting from it, "you're blessed in not knowing the plague of a silent house."

It occurred to her then that he was exploring the situation. She would give him small satisfaction. "Yes, I count that among my blessings."

There was a kind of amusement in his eyes. You're as lonesome as me, old girl, they seemed to say, and their frankness bade her to add: "But I do wish Gerald was home more of the time."

"Ah, well, he's at the age when most men look to a last trot around the paddock," he said, squinting at her through the smoke.

"Gerald is only forty-three," she said, losing the words before she knew it.

"There's some take it at forty, and others among us leaping after it from the rocking chair."

The conversation had taken a turn she certainly had not intended, and she found herself threshing around in it. Beating a fire with a feather duster. "There's the moon," she said, charging to the window as though to wave to an old friend.

"Aye," he said, "there's the moon. Are you up to a trot in it?"

"What did you say, Mr. Joyce?"

"I'd better say what I was thinking first. If I hitch

Micky to the old rig, would you take a turn with me on the Mill Pond Road?''

She saw his reflection in the window, a smug, daring little grin on his face. In sixteen years of settling she had forgotten her way with men. But it was something you never really forgot. Like riding a bicycle, you picked it up again after a few turns. "I would," she said.

The horse ahead of the rig was a different animal from the one on the plow that morning. Mr. Joyce had no more than thrown the reins over his rump than he took a turn that almost tumbled Sarah into the sun frames. But Mr. Joyce leaped to the seat and pulled Micky up on his hind legs with one hand and Sarah down to her cushion with the other, and they were off in the wake of the moon. . . .

The sun was full in her face when Sarah awoke the next morning. As usual, she looked to see if Gerald were in his bed by way of acclimating herself to the day and its routine. With the first turn of her body she decided that a gallop in a rusty-springed rig was not the way to assert a stay of youth. She lay a few moments thinking about it and then got up to an aching sense of folly. It remained with her through the day, giving way at times to a nostalgia for her bric-a-brac. She had never realized how much of her life was spent in the care of it.

By the time Gerald came home she was almost the person he had left the day before. She had held out against the ornaments, however. Only the flowers decorated the living-room. It was not until supper was over and Gerald had settled with his book that he commented

"Sarah, what happened to the old Chinese philosopher?''

"I put him away. Didn't you notice? I took all the clutter out of here.''

He looked about him vacantly as though trying to recall some of it. "So you did. I'll miss that old boy. He gave me something to think about.''

"What?''

"Oh, I don't know. Confucius says . . . that sort of thing."

"He wasn't a philosopher at all," she said, having no notion what he was. "He was a farmer."

"Was he? Well, there's small difference." He opened the book.

"Aren't the flowers nice, Gerald?"

"Beautiful."

"Mr. Joyce gave them to me, fresh out of his garden."

"That's nice."

"Must you read every night, Gerald? I'm here all day with no one to talk to, and when you get home you stick your nose into a book . . ." When the words were half out she regretted them. "I didn't tell you, Gerald. I had Mr. Joyce to dinner last night."

"That was very decent of you, dear. The old gentleman must find it lonesome."

"I don't think so. It was a relief to him when his wife died."

Gerald looked up. "Did he say that?"

"Not in so many words, but practically."

"He must be a strange sort. What did she die of?"

"I don't remember. A heart condition, I think."

"Interesting." He returned to his book.

"After dinner he took me for a ride in the horse and buggy. All the way to Cos Corner and back."

"Ha!" was his only comment.

"Gerald, you're getting fat."

He looked up. "I don't think so. I'm about my usual weight. A couple of pounds maybe."

"Then you're carrying it in your stomach. I noticed you've cut the elastic out of your shorts."

"These new fabrics," he said testily.

"They're preshrunken," she said. "It's your stomach. And haven't you noticed how you pull at your collar all the time?"

"I meant to mention that, Sarah. You put too much starch in them."

"I ran out of starch last week and forgot to order it. You can take a size fifteen-and-a-half now."

"Good Lord, Sarah, you're going to tell me next I should wear a horse collar." He let the book slide closed between his thighs. "I get home only three or four nights a week. I'm tired. I wish you wouldn't aggravate me, dear."

She went to his chair and sat on the arm of it. "Did you know that I was beginning to wonder if you'd respond to the poke of a hat-pin?"

He looked directly up at her for the first time in what had seemed like years. His eyes fell away. "I've been working very hard, dear."

"I don't care what you've been doing, Gerald. I'm just glad to find out that you're still human."

He slid his arm around her and tightened it.

"Aren't spring flowers lovely?" she said.

"Yes," he said, "and so is spring."

She leaned across him and took a flower from the vase. She lingered there a moment. He touched his hand to her. "And you're lovely, too."

This is simple, she thought, getting upright again. If the rabbit had sat on a thistle, he'd have won the race.

"The three most beautiful things in the world," Gerald said thoughtfully, "a white bird flying, a field of wheat, and a woman's body."

"Is that your own, Gerald?"

"I don't know. I think it is."

"It's been a long time since you wrote any poetry. You did nice things once."

"That's how I got you," he said quietly.

"And I got you with an old house. I remember the day my mother's will was probated. The truth, Gerald—wasn't it then you made up your mind?"

He didn't speak for a moment, and then it was a continuance of some thought of his own, a subtle twist of association. "Do you remember the piece I wrote on the house?"

"I read it the other day. I often read them again."

"Do you, Sarah? And never a mention of it."

It was almost all the reading she did these days. His devotion to books had turned her from them. "Remember how you used to let me read them to you. Gerald? You thought that I was the only one besides yourself who could do them justice."

"I remember."

"Or was that flattery?"

He smiled. "It was courtship, I'm afraid. No one ever thinks anybody else can do his poetry justice. But Sarah, do you know—I'd listen tonight if you'd read some of them. Just for old time's sake."

For old time's sake, she thought, getting the folder from the cabinet and settling opposite him. He was slouched in his chair, pulling at his pipe, his eyes half-closed. Long ago this same contemplativeness in him had softened the first shock of the difference in their ages.

"I've always liked this one best—*The Morning of My Days.*"

"Well you might," he murmured. "It was written for you."

She read one piece after another, wondering now and then what pictures he was conjuring up of the moment he had written them. He would suck on his pipe at times. The sound was like a baby pulling at an empty bottle. She was reading them well, she thought, giving them a mellow vibrancy, an old love's tenderness. Surely there was a moment coming when he would rise from the chair and come to her. Still he sat, his eyes almost closed, the pipe now in hand on the chair's arm. A huskiness crept into her voice, so rarely used to this length any more, and she thought of the nightingale's singing, the thorn against its breast. A slit of pain in her own throat pressed her to greater effort, for the poems were almost done.

She stopped abruptly, a phrase unfinished, at a noise in the room. The pipe had clattered to the floor, Gerald's hand still cupped its shape, but his chin was now on his breast. Laying the folder aside, she went over and picked up the pipe with a rather empty regret, as she would pick up a bird that had fallen dead at her feet.

Gerald's departure in the morning was in the tradition of all their days, even to the kiss upon her cheek and the words, "Till tomorrow evening, dear, take care."

Take care, she thought, going indoors. Take care of what? For what? Heat a boiler of water to cook an egg? She hurried her chores and dressed. When she saw Mr. Joyce hitch the wagon of flowers, she locked the door and waited boldly at the road for him.

"May I have a lift to the highway?" she called out, as he reined up beside her.

"You may have a lift to the world's end, Mrs. Shepherd. Give me your hand." He gave the horse its rein when she was beside him. "I see your old fella's taken off again. I daresay it gave him a laugh, our ride in the moonlight."

"It was giddy business," she said.

"Did you enjoy yourself?"

"I did. But I paid for it afterwards." Her hand went to her back.

"I let out a squeal now and then bending over, myself. But I counted it cheap for the pleasure we had. I'll take you into the village. I've to buy a length of hose anyway. Or do you think you'll be taken for a fool riding in on a wagon?"

"It won't be the first time," she said. "My life is full of foolishness."

"It's a wise fool who laughs at his own folly. We've that in common, you and me. Where'll we take our supper tonight?"

He was sharp as mustard.

"You're welcome to come over," she said.

He nodded. "I'll fetch us a steak, and we'll give Micky his heels again after."

Sarah got off at the post office and stayed in the building until Joyce was out of sight—Joyce and the gapers who had stopped to see her get out of the wagon. Getting in was one thing, getting out another. A bumblebee after a violet. It was time for this trip. She walked to the doctor's office and waited her turn among the villagers.

"I thought I'd come in for a check-up, Dr. Philips," she said at his desk. "And maybe you'd give me a diet?"

"A diet?" He took off his glasses and measured her with the naked eye.

"I'm getting a little fat," she said. "They say it's a strain on the heart at my age."

"Your heart could do for a woman of twenty," he said, "but we'll have a listen."

"I'm not worried about my heart, Doctor, you understand. I just feel that I'd like to lose a few pounds."

"Uh-huh," he said. "Open your dress." He got his stethoscope.

Diet, apparently, was the rarest of his prescriptions. Given as a last resort. She should have gone into town for this, not to a country physician who measured a woman by the children she bore. "The woman next door to us died of a heart condition," she said, as though that should explain her visit.

"Who's that?" he asked, putting away the instrument.

"Mrs. Joyce. Some years ago."

"She had a heart to worry about. Living for years on stimulants. Yours is as sound as a bullet. Let's have your arm."

She pushed up her sleeve as he prepared the apparatus for measuring her blood pressure. That, she felt, was rising out of all proportion. She was ashamed of herself before this man, and angry at herself for it, and at him for no reason more than that he was being patient with her. "We're planning insurance," she lied. "I wanted our own doctor's opinion first."

"You'll have no trouble getting it, Mrs. Shepherd. And no need of a diet." He grinned and removed the apparatus. "Go easy on potatoes and bread, and on the sweets. You'll outlive your husband by twenty years. How is he, by the way?''

"Fine. Just fine, Doctor, thank you.''

What a nice show you're making of yourself these days, Sarah, she thought, outdoors again. Well, come in or go out, old girl, and slam the door behind you . . .

Micky took to his heels that night. He had had a day of ease, and new shoes were stinging his hooves by nightfall. The skipping of Joyce with each snap of the harness teased him, the giggling from the rig adding a prickle. After the wagon, the rig was no more than a fly on his tail. He took the full reins when they slapped on his flanks and charged out from the laughter behind him. It rose to a shriek the faster he galloped and tickled his ears like something alive that slithered from them down his neck and his belly and into his loins. Faster and faster he plunged, the sparks from his shoes like ocean spray. He fought a jerk of the reins, the saw of the bit in his mouth a fierce pleasure. He took turns at his own fancy and only in sight of his own yard again did he yield in the fight, choking on the spume that lathered his tongue.

"By the holy, the night a horse beats me, I'll lie down in my grave," Joyce cried. "Get up now, you buzzard. You're not turning in till you go to the highway and back. Are you all right, Sarah?''

Am I all right, she thought. When in years had she known a wild ecstasy like this? From the first leap of the horse she had burst the girdle of fear and shame. If the wheels had spun out from beneath them, she would have rolled into the ditch contented.

"I've never been better,'' she said.

He leaned close to her to see her, for the moon had just risen. The wind had stung the tears to her eyes, but they were laughing. "By the Horn Spoon,'' he said, "you liked it!'' He let the horse have his own way into the drive after all. He jumped down from the rig and held his hand up to her. "What a beautiful thing to be hanging in the back of the closet all these years."

"If that's a compliment," she said, "it's got a nasty bite."

"Aye. But it's my way of saying you're a beautiful woman."

"Will you come over for a cup of coffee?"

"I will. I'll put up the horse and be over."

The kettle had just come to the boil when he arrived.

"Maybe you'd rather have tea, Mr. Joyce?"

"Coffee or tea, so long as it's not water. And I'd like you to call me Frank. They christened me Francis but I got free of it early."

"And you know mine, I noticed," she said.

"It slipped out in the excitement. There isn't a woman I know who wouldn't of collapsed in a ride like that."

"It was wonderful." She poured the water into the coffee pot.

"There's nothing like getting behind a horse," he said, "unless it's getting astride him. I wouldn't trade Micky for a Mack truck."

"I used to ride when I was younger," she said.

"How did you pick up the man you got, if you don't mind my asking?"

And you the old woman, she thought; where did you get her? "I worked for a publishing house and he brought in some poetry."

"Ah, that's it." He nodded. "And he thought with a place like this he could pour it out like water from a spout."

"Gerald and I were in love," she said, irked that he should define so bluntly her own thoughts on the matter.

"Don't I remember it? In them days you didn't pull the blinds. It used to put me in a fine state."

"Do you take cream in your coffee? I've forgotten."

"Aye, thank you, and plenty of sugar."

"You haven't missed much," she said.

"There's things you see through a window you'd miss

sitting down in the living-room. I'll wager you've wondered about the old lady and me?''

"A little. She wasn't so old, was she, Mr. Joyce?" Frank, she thought. Too frank.

"That one was old in her crib. But she came with a greenhouse. I worked for her father.''

Sarah poured the coffee. "You're a cold-blooded old rogue," she said.

He grinned. "No. Cool-headed I am, and warm-blooded. When I was young, I made out it was the likes of poetry. She sang like a bird on a convent wall. But when I caged her she turned into an old crow.''

"That's a terrible thing to say, Mr. Joyce.''

The humor left his face for an instant. "It's a terrible thing to live with. It'd put a man off his nut. You don't have a bit of cake in the house, Sarah, to go with this?''

"How about muffins and jam?''

"That'll go fine." He smiled again. "Where does your old fella spend the night in his travels?''

"In the hotel in whatever town he happens to be in.''

"That's a lonesome sort of life for a married man," he said.

She pulled a chair to the cupboard and climbed up to get a jar of preserves. He made no move to help her although she still could not reach the jar. She looked down at him. "You could give me a hand.''

"Try it again. You almost had it that time." He grinned, almost gleeful at her discomfort.

She bounced down in one step. "Get it yourself if you want it. I'm satisfied with a cup of coffee.''

He pounded his fist on the table, getting up. "You're right, Sarah. Never fetch a man anything he can fetch himself. Which bottle is it?''

"The strawberry.''

He hopped up and down, nimble as a goat. "But then maybe he doesn't travel alone?''

"What?''

"I was suggesting your man might have an outside interest. Salesmen have the great temptation, you know."

"That's rather impertinent, Mr. Joyce."

"You're right, Sarah, it is. My tongue's been home so long it doesn't know how to behave in company. This is a fine cup of coffee."

She sipped hers without speaking. It was time she faced that question, she thought. She had been hedging around it for a long time, and last night with Gerald should have forced it upon her. "And if he does have an outside interest," she said, lifting her chin, "what of it?"

"Ah, Sarah, you're a wise woman, and worth waiting the acquaintance of. You like me a little now, don't you?"

"A little."

"Well," he said, getting up, "I'll take that to keep me warm for the night."

And what have I got to keep me warm, she thought. "Thank you for the ride, Frank. It was thrilling."

"Was it?" he said, coming near her. He lifted her chin with his forefinger. "We've many a night like this ahead, Sarah, if you say the word." And then when she left her chin on his finger, he bent down and kissed her, taking himself to the door after it with a skip and a jump. He paused there and looked back at her. "Will I stay or go?"

"You'd better go," she choked out, wanting to be angry but finding no anger in herself at all.

All the next day Sarah tried to anchor herself from her peculiar flights of fancy. She had no feeling for the man, she told herself. It was a fine state a woman reached when a kiss from a stranger could do that to her. It was the ride made you giddy, she said aloud. You were thinking of Gerald. You were thinking of . . . the Lord knows what. She worked upstairs until she heard the wagon go by. She would get some perspective when Gerald came home. It seemed as though he'd been gone a long time.

The day was close and damp, and the flies clung to the screens. There was a dull stillness in the atmosphere. By late afternoon the clouds rolled heavier, mulling about one another like dough in a pan. While she was peeling potatoes for supper, Frank drove in. He unhitched the horse but left him in the harness, and set about immediately building frames along the rows of flowers. He was expecting a storm. She looked at the clock. It was almost time for Gerald.

She went out on the front porch and watched for the bus. There was a haze in the sweep of land between her and the highway, and the traffic through it seemed to float thickly, slowly. The bus glided toward the intersection and past it without stopping. She felt a sudden anger. Her whole day had been strung up to this peak. Since he had not called, it meant merely he had missed the bus. The next one was in two hours. She crossed the yard to the fence. You're starting up again, Sarah, she warned herself, and took no heed of the warning.

Frank looked up from his work. "You'd better fasten the house," he said. "There's a fine blow coming."

"Frank, if you're in a hurry, I'll give you something to eat."

"That'd be a great kindness. I may have to go back to the stand at a gallop."

He was at the kitchen table, shoveling in the food without a word, when the heavy sky lightened. He went to the window. "By the glory, it may blow over." He looked around at her. "Your old boy missed the bus, did he?"

"He must have."

Frank looked out again. "I do like a good blow. Even if it impoverished me, there's nothing in the world like a storm."

An automobile horn sounded on the road. It occurred to Sarah that on a couple of occasions Gerald had received a ride from the city. The car passed, but watching its dust she was left with a feeling of suspended urgency. Joyce was chatting now. He had tilted back in the chair and for the first time since she had known him, he was rambling on about weather, vegetables, and the price of eggs. She found it more disconcerting than his bursts of intimate comment, and she hung from one sentence to the next waiting for the end of it. Finally she passed in back of his chair and touched her fingers briefly to his neck.

"You need a haircut, Frank."

He sat bolt upright. "I never notice it till I have to scratch. Could I have a drop more coffee?"

She filled his cup, aware of his eyes on her. "Last night was something I'll never forget—that ride," she said.

"And something else last night, do you remember that?"

"Yes."

"Would you give me another now to match it if I was to ask?"

"No."

"What if I took it without asking?"

"I don't think I'd like it, Frank."

He pushed away from the table, slopping the coffee into the saucer. "Then what are you tempting me for?"

"You've a funny notion of temptations," she flared up, knowing the anger was against herself.

Joyce spread his dirt-grimed fingers on the table. "Sarah, do you know what you want?"

The tears were gathering. She fought them back. "Yes, I know what I want!" she cried.

Joyce shook his head. "He's got you by the heart, hasn't he, Sarah?"

"My heart's my own!" She flung her head up.

Joyce slapped his hand on the table. "Ho! Look at the spark of the woman! That'd scorch a man if there was a stick in him for kindling." He moistened his lips and in spite of herself Sarah took a step backwards. "I'll not chase you, Sarah. Never fear that. My chasing days are over. I'll neither chase nor run, but I'll stand my ground for what's coming to me." He jerked his head toward the window. "That was only a lull in the wind. There's a big blow coming now for certain."

She watched the first drops of rain splash on the glass. "Gerald's going to get drenched in it."

"Maybe it'll drown him," Joyce said, grinning from the door. "Thanks for the supper."

Let it come on hail, thunder, and lightning. Blow the roof from the house and tumble the chimney. I'd go out from it then and never turn back. When an old man can laugh at your trying to cuckold a husband, and the husband asking it, begging it, shame on you. She went through the house clamping the locks on the windows. More pleasure putting the broom through them.

An early darkness folded into the storm, and the walls of rain bleared the highway lights. There was an ugly yellow tinge to the water from the dust swirled into it. The wind sluiced down the chimney, spitting bits of soot on the living-room floor. She spread newspapers to catch it. A sudden blow, it would soon be spent. She went to the hall clock. The bus was due in ten minutes. What matter? A quick supper, a good book, and a long sleep. The wily old imp was right. A prophet needing a haircut.

The lights flickered off for a moment, then on again. Let them go out, Sarah. What's left for you, you can see by candlelight. She went to the basement and brought up the kerosene lamp and then got a flashlight from the pantry. As she returned to the living-room, a fresh gust of wind sent the newspapers out of the grate like scud. The lights flickered again. A sound drew her to the hall. She thought the wind might be muffling the ring of the telephone. When she got there, the clock was striking. The bus was now twenty minutes late. There was something about the look of the phone that convinced her the line was dead. It was unnerving to find it in order. Imagination, she murmured. Everything was going perverse to her expectations. And then, annoyed with herself, she grew angry with Gerald again. This was insult. Insult on top of indifference.

She followed a thumping noise upstairs. It was on the outside of the house. She turned off the light and pressed her face against the window. A giant maple tree was rocking and churning, one branch thudding against the house. There was not even a blur of light from the highway now. Blacked out. While she watched, a pinpoint of light shaped before her. It grew larger, weaving a little. A flashlight, she thought, and wondered if Gerald had one. Then she recognized the motion: a lantern on a wagon. Frank was returning.

When she touched the light switch there was no response. Groping her way to the hall she saw that all the lights were out now. Step by step she made her way downstairs. A dankness had washed in through the chimney, stale and sickening. She lit the lamp and carried it to the kitchen. From the window there, she saw Frank's lantern bobbing as he led the horse into the barn. She could not see man or horse, only the fading of the light until it disappeared inside. When it reappeared she lifted her kerosene lamp, a greeting to him. This time he came around the fence. She held the door against the wind.

"I've no time now, Sarah. I've work to do," he shouted. "He didn't come, did he?"

"No!"

"Is the phone working?"

She nodded that it was and waved him close to her. "Did the bus come through?"

"It's come and gone. Close the door or you'll have the house in a shambles." He waved his lantern and was gone.

She put the pot roast she had prepared for Gerald in the refrigerator and set the perishables close to the freezing unit. She wound the clock and put away the dishes. Anything to keep busy. She washed the kitchen floor that had been washed only the day before. The lantern across the way swung on a hook at the barn, sometimes moving toward the ground and back as Joyce examined the frames he was reinforcing.

Finally she returned to the living-room. She sat for a long time in Gerald's chair, watching the pattern of smoke in the lamp-chimney. Not even a dog or cat to keep her company. Not even a laughing piece of delft to look out at her from the mantlepiece; only the cold-eyed forebears, whom she could not remember, staring down at her from the gilt frames, their eyes fixed upon her, the last and the least of them who would leave after her—nothing.

It was not to be endured. She lunged out of the chair. In the hall she climbed to the first landing where she could see Joyce's yard. He was through work now, the lantern hanging from the porch although the house was darkened. It was the only light anywhere, and swayed in the wind like a will-o'-the-wisp.

She bounded down the stairs and caught up her raincoat. Taking the flashlight she went out into the storm. She made her way around the fence, sometimes pushing into the wind, sometimes resting against it. Joyce met her in his driveway. He had been waiting, she thought, testing his nerves against her own, expecting her. Without a word, he caught her hand and led her to his back steps and into the house. "I've an oil lamp," he said then. "Hold your light there till I fix it."

She watched his wet face in the half-light. His mouth was lined with malicious humor, and his eyes as he squinted at the first flame of the wick were fierce, as fierce as the storm, and as strange to her. When the light flared up, she followed its reaches over the dirty wall, the faded calendar, the gaping cupboards, the electric cord hanging from a naked bulb over the sink to the back door. There were dishes stacked on the table where they no doubt stood from one meal to the next. The curtains were stiff with dirt, three years of it. Only then did she take a full glimpse of the folly that had brought her here.

"I just ran over for a minute, Frank . . ."

"A minute or the night, sit there, Sarah, and let me get out of these clothes."

She took the chair he motioned her into, and watched him fling his coat into the corner. Nor could she take her eyes from him as he sat down and removed his boots and socks. Each motion fascinated her separately, fascinated and revolted her. He wiped between his toes with the socks. He went barefoot toward the front of the house. In the doorway he paused, becoming a giant in the weird light.

"Put us up a pot of coffee, dear woman. The makings are there on the stove."

"I must go home. Gerald . . ."

"To hell with Gerald," he interrupted. "He's snug for the night, wherever he is. Maybe he won't come back to you at all. It's happened before, you know, men vanishing from women they don't know the worth of."

Alone, she sat stiff and erect at the table. He was just talking, poisoning her mind against Gerald. How should she get out of here? Run like a frightened doe and never face him again? No, Sarah. Stay for the bitter coffee. Scald the giddiness out of you once and for all. But on top of the resolve came the wish that Gerald might somehow appear at the door and take her home. Dear, gentle Gerald.

She got up and went to the sink to draw the water for coffee. A row of meidcine bottles stood on the windowsill, crusted with dust. Household remedies. She leaned close and examined a faded label: "Mrs. Joyce—take immediately upon need."

She turned from the window. A rocker stood in the corner of the room. In the old days the sick woman had sat in it on the back porch, rocking, and speaking to no one. The stale sickness of her was still about the house, Sarah thought. What did she know of people like this?

He was threshing around upstairs like a penned bull. His muddy boots lay where he had taken them off, a pool of water gathering about them. Again she looked at the windowsill. No May wine there. Suddenly she remembered Dr. Philips's words: "Lived on stimulants for years.'' She could almost see the sour woman, even to her gasping for breath . . . "Take immediately."

Fix the coffee, Sarah. What kind of teasing is this? Teasing the dead from her grave before you. Teasing. Something in the thought disturbed her further . . . an association: Joyce watching her reach for the preserves last night, grinning at her. "Try it again, Sarah. You almost had it that time." And she could still hear him asking, "Which bottle?" Not which jar, but which bottle.

She grabbed the kettle and filled it. Stop it, Sarah. It's the storm, the waiting, too much waiting . . . your time of life. She drew herself up against his coming, hearing his quick step on the stairs.

"Will you give us a bit of iodine there from the window, Sarah? I've scratched myself on those blamed frames."

She selected the bottle carefully with her eyes, so that her trembling hand might not betray her.

"Dab it on here," he said, holding a white cuff away from his wrist.

The palm of his hand was moist as she bent over it and she could smell the earth and the horse from it. Familiar. Everything about him had become familiar, too familiar. She felt his breath on her neck, and the hissing sound of it was the only sound in the room. She smeared the iodine on the cut and pulled away. His lips tightened across his teeth in a grin.

"A kiss would make a tickle of the pain," he said.

Sarah thrust the iodine bottle from her and grabbed the flashlight. "I'm going home."

His jaw sagged as he stared at her. "Then what did you come for?"

"Because I was lonesome. I was foolish . . ." Fear choked off her voice. A little trickle of saliva dribbled from the corner of his mouth.

"No! You came to torture me!"

She forced one foot toward the door and the other after it. His voice rose in laughter as she lumbered away from him. "Good Lord, Sarah. Where's the magnificent woman who rode to the winds with me last night?"

She lunged into the electric cord in her retreat, searing her cheek on it. Joyce caught it and wrenched it from the wall, its splayed end springing along the floor like a whip. "And me thinking the greatest kindness would be if he never came home!"

The doorknob slipped in her sweaty hand. She dried it frantically. He's crazy, she thought. Mad-crazy.

"You're a lump, Sarah," he shouted. "And Mr. Joyce is a joker. A joker and a dunce. He always was and he will be till the day they hang him!"

The door yielded and she plunged down the steps and into the yard. In her wild haste she hurled herself against the rig and spun away from it as though it were something alive. She sucked in her breath to keep from screaming. She tore her coat on the fence hurtling past it, leaving a swatch of it on the wire. Take a deep breath, she told herself as she stumbled up the steps. Don't faint. Don't fall. The door swung from her grasp, the wind clamoring through the house. She forced it closed, the glass plate tingling, and bolted it. She thrust the flashlight on the table and caught up the phone. She clicked it wildly.

Finally it was the operator who broke through. "I have a call for you from Mr. Gerald Shepherd. Will you hold on, please?"

Sarah could hear only her own sobbing breath in the hollow of the mouth piece. She tried to settle her mind by pinning her eyes on the stairway. But the spokes of the stairway seemed to be shivering dizzily in the circle of light, like the plucked strings of a harp. Even the sound of them was vibrant in her head, whirring over the rasp of her breath. Then came the pounding footfalls and Joyce's fists on the door. Vainly she signaled the operator. And somewhere in the tumult of her mind she grasped at the thought that if she unlocked the door, Joyce would come in and sit down. They might even light the fire. There was plenty of wood in the basement. But she could not speak. And it was too late.

Joyce's fist crashed through the glass and drew the bolt. With the door's opening the wind whipped her coat over her head; with its closing, her coat fell limp, its little pressure about her knees seeming to buckle them.

"I'm sorry," came the operator's voice, "the call was canceled ten minutes ago."

She let the phone clatter onto the table and waited, her back still to the door. Ten minutes was not very long ago, she reasoned in sudden desolate calmness. She measured each of Joyce's footfalls toward her, knowing they marked all of time that was left to her. And somehow, she felt, she wanted very little more of it.

For only an instant she saw the loop he had made of the electric cord, and the white cuffs over the strong, gnarled hands. She closed her eyes and lifted her head high, expecting that in that way the end would come more quickly . . .

1952

Born Killer

There is a sort of legend about Corporal George Orbach. More than one man of his outfit has summed him up as the only person he ever met who didn't know what fear was. They have a good many pat explanations, the way men will when they have nothing to do between patrols but pin labels on one another. "A born killer" is a favorite. A lieutenant called it "a suicidal complex." This particular phrase did not take with the men. A handful of sleeping pills, a loaded .32, they figure, and he could have died in bed without scurvy, without frostbite, and without Migs.

He was up once for rotation and asked to stay. Forced into regulation five-day leaves in Japan, he walks the streets there, striding along them like a farmer behind a plow who sees neither birds nor trees nor sky except to measure the daylight left in them. The one piece of information about himself which he ever volunteered was the remark: "I bet I've walked more than any goddamn soldier in the infantry."

No one doubted it, which is strange only in the fact that George Orbach is just nineteen years old. He lied about his age when he signed up. At sixteen he said he was twenty-one, and the recruiting officer studied him trying to decide which way he was lying. He was bent like a man with something on his back and his eyes were old; but his skin was smooth and his dirty, nervous hands boy's hands.

"Home?"

"U.S.A."

"Where were you born, wise guy?"

"Masonville, Wisconsin. Ever hear of it? '

"They'll clip your tongue in the army, farm boy. Why don't you take a haircut?"

"I don't have any money."

"Family?"

"Don't have any."

"That's a shame. You ought to have an insurance beneficiary."

"What insurance?"

"What they make you take out before you go overseas."

"Look, Mister . . ."

"Sir!"

"Sir. I got a sister. Put her down for it. Elizabeth Orbach, Route 3, Masonville, Wisconsin."

"That's better. How did you get to New York?"

"I walked."

"Fair game for the infantry. Got a police record, Orbach?"

"No, sir."

The recruiting sergeant watched him closely. "They'll extradite you if you have."

George slurred the word wearily. "I don't think they'll extradite me."

"Think it over." The sergeant gave him a card. "If you still want to join up, be at this address at 8 o'clock tomorrow morning."

George was born in violence, in a storm that tore great pines out by the roots and so flattened the tall white birches that ten years later George himself, then given to visualizing good and evil, counted the stricken birches pure white souls bowed by the devil, as he scrambled over them on his shortcut home from Sunday school. But on the night he was born, his father killed a horse racing him to Masonville to bring the doctor. Electric wires were down, the phone dead, the truck useless on the washed-out road. George and his mother were attended by Elizabeth, twelve years old. George lived. His mother died.

Elizabeth learned more in going over George's lessons with him than she had in attending school herself. She was more delighted with his first, second, and third readers than he was, and when he was nine or so, he could not quite understand her pleasure in them. By then Elizabeth was over twenty, which to Geroge meant that there was less difference in age between Elizabeth and their father than between his sister and himself.

"Do you believe all that about giants and princes?" he asked her more than once.

"They're nice," she would say. "They're real pretty. I like them."

Mike Orbach, who read only the Masonville weekly, *Hoard's Dairyman,* and the Bible, would shake his head. He should have liked to see her reading the Bible, but all he ever said was, "You just read whatever you like, honey. You got it coming to you."

George was further puzzled when, bringing home a geography and then a history, and books called literature which he could now read himself, he found Elizabeth still smiling over his tattered primers.

The world was at war then, and even to the backwoods of Wisconsin the mobile blood-bank units came. Across the lake, five of the Bergson boys went into service, but four were left and nothing changed very much. At the church basket-suppers there were more women than men, and Elizabeth was not unusual in having her father take her to dances. Nor did she mind sitting them out. She smiled and nodded as the dancers passed her and clapped her hands when a couple did an elaborate bow before her.

"She's so good-natured," George overheard Mrs.

Bergson say once. "God's been kinder to them than he has to lots of us."

George could not see where the kindness of God had much to do with it. He was fourteen and going by bus to the township high school. Every day when he came home Elizabeth would have his dinner warm on the back of the stove—meat, potatoes, and vegetables, always in the one pot. It didn't have much taste, he discovered, after his lunches in the school cafeteria.

"Can't you put some sugar or salt or something in it, Liz?" he said one day.

The next day there were both sugar and salt, and more of them than his stomach could take. His father had come in from the barn for a cup of tea, for he liked to hear George tell of school as much as Elizabeth did. He scowled when George pushed the plate away.

"For Cripe's sake, Liz, what did you do to this?"

"Eat it," his father said quietly.

Elizabeth went out to the icebox in the back kitchen.

"I can't, Pa," George said.

"God damn you, eat it and keep your mouth shut!"

He had not heard his father swear before. He pulled the plate back and swallowed one mouthful after another, trying to deaden the taste with tea.

Elizabeth returned and watched him. "Sugar and salt," she said.

"It's swell," George murmured.

He went to his room to change his clothes, and changing them, caught sight of himself in the mirror. He moved closer to it and examined his face. There was fuzz on his upper lip and on his chin. He twisted his neck that he might see himself from other angles. He was blond like his sister, but there all resemblance that he could find ended. He wondered which one—his sister or himself—did not belong in the family. The possibility that he might be an orphan did not hurt so much as the thought that there might be no bond of family between Elizabeth and him. But there was; he was sure of that. As long as he could remember, Liz had been taking care of him. He could remember her brushing his hair. Then he distinctly remembered his father taking the comb to part it. Liz put his shoes on when he was a child. His father tied the laces.

His face, as he stared at it, seemed to quiver—as though someone were jiggling the glass. He thrust himself into his work clothes and rushed out of the house. His father had already let the cows in and now was in the loft shoveling hay down the chute. The cows nearest it were straining in their stanchions, the metal of their collars jangling.

George measured their grain, and until the last one was fed they snorted and bellowed greedily. It was his practice to start at opposite ends on alternate days, and he was always annoyed that they had no appreciation of his fairness. That day he didn't care.

His father eased himself down the chute, dropping on the hay.

"You'll hurt yourself doing that, Pa. You should walk around."

"I was doing that before you was born."

"Where was I born?"

"Better get the milking pails."

"It's early. Where, Pa?"

"Right in the house there." The old man motioned toward it. The early darkness of winter was coming down fast.

"Was that when my mother died?"

"It was. Your sister took care of you till I got home. It was a terrible storm and I couldn't get Doc Blake to come. He was drunk. That's why I'll whip you if you ever take to liquor. Now get the buckets."

"Pa, what's the matter with Liz?"

His father looked at him. Even in the half-darkness he could see the anger in the old man's eyes.

"Who told you that?"

"Nobody. I can see. Maybe you told me something when you swore at me."

"She's raised you like she was your mother. There ain't ever going to be a woman love you like she's done." The old man drove the pitchfork down on the cement floor, striking sparks. "You've been hanging around that Jennie Bergson . . ."

"No, Pa."

"Don't 'no pa' me. I seen you cutting out across the lake. Don't you go touching that girl, Goerge. I've been watching her. She's just asking you to get her in trouble. That'd suit Neil Bergson fine. He's got too many girls to home now." He poked his finger into the boy's chest. "You don't touch a girl till you get one you want to marry. If you get feeling queer, you tell me about it, George. Maybe I can help you. I don't know. You can chop down trees." He made a wild gesture toward the woods. "We can read the holy Bible like I did. Now I'm going for the milking pails."

"Pa, what's all this got to do with Liz?"

"She's your sister, ain't she?"

The old man's voice cracked on the words, and George let him go, not wanting to see him cry. Their conversation never did make sense to the boy, although he thought about it many times. He did not try to talk about it to his father again, but he tried to be kinder toward his sister. He did not comment further upon her cooking, and sometimes, making a sort of game of it, he let her wash his hair, and then in turn washed and braided hers.

"Don't you tell," he'd say. "I don't want them calling me sissy."

"It's a secret," Elizabeth agreed. "I like secrets." She would examine herself at the mirror over the kitchen sink, smiling vacantly into it.

Now and then, after staying overnight in town with a schoolmate because of a late basketball game or class play, George would say to his father, "Pa, I need $10 for the house."

"Do you?" the old man always said, but it was not a question. He led the way into the parlor where his rolltop desk stood and from the window ledge above it took the key and unlocked the desk. Within it he kept a strong box, also locked, and within that his cash and milk receipts, and over them a pearl-handled revolver.

"That's like giving a burglar a gun, keeping it there, Pa."

"Guns ought to be locked up," the old man said. He carried the revolver in his pocket once a month when he collected on the milk receipts and took the money into Masonville to the bank. Giving the boy $10, he would say: "Something special?"

"I want to surprise Liz and you."

Thus George brought home now a table lamp, again a cover for the daybed, curtains, and sometimes a dress for his sister. He went alone and picked them out, and watched furtively while he did it that a schoolmate did not come upon him unawares.

His friends began to come to the house, some of them old enough to drive a car, and George had learned to play the mouth organ. In the summertime they swam in the lake below the Orbach farm, and afterwards roasted hot dogs on the beach. George played the tunes he knew, and all of them sang loudly, their voices carrying up to the house so that Elizabeth and her father felt compelled to go down to where they were. They sat quietly, father and daughter, in the shadows, and only when the fire blazed up, were they to be seen and waved at, but not heard.

But one night, above a rollicking song, Elizabeth raised her voice in a high sweet reverie of her own. It was like a bird's song, native to the night and the great high pine trees and the stars. There was no one there who could have said what happened to them, hearing it, but afterwards, the boys always inquired of George about his sister. They did it reverently, as they might point out the moon's rising or a shooting star. They thought her very shy. Some nights she did not make a sound, as if there was no one song which seemed especially to tempt her. But when she sang, all of them felt happier and somehow wiser, and George thought that it was her way of saying things she never managed to get out in words.

Mike Orbach had never known such prosperous days. He often remarked that things were bound to bust wide open soon. "When a farmer makes a living," he would say, "the rest of the country must be making fortunes." He bought a new car and a good bull, and was at last able to breed his own cattle.

In the late spring the usual migratory strays started dropping off the freight train and applying for work by the day. They would come and go until harvest time. Mostly they were men of George's father's age, lean and grimed with the dust of many roads, and all of them with one habit in common: they were always in search of a place to spit, as though the chaff of a thousand threshings was in their throats. The only qualifications on which Orbach ever questioned a man was his sobriety. None of them admitted drinking, and most all of them drank, which he knew, but Orbach calculated his question to have a restraining influence. His only real measurement of a man was his day's work. The summer before George was to enter his third year of high school, Al Jackson came. He was at the breakfast table when George came in from chores one morning.

"This is George, my son," the old man said.

"My name's Jackson. Al Jackson. Glad to meet you, George." He half rose from the chair and extended his hand.

George was pleased at that, the handshake offered him as between men, and in itself a rare custom among the day workers. The handshake was firm but the hand soft, and George made up his mind then to keep his distance when this rookie started to wield a pitchfork.

"Al, here," his father said, "he's been in the army. He's going to take a day or so getting into shape. Man, how your back's going to ache."

There were plenty of men around already in good shape, George thought. There was not even the look of weather about Jackson. His face was newly sunburned, his nose peeling. Still, he was a big man, good-looking, and it might be fun to have someone around whose tongue wasn't wadded in his throat like a plug of tobacco.

"Can you milk?" George asked, for he did love to be relieved of that chore.

"Beg pardon?"

"Cows. Can you milk them?"

Jackson shook his head doubtfully. "I broke my arm a year back. It stiffened up on me. I don't think I'd do 'em justice."

This amused the old man, and Elizabeth, bringing the coffee pot, giggled. Jackson looked up at her and smiled. "That's the best oatmeal I've had since I left home."

Elizabeth blushed and had to set the pot on the table to get a better hold on it.

George, trying to blend his cereal with the milk, said, "It's got lumps in it."

"Maybe it's got lumps," Jackson said, "but the stuff I've been having could've been chipped off a rock pile." He reached across the table for the coffee pot. "Here, let me pour that for you. Sit down, Miss."

"Her name's Elizabeth," the old man said.

"Really? That was my mother's name."

The right arm was limber enough with the coffee pot, George noticed.

But that summer George obtained his driver's license, and in the month between haymaking and threshing, and again between threshing and silo-filling, he spent his spare time in Masonville. His father paid him the wage of a hired hand on condition that he outfit himself for school that fall and buy his own books. It left him ample change for the juke box and the trivia he needed to bolster his attentions to Thelma Sorinson, a classmate of whom he had grown very fond.

Many times, with Thelma sitting beside him in the Ford, he remembered his father's outbreak when he had asked him about Elizabeth, his warning that George was not to touch a girl he didn't intend to marry. George reasoned that he might be willing to marry Thelma some day if she would have him. She was pretty and she could dance like a feather in a whirlwind. Thelma didn't care much what George reasoned, for he had grown tall and he shaved now once a week.

More and more at home he talked about her. His father nodded and asked such questions as what church she attended and what her father did for a living. Al, who had a bedroom in the attic, played a lot of checkers with the old man and a card game called "War" with Elizabeth, so that he was around often enough to take his turn in conversation.

"You ought to invite her out sometime so we can take a look at her, George," Al said one morning.

It was the first time since Al's arrival that George had felt one way or another about him. Now he measured how much a part of the family Al had become. He went to church with them Sundays, having bought a suit with his first pay; he took his bath in the family tub where other hands had always scrubbed down at the dairy pump; his shirts and underwear hung on the line with the household wash every Monday. More than any one thing, it suddenly irked George that Elizabeth should do his underwear.

"What do you mean, 'we'?"

Al shrugged and winked at the old man. "I like to see a pretty girl as much as the next guy."

"I'll say you do."

"That's enough, George," his father interrupted.

"Who's coming?" Elizabeth asked.

"A pretty girl like you," Al said soothin .

Elizabeth clapped her hands.

The old man was still talking through it. ". . . getting too big for your britches, driving off in a car and your pockets jingling . . ."

"For God's sake, Pa."

"You'll not swear in this house, boy."

George pushed back from the table, the anger choking him.

"He didn't mean no harm," Al said.

"I meant plenty!" George shouted.

Still Elizabeth clapped her hands. "When's she coming, George?"

"She's not coming ever, not here she's not!"

"Out! Outdoors with you." His father pointed, his finger trembling.

"I'll go when I'm ready," George said. "I live here, too."

But he went quickly and strode down the path to the chicken house. He caught up the scraper and basket and flung into the coop with such violence that the birds indoors fled screeching to the entry.

"His arm's not strong enough," George screamed after them, "to clean out a chicken coop, but he can bounce his backside on a tractor seat all day!"

It was milking time before George saw his father, for he did not go into the house at noon, tearing a few ears of corn from the stalks and eating them raw in the field.

"What have you got against him, George?" the old man asked when they met at chores.

"I don't know, Pa. All of a sudden it just seemed to me there was something bad about him. Maybe the way he looks at Liz."

"And maybe the way you're jealous, son?"

George did not look up. He had been afraid all afternoon that that was it. "Maybe," he admitted.

The old man weighed the words before he said them. "I'm hoping he's going to marry Elizabeth."

George could feel a sickness rising in him. "Oh no, Pa!"

"She isn't going to have you and me to look out for her always. Already you got a girl."

"And you?"

The old man squinted at him. "There's a place for me

beside your mother. It's just looking at things straight. Nobody lives forever.''

George thought about it. ''But him, Pa. What's he see in Liz?''

He knew he had put it wrong the moment the words were out, for the anger flickered up in his father's eyes. But he spoke slowly and the anger eased away. ''Can you tell me why you think a sunset's pretty and you wouldn't look up at the sun at noon? Can you tell me why?''

George shrugged.

''I couldn't tell you either. I think that a shock of corn is beautiful. But there's some folks who'd tell you it reminded them of scarecrows. Now I think Elizabeth is beautiful.''

''So do I, Pa.''

''Do you, boy? Do you really? You better look down deep inside yourself. I ain't waiting for the answer, but you better look.''

George tried to look while he went about the chores, but he knew he was missing the heart of the matter. Still, he searched his memory for moments when he had loved his sister best. He dwelt especially on her singing near the campfire, and since he had not brought about such occasions this summer, he thought he had struck upon his father's meaning. It was true, he had neglected the most beautiful thing about her.

Going into the house at suppertime, he decided that an apology was due Al for the morning's incident. He tried to summon the courage for it. But Al greeted him heartily as though he had been off on a vacation, and because he had decided Al deserved an apology he disliked and distrusted him for not expecting it.

Within the week George arranged a beach party. It was too late in the season for swimming, but the full moon rose early over the lake, and as they huddled near the fire, boys and girls, their song was like a serenade to its great gold face. They were a long time singing before Elizabeth joined her melody to theirs, and her voice came faint and tentative at first, like a bird's mimicry. George, his arm in Thelma's as they swayed to the music, felt a startled pressure from her, and glanced up to see her smile as she withdrew from him. She was not sharing her discovery with him. It was a quick and private ecstasy, and he realized this must happen to everyone. Catching beauty was a selfish thing. A person had to catch it alone before he could share it. Elizabeth had found the courage of her voice now; she sang out her wordless music as she had never done before. And George had never felt so lonely.

He got up and moved away from the fire. He watched in the shadows while another boy filled his place. He saw that boy pull Thelma down backwards and kiss her quickly, as one couple and then another were doing.

He turned away and his eyes grew accustomed to far images lighted only by the moon. Elizabeth stopped her song abruptly, and George climbed up from the beach. He trod amid the debris cautiously and searched the shadows. His eyes found her and Al, except that they were almost one person, so close was their embrace. He started toward them. Soundlessly, his father caught him from behind, whirled him around to face his own party and shoved him toward it. George went, but he sat apart and joined no more songs that night, blaming himself for having opened the full measure of his sister's beauty to her lover.

He stayed at home more after that and tried to pretend to a camaraderie with Al, asking him all sorts of questions about the army, his family, his schooling. Al parried the questions like an experienced boxer would an amateur, always keeping him at arm's length. He could tell him he'd served in Afghanistan, George realized, and he could not prove otherwise. On an inquiry about his family, Al said he was an orphan. George remembered the day he came: his saying that his mother's name was Elizabeth. Apparently Goerge showed triumph in his face, because Al drawled: "When you don't have one of your own, you're liable to call any woman who's good to you 'mother.' Ain't that a fact, George?''

He retreated, bested in that as he was in all such encounters, and hated himself for it. He grew sullen, and now when Elizabeth sang often, even about the house as she had never done before, he snapped at her for it. She merely laughed and was still for a few moments. Then, her happiness bubbling up like spittle in a baby's mouth, she would have to let out the sound of it. He fled outdoors.

His father spent almost every evening poring over the Bible. Sometimes, coming on a phrase especially to his liking, he would read it aloud. "Ah," he would say as though he had discovered something for which he had been searching, "ah, listen to this." And he would read a passage, most often describing monumental sins true penitents had been forgiven.

From this, too, George fled.

His father came on him shivering in the pumphouse one night when it was time for him to start back to school. Cornered there, George took a screwdriver to the pump motor.

"There's nothing wrong with that," the old man said, watching him tinker in hurried clumsiness. "Put down your tools for a minute."

George obeyed him.

"A few years back," the old man started, "I was thinking serious of marrying Miss Darling . . .''

Miss Darling had been George's Sunday-school teacher.

". . . I figured we'd go away a while, her and me, and then come back to the farm. That way I thought you and Liz would be so glad to see me, you'd like her here, too . . .''

George felt something drop down inside him like a plunger.

"But things weren't as good as now, and it just got put off until it was too late. I'm going to send you away to school this year, son. I talked to Reverend Johns about it. He's recommending me a school after service tonight.''

''Pa, I don't want to go.''

''You always took to books. Now's your chance. No chores, no milking. You can go to the University then.''

''No, Pa.''

The old man looked at him. ''Elizabeth and Al's getting married next week. I don't want you around then, George, the way you're acting.''

George could not hold back the tears. ''Pa, wait. Make them wait. Ask him where he came from. What does he want with us? Maybe he's got a wife already some place . . . He's 30, Pa . . .''

''He's being baptized tonight,'' the old man interrupted. ''The Lord is cleansing him whatever sins he's done. I'm satisfied in that. He's seen salvation.''

''He's seen a farm and a sucker!'' George shouted.

The old man struck him hard across the face, the force of the blow knocking the boy backwards. The fan belt broke his fall, but before he got to his feet the old man was at the door. He turned and looked back at his son, his eyes streaming. ''All we seem to do any more is hurt each other.''

When he was gone, the stench of sulphur from the well added to George's nausea. He went outdoors and retched. He was sitting on the stone hedge when he heard the car drive out. He watched for the taillight to appear on the highway, and seeing it, went into the house.

He could hear the clock tick in the stillness, and the water dripping at the sink. There was no other sound and he went up the steps to Al's room. He searched every drawer, finding nothing but clothes; not a letter, not a paper nor a picture, not even an army ''dog tag.'' He almost tore the bed apart, and that search, too, was futile.

''Satisfied, kid?''

The boy whirled around. Al had climbed the stairs without a sound.

"You're supposed to be in church," George blurted out.

"And you're past due for hell," Al said, drawling the words as though there were no threat in them. "What did you find against me, George?"

Everything, George thought, but he could name nothing. He stood, stiff-tongued and awkward in every limb, while Al sauntered to the window and looked out. "I work hard, I go to church regular, and I'm going to marry your sister. I don't know another guy who'd do that."

George clenched his fists and managed but one step forward. Al spun around, holding in his hand the pearl-handled revolver.

"That's Pa's gun," George said.

"Pa's gun and Pa's bullets. You're a fool, kid. We could've got along fine, the four of us."

George was near to tears, fear and hatred torturing him. "Liz," he cried. "You don't love her. I know it. I can't prove it, but I know it."

"So what? Just so what? I never saw the beat of you and your old man for playing God almighty."

Al moved a step toward him, the gun real and steady in his hand.

The fear grew thick in George's throat. "What are you going to do?" he managed.

"You've been on your way to suicide a long time. I'm going to help you."

"Oh no," George moaned.

"Oh yes. Think about it, kid, the way you've been carrying on. Can't you just hear the old man saying, 'I should've put the gun away. I never should've left it where he could get at it.' "

Oh God, George thought, please God, help me. "Pa!" he called out, with the only responding sound the twitter of nesting birds. "Liz!"

"For just once we're going to be real close," Al mocked, coming on.

And at that instant, from the oak tree just outside the window, a bird sounded one last high burst of song.

Al started at the sound and jerked his head. George scarcely knew the impulse, but he leaped at the farmhand, striking the gun from his hand and following it to the floor. Even from there he started firing, the first shots wild, but one finding Al as he plunged toward him. The boy emptied the gun into the fallen body. Then he flung the revolver from him and groped his way through the smoke. Downstairs, he called the county sheriff's office and waited, his mind as empty as the gun.

The sheriff came a few minutes before his father and sister, and he told what he had done while a deputy intercepted the family outdoors. He repeated the circumstances, and took the sheriff to his father's desk to show him where the gun was kept. It had been taken out in haste the moment of his father's departure, George realized, for the rolltop was up and the strong box gaping. The sheriff shook his head, studying the boy, and George thought vaguely that the truth was not so apparent to the sheriff as it was to him.

Then the sheriff went upstairs, and George heard a car drive out. Presently another, or the same car, drove in again. His father must have taken Elizabeth somewhere. To the Bergsons', he thought. The old man came in. He didn't look at George where he was sitting on the daybed in the parlor. He went to his desk and stared at it without touching anything. He, too, was thinking George had taken the gun and gone upstairs to find Al, the boy reasoned.

The sheriff came down. "Sorry, Orbach," he said to George's father.

The old man looked at him.

The sheriff rubbed his neck. "He was marrying your daughter, was he?"

Orbach nodded, his face a dumb mask of pain.

"You got to believe me," George said then. He knew

he was whining, but he couldn't help it. "He'd of killed me. I didn't take the gun, *he* did."

"I believe you, boy," the sheriff said. "Maybe this is all for the best. I just got an alarm on that guy at the office. Murder, while committing robbery. I think he was holing in here."

The old man raised his head and cried out: "It is not all for the best!"

George forced himself to his feet, a terrible realization striking through his sick relief. "Pa! Did you know about him? Did you know that?"

His father lifted his eyes and his voice to the ceiling: "There's things we are not meant to know. God's mercy should not be thwarted by the vengeance of men. Vengeance is Mine, sayeth the Lord."

George stumbled from the room and then outdoors.

"Let him go," he heard the sheriff call. "He'll come back in soon."

But George did not go back. They may not understand him in the army, not knowing all these things. But his buddies are agreed on one thing: he makes a good soldier.

1953

Sweet William

"It's a fine story we'll have to tell, and them meeting us at the boat to hear it." She let the drapes fall into place and turned from the window brushing the dust from her hands. " 'What did you see of New York?' they'll ask. 'A galaxy of lights,' I'll tell them. 'A reflection of the sky under our feet from a dusty window, and four of the dirtiest walls which ever surrounded an actress.' "

"And an actor," he added from the bed. "I'm an actor as well as your husband."

"Wasn't I the stupid girl to accept an arrangement like that?" she said, coming near him.

He looked up at her and lifted an eyebrow. "Accepted? Promoted it, and me the silly gobeen to fall in with the scheme when I could've married the daughter of a jewelry merchant." He sat up and swung his feet to the floor. "Aye, and maybe come to New York on a buying trip—with an expense account."

She sat down beside him on the edge of the bed. "It wouldn't be so bad if we weren't a success, Denny." She picked up the newspaper and read aloud for at least the tenth time: " 'The great Irish Players have invaded Broadway and taken over its heart.' "

"I'd rather a chance at its pocketbook," Denny said. "But the truth of the matter is we read our contracts in Dublin. We've ourselves to thank for the terms we took. So what are we grousing for?"

"I'd no notion of the difference in costs. Did you?"

"Well, I'd some intimation of it. But I put it far back in my mind, I was that eager to see New York."

"I did the same thing," she admitted. "But instead of a feast day, here's our one day off in the week turned into a fast." She plucked a thread from his coat. "Why do you lie down with your coat on, Denny? There's more lint on you than there is on the blanket."

He got up and went through the motions of brushing himself. "If you'd part with that $20 you laid away, Peg, we could own the town tonight."

"What $20? Didn't I pay the rent with it?"

"Was that what you paid it with?"

"They weren't taking a smile on deposit, or a turn of the ankle . . ."

"All right, all right. I'd the notion you hid it, and paid it out of mine. You've done that to me before, you know, Peg—putting away for an emergency. An emergency? Ha! A catastrophe wouldn't pry it from you."

She threw her head back in impatience. "Just answer me this: didn't we owe the twenty out of yours to the stage manager?"

"We did and I intended to still. He's relatives living in Bronx, Brooklyn, and Ballyqueens, and us with no more here than my cousin Richard."

"What again was it Richard said when you rang him up, Denny?"

Denny paced the length of the room and back, mimicking Richard's voice: " 'We must go out to our supper together one night while you're here,' he says. 'I've no more than a bachelor apartment and it's no place to be bringing your bride.' "

"By that did he mean him taking us or us taking him out to the supper?"

"From what I remember of Richard, all we'd do is go hungry together. Peg, are you sure about paying back the twenty? I thought . . ."

"Yes, I'm sure. Was I to get a receipt from him?"

"It's only your temper makes me suspicious."

"It's the short temper goes with the long appetite."

"That settles it." He snatched his hat from the dresser. "I'm going to have a look at Richard and his bachelor apartment. If there's a breath of prosperity about him, I'm going to claim an early inheritance."

"What am I to do while you're gone?"

He tossed his wallet on the bed beside her. "Here. There's 50 cents in it and a St. Christopher's medal. If I'm not back in an hour, eat on the one and pray on the other."

"Don't do anything desperate, Denny," she called as he reached the door. "And give me a kiss to sustain me."

"It's me that'll need sustaining. Amn't I leaving you the 50 cents?" But he gathered her into his arms.

"We'll both have nourishment from that," she whispered after the kiss. "And Denny, remember, our troubles are no more than'll be behind us when this day is over."

"Or ahead of us till we get on the boat again."

A few minutes later he was halfway across town, shortening the distance between the West Fifties and the East Fifties in long determined strides. It was warmer outdoors than it was in the hotel, which was the way of a late October afternoon, he thought. To staple his courage at its peak he recalled his own boyhood and his cousin Richard's. They were of an age, and the one woman raised them both, Denny's mother, for Richard's passed away when he was an infant. He reminded himself of the shoes that were bought for Richard when he got a pair, and the chop that was slivered in two when there was but one on the table. That was no more than fair in a charitable house, he thought. But Richard's behavior in manhood was small thanks for it. He shipped on the first boat he could for America, and thereafter sent word but no evidence of his success, while Denny divided his actor's pittance between the old lady and his own dreams.

His small confidence in Richard rose when he reached the block of the address. It fell again when he saw the side of the street Richard lived on. He climbed the steps of the dilapidated brownstone and watched an overdressed and overweight woman come from the rear of the hall in answer to his ring. It wasn't a bachelor apartment that one ran, he thought.

"Is Mr. Tully at home, madame?" he asked. "Mr. Richard Tully."

She let the door swing open, presumably for him to enter, and went to the stairs. "Dick?" she called out like a harbor whistle. "Dicky Boy!"

There was no answer from the dim passageway above, only a board creaking in a building that might have trembled with the trot of a mouse across the floor.

"It's no sign he's not there, not answering me," she said, turning around on Denny. "What is it you want with him?"

"No more than a civil word," Denny said. "I'm his cousin from Ireland."

She grunted. "Number Eight at the rear." Without waiting to see him up she waddled out of sight, the lamp jingling as she passed the table on which it stood.

Denny climbed the stairs two at a time. In the upstairs hall there was the smell of dust and disinfectant, and only enough light from a wall fixture to be reflected on the tarnished numerals. He knocked at Number Eight, and then called out his cousin's name. His own voice bounced back at him. He thought himself a fool then to expect that any man would stay in a place like this when he could be out of it. Since nothing stirred within or without, he tried the door. It opened as though it recognized him.

The whole feeling of Richard came back to him when he touched the wall switch and saw the room. For all its tacky furnishings it was as neat as a star, and he could hear his mother's pleading with him as he had heard it so often as a boy: "Denny, just look at Richard's room. Couldn't you take a page from his book and gather your things in a piece?"

"To hell with Richard's room," he said aloud and

laughed at his childishness. He moved from one piece to the next trying to feel comfortable and thinking about what he should say at that moment if Richard walked in—or anyone else for that matter. There was only one reason to leave a door open: you were expecting someone who hadn't a key. "I'm just leaving," he said, testing the words. "I'm looking for a scrap of paper to leave Richard a note."

With that intention he went to the one table in the room with a drawer in it and drew it open. He found a writing tablet and a stub of a pencil. Flipping open the cover of the tablet, he found a note already on the first page, and in the neat round letters Richard had mastered while he was making O's the shape of raisins.

With no other thought save that it might reveal the hour of Richard's return, Denny read the note. Indeed, he had read it before he had time for intentions:

> *Jimmie*
> *Sweet William in the second*
> > *Dick*

Well, he thought: there's small change in Richard. He had come to America on a horse—a 40-to-1 shot in the Grand National, and without so much as paying back the pound he had borrowed to put on her nose.

He was about to tear a back sheet from the tablet when something fluttered from between the pages. Fascinated, he watched it waft to the floor: a $20 bill.

In an instant he blessed temptation and pocketed the money. He grabbed the pencil and scribbled:

> *Dear Richard*
> *I'll be home ahead of Sweet William. But*
> *don't wait up for me or the twenty.*
> > *Your cousin,*
> > *Poor Dennis*

He reached the street without sight or protest of the landlady. Striding across Manhattan again he began to

think of how he would explain to Peg. She did not know
Richard, and was therefore entitled to her qualms. Altogether, he decided, his best chance would be if she had
not tempered her hunger. He had not been gone the hour
yet.

When he reached Eighth Avenue and turned down it
toward the hotel, he found himself heading straight into a
man who seemed to have no more power to avoid their
colliding than he did. They dodged and swayed as though
one was the mirror to the other until they were noses
apart. Even their recognition of each other was simulta-
neous.

"Dennis!"

"Richard!"

"How the hell are you?" cried Richard.

"Were you visiting us?" Denny asked, thinking of
more than his health.

"I stopped by for a minute's palaver with your lovely
lady." He nudged Denny with his elbow. "Ah, laddie,
you must've plucked her from the very top of the tree."
Denny began to think of the fun it would be to treat
Richard on his own $20. Before he got the invitation out,
however, his cousin added: "Well, I must be off till the
next time. I'm in a terrible rush to see a man on a transac-
tion."

You'll be in a greater rush after seeing him, Denny
thought, but he said: "You'll be getting in touch with us
Richard."

"Oh, I will that. Or you with me, Dennis. Good day to
you. And welcome to New York."

Denny watched him hurry out of sight, and then quickened his own pace. New York was half the size of
Dublin, he thought, for all its population. He tipped his
hat to an old lady selling flowers at the hotel entry and
gathered his thoughts again to the persuasion of Peg on
the twenty. He was halfway through the lobby when it
occurred to him that she would be easier persuaded if the
money were not in one piece, and a flower for her hair

would ease the introduction. He turned around and
started back to the door. But the old flower woman was
not likely to have that much change. He swung across the
lobby to the cigar stand and asked the clerk to break down
a $20 note for him.

The clerk snickered. "It's a bill," he said. "In this
country, my friend, you call it a $20 bill."

"Bill," Denny mused aloud, fondling the crisp money
for an instant. "Sweet William."

Before the clerk took the money from his hand, Denny
felt a hard clap on his shoulder.

"Come into the manager's office, buddy."

He stuck the money in his pocket and swung around on
the man who had spoken.

"Come quiet unless you want to be carted," he added
flatly.

Looking up at him, Denny realized his muscles were
as thick as his brogue and he had never heard one thicker
in Ireland. He did as he was told. In that small office, he
was almost in a chair when the big man yanked him up
again.

"Let's have your identification."

"Let's have yours," Denny said, trying for boldness.

"I'm the house detective," the big one roared glaring
at him angrily.

Denny shook himself free. "What the hell is this all
about? I'm with the Irish Players here on a visit."

"Isn't that lovely. You're an actor, are you?"

"I am."

"Then let's see you act. Gimme your wallet."

"It's upstairs with my wife. Keep your fist out of my
pocket."

"I'll put it down your throat in a minute. You're a fine
credit to Ireland." He pulled the bill from Denny's
pocket.

"That's mine," Denny cried.

"Is it now? All that money on an actor." He picked up
the phone on the desk. "Gimme the woman who put in

the complaint.'' He looked Denny over with contempt.
''They're raising the fine ones over there now, for all
they're learning them Gaelic.''

Denny stared at the $20 as the detective pressed it
smooth on the desk. ''Madame,'' he said into the phone,
''I've got him and your $20.''

Denny's heart leaped at the sound of her voice. Even
from where he sat he could hear the fine, crooning lilt of
it: ''That was wonderful quick, officer. Just take the
twenty off him for me and let him go.''

Peg called into the phone as though she were trying for
an echo across the hills. The detective had to hold the instrument at near arm's length. But he brought it up quick
to say: ''It isn't that easy, ma'am. You'll have to identify
him. Come down now to the office.''

''Will it take long?'' Peg crooned. ''My husband'll
soon be home, and I'd as soon he didn't know. It's his
family, you know.''

So, Denny thought, Richard had more with Peg than
palaver.

The detective was as soft as butter with her. ''There's
a rogue in my wife's family, too,'' he purred, ''but I
never cast it up to her though it was me turned him in.''
He hung up the phone and glowered at Denny. ''A nice
little girl like that. You're the fine bucko.''

Denny sat very still and thought about it all until Peg
arrived. She looked from one to the other of the men,
speechless.

''Well?'' the detective demanded.

''That's my husband,'' she burst out.

For only a second did the detective waver. He fitted
the tips of his fingers together as he added one thing to
another. His face lengthened in sympathy. ''You can
thank your stars you found him out before you had a
string of childer' to worry about.''

''You don't understand,'' Peg said.

The detective threw his arms in the air. ''Didn't you
tell me he threatened you? Didn't you say he promised to

stand up in the Crown Theatre and proclaim you a wanton woman if you didn't cough up?"

"Yes, but . . ."

"And didn't you say he was mad to match a twenty he'd lost on a horse?"

"That was his cousin Richard said that," Peg cried.

Denny grinned, having the gist of it. Sweet William had run and lost early, but whoever was collecting from Richard was late on his rounds.

The detective smashed his fist down on the desk. "But this is the one I caught placing the bet! Right out there." He waved his hand toward the lobby. "Sweet William,' he says, holding out the twenty and I nabbed him."

"Hold on a minute," Denny shouted. "Sweet William ran in the second race. What would I be doing betting on a horse already in the pasture?"

"There! That's what I'm trying to tell you," the detective triumphantly cried. "They were in it together!"

"Oh," Peg said, after a second, a look of great understanding lighting her face. "They were in it together, were they? What mischief, the two of them."

What mischief indeed, Denny thought. "I was not placing a bet," he said with great deliberateness. "I wouldn't know a bookmaker from a cobbler in this country. I was getting change of the twenty."

"And where, love, did you get the twenty?" said Peg. As though she could be persuaded now. "I shook it out of Richard."

"After he shook down your wife for it," the detective put in harshly.

"She was a hell of a lot more shakeable for him than ever she was for me then," Denny shouted. He turned on the big man and faced up to him. "Since you're so set on patching us up, let me ask you a question: who carries the purse in your house?"

The detective's mouth fell open. "My wife Norah does," he said in no more than a whisper.

"And I suppose your pockets are bulging?"

The detective smiled wanly. "The sad truth is, she's so tight she could squeeze a ha'penny out of a mouse."

Peg reached for the money, but Denny clamped his hand over it first. "I've earned this twice," he said. "I want to spend it before I've got to go out and earn it over again."

Peg threw her head back. "I suppose we're treating Richard on it, too, since he was such a help to you getting it out of me?"

"No," Denny said, "but you might say we're treating each other."

"That was a mean prank," Peg said. "I'd never've suspected you of conspiring like that, Denny."

"Nor did I think you'd tell me the story you did, love, of paying the rent with it."

" 'Twas just for today, dear, to save the money. Tomorrow I'd have told you the truth."

"Then tomorrow I'll tell it to you," said Denny. "Tonight we'll celebrate the conspiracy."

1953

Backward, Turn Backward

Sheriff Andrew Willets stood at the living-room window and watched his deputies herd back from the lawn another surge of the curious, restive people of Pottersville. Some had started out from their houses, shops, or gardens at the first sound of his siren, and throughout the long morning the crowd had swelled, winnowed out, and then swelled again.

Behind him in the kitchen, from which the body of Matt Thompson had been recently removed, the technical crew of the state police were at work with microscope and camera, ultraviolet lamp and vacuum cleaner. He had full confidence in them but grave doubts that their findings would add much weight to, or counterbalance by much, the spoken testimony against Phil Canby. They had not waited, some of those outside, to give it to police or state's attorney; they passed it to one another, neighbor to stranger, stranger sometimes back again to neighbor.

It was possible to disperse them, the sheriff thought, just as a swarm of flies might be waved from carrion; but they would as quickly collect again, unless it were possible to undo murder—unless it were possible to go out and say to them: "It's all a mistake. Matt Thompson fell and hit his head. His daughter Sue got hysterical when she

54

found him . . ." Idle conjecture. Even had he been able
to say that to the crowd they would not have dispersed.
They would not have believed it. Too many of them were
now convinced that they had been expecting something
like this to happen.

There was one person in their midst responsible in
large measure for this consensus, a lifetime neighbor of
both families, Mrs. Mary Lyons, and she was prepared
also to give evidence that Phil Canby was not at home
with his grandson the night before, at the hour he swore
he was at home and asleep.

Sheriff Willets went outdoors, collected Mrs. Lyons,
and led her across the yard between the Thompson house
and the house where Phil Canby lived with his daughter
and son-in-law, and up her own back steps. From the
flounce of her skirts and the clack of her heels he could
tell she didn't want to come. She smiled when she looked
up at him, a quick smile in which her eyes had no part.

"I hope this won't take long, Andy," she said when
he deliberately sat down, forcing her hospitality. "I
should give the poor girl a hand."

"In what way, Mrs. Lyons?"

"With the house," she said, as though there would be
nothing unusual in her helping Sue Thompson with the
house. "It must be a terrible mess."

"You've got lots of time," he said. "There's nobody
going to be in that house for quite a while except the police."

Mrs. Lyons made a noise in her throat, a sort of moan,
to indicate how pained she was at what had happened
across her back yard.

"You were saying over there," Willets went on, "that
you knew something terrible was going to happen."

"Something terrible did happen, even before this,"
she said, "Phil Canby taking after that girl. Sue Thompson's younger than his own daughter."

"Just what do you mean, taking after her?"

"I saw him kiss her," she said. Then, as though it had

hurt her to say it in the first place, she forced herself to be explicit. "A week ago last night I saw Phil Canby take Sue in his arms and kiss her. He's over sixty, Andy."

"He's fifty-nine," the sheriff said, wondering immediately what difference a year or two made, and why he felt it necessary to defend the man in the presence of this woman. It was not that he was defending Canby, he realized; he was defending himself against the influence of a prejudiced witness. "And he gave it out the next day that he was going to marry her, and she gave it out she was going to marry him. At least, that's the way I heard it."

"Oh, you heard it right," Mrs. Lyons said airily, folding her hands in her lap.

If it had been of her doing, he should not have heard it right, the sheriff thought. But Phil Canby had passed the age in life, and had lived too much of that life across the hedge from Mary Lyons, to be either preprecipitated into something or forestalled from it by her opinions. Had he looked up on the night he proposed to Sue Thompson and seen her staring in the window at them, likely the most he would have done would be to pull the windowshade in her face.

"Would you like your daughter to marry a man of fifty-nine, Andy?"

"My daughter's only fifteen," the sheriff said, knowing the answer to be stupid as soon as he had made it. He was no match for her, and what he feared was that he would be no match for the town, with her sentiments carrying through it as they now were carrying through the crowd across the way. They would want Phil Canby punished for courting a young girl, whatever Canby's involvement in her father's murder. "How old is Sue Thompson, Mrs. Lyons?"

"Nineteen, she must be. Her mother died giving birth to her the year after I lost Jimmie."

"I remember about Jimmie," the sheriff said, with relief. Remembering that Mary Lyons had lost a boy of four made her more tolerable. He wondered now how close she had got to Matt Thompson when his wife died. Nobody had been close to him from then on that Willets could remember. He had been as sour a man as ever gave the devil credence. A gardener by trade, Thompson had worked for the town of Pottersville, tending its landscape. A lot of people said that whatever tenderness he had went into the care of his flowers. One thing was agreed upon by all of them, it didn't go into the care of his daughter. As he thought about it now, Willets caught a forlorn picture from memory: Sue as a child of five or six trotting to church at her father's side, stopping when he stopped, going on when he went on, catching at his coattail when she needed balance but never at his hand, because it was not offered to her. Would no one but himself remember these things now?

"How long has it been since you were in the Thompson house, Mrs. Lyons?"

Her eyes narrowed while she weighed his purpose in asking it. "I haven't been in the house in fifteen years," she said finally.

He believed her. It accounted in part for her eagerness to get into it now. "She isn't much of a housekeeper, Sue," he said, to whet her curiosity further and to satisfy his own on what she knew of her neighbors. "Or maybe that's the way Matt Thompson wanted it."

She leaned forward. "What way?"

"It has a funny dead look about it," he said. "It's not dirty, but it just looks like nothing has been put in or taken out in fifteen years."

"He never got over his wife's death," Mrs. Lyons said, "and he never looked at another woman."

Her kind had no higher praise for any man, he thought. "Who took care of Sue when she was a baby?"

"Her father."

"And when he was working?"

"I don't know."

"From what I've heard," he lied, for he had not yet had the opportunity to inquire elsewhere, "you were very good to them, and so was Phil Canby's wife in those days.''

"Mrs. Canby was already ailing then," she snapped. "I was good to both families, if I say it myself."

"And if you don't," the sheriff murmured, "nobody else will."

"What?"

"People have a way of being ungrateful," he explained.

"Indeed they do."

"You know, Mrs. Lyons, thinking about it now, I wonder why Matt Thompson didn't offer Sue for adoption."

"You might say he did to me once." A bit of color tinged her bleached face after the quick, proud answer. She had probably been at the Thompson house night and day then with solicitudes and soups, when Matt was home and when he wasn't home.

Assuming Thompson to have been sarcastic with her—and he had had a reputation for sarcasm even that far back—the sheriff said: "Would you have taken the child? You must've been lonesome . . . after Jimmie."

For once she was candid with him, and soft as he had not known her to be since her youth. "I'd have thought a good deal about it. I had a feeling there was something wrong with her. She was like a little old maid, all to herself. She's been like that all her life—even in school, they say."

"It makes you understand why she was willing to marry Phil Canby," the sheriff said quietly. "Don't it?"

"Oh, I don't blame her," Mrs. Lyons said. "This is one case where I don't blame the woman."

Willets sighed. Nothing would shake her belief that there was something immoral in Phil Canby's having proposed marriage to a girl younger than his own daughter. "Last night," he said, "your husband was away from home?"

"He was at the Elks' meeting. I was over at my sister's

and then I came home about 10:30. I looked at the clock. I always do. It takes me longer to walk home than it used to.''

''And that was when you heard the baby crying?''

''It was crying when I came up the back steps.''

Phil Canby had been baby-sitting with his grandson while his daughter, Betty, and his son-in-law, John Murray, were at the movies. It was his custom to stay with young Philip every Thursday night, and sometimes oftener, because he lived with them; but on Thursdays Betty and her husband usually went to the movies.

''And you're sure it was the Murray baby?''

''Who else's would it be over that way? I couldn't hear the Brady child from here. They're five houses down.''

The sheriff nodded. Phil Canby swore that he was in bed and asleep by that time, and he swore that the baby had not cried. He was a light sleeper, in the habit of waking up if little Philip so much as whimpered. The neighbors to the south of the Murray house had not heard the crying, nor for that matter the radio in the Murray house, which Canby said he had turned on at 10 o'clock for the news. But they had been watching television steadily until 11:30. By that time the Murrays had come home and found Phil and the baby Philip each asleep in his own bed.

But to the north of the Murrays, in the corner house where Sue Thompson claimed she was asleep upstairs, her father Matt had been bludgeoned to death some time between 10 o'clock and midnight.

''And you didn't hear anything else?'' the sheriff asked.

''No, but then I didn't listen. I thought maybe the baby was sick and I was on the point of going down. Then I remembered it was Thursday night and Mr. Canby would be sitting with him. He wouldn't take the time of day from me.''

Not now he wouldn't, the sheriff thought. ''Have you any idea how long the baby was crying, Mrs. Lyons?''

"I was getting into bed when he stopped. That was fifteen minutes later maybe. I never heard him like that before, rasping like for breath. I don't know how long the poor thing was crying before I got home."

If Phil Canby had murdered Matt Thompson and then reached home by a quarter to 11, he would have had time to quiet baby Philip and to make at least a pretense of sleep himself before his family came home. Betty Murray admitted that her father was in the habit of feigning sleep a good deal these days, his waking presence was so much of an embarrassment to all of them. Scarcely relevant except as practiced art.

Willets took his leave of Mrs. Lyons. What seemed too relevant to be true, he thought, striding over the hedge which separated her yard from the Thompsons's, was that Phil Canby admitted quarreling with Thompson at 9 o'clock that night, and in the Thompson kitchen.

After the first exchange of violent words between the two households, when Phil Canby and Sue Thompson made known their intentions of marriage, an uneasy, watchful quiet had fallen between them. Sue Thompson had not been out of the house except with her father, and then to Sunday prayer meeting. Matt Thompson had started his vacation the morning his daughter told him. Vacation or retirement: he had put the hasty choice up to the town supervisor. Thompson then had gone across to Betty Murray. He had never been in Betty's house before, not once during her mother's long illness or at her funeral; and if he had spoken to Betty as a child, she could not remember it. But that morning he spoke to her as a woman, and in such a manner and with such words that she screamed at him: "My father is not a lecher!" To which he had said: "And my daughter is not a whore. Before she takes to the bed of an old man, I'll shackle her!" When John Murray came home from the office that night and heard of it, he swore that he would kill Matt Thompson if ever again he loosed his foul tongue in Betty's presence.

But Matt Thompson had gone into his house and pulled down all the shades on the Murray side, and Phil Canby had gone about the trade he had pursued in Pottersville since boyhood. He was a plumber, and busier that week for all the talk about him in the town. All this the sheriff got in bits and pieces, mostly from Betty Murray. When Thursday night had come around again, she told him, she felt that she wanted to get out of the house. Also, she had begun to feel that if they all ignored the matter, the substance of it might die away.

So she and John had gone to the movies, leaving her father to sit with the baby. About 8:30, Sue Thompson had come into the yard and called to Phil. He went out to her. She had asked him to come over and fix the drain to the kitchen sink. Her father was sleeping, she told him, but he had said it would be all right to ask him. Canby had gone back into the house for his tools and then had followed her into the Thompson house, carrying a large plumber's wrench in his hand. When Phil Canby had told this to the sheriff that morning—as frankly, openly, as he spoke of the quarrel between himself and Thompson, a quarrel so violent that Sue hid in the pantry through it—Willets got the uncanny feeling that he had heard it all before and that he might expect at the end of the recitation as candid and calm a confession of murder.

But Canby had not confessed to the murder. He had taken alarm, he said, when Matt Thompson swore by his dead wife to have him apprehended by the state and examined as a mental case. He knew the man to do it, Thompson had said, and Canby knew the man of whom he spoke: Alvin Rhodes, the retired head of the state hospital for the insane. Thompson had landscaped Rhodes's place on his own time when Rhodes retired, borrowing a few shrubs from the Pottersville nursery to do it. This the sheriff knew. And he could understand the extent of Canby's alarm when Canby told about the confinement of a friend on the certification of his children, and on no more grounds apparent to Canby than that the man had become cantankerous, and jealous of the house which he had built himself and in which he was becoming, as he grew older, more and more of an unwelcome guest. Phil Canby had bought the house in which he now lived with his daughter. He had paid for it over 30 years, having had to add another mortgage during his wife's invalidism. Unlike his friend, he did not feel a stranger in it. The baby had even been named after him, but he was well aware the tax his wooing of Sue Thompson put upon his daughter and her husband.

All this the sheriff could understand very well. The difficulty was to reconcile it with the facts of the crime. For example, when Canby left the Thompson house, he took with him all his tools save the large wrench with which Thompson was murdered. Why leave it then—or later—except that to have taken it from beside the murdered man and to have had it found in his possession (or without it when its ownership was known) was to leave no doubt at all as to the murderer? All Canby would say was that he had forgotten it.

Willets went to the back door of Canby's house. He knocked, and Betty Murray called out to him to come in. Little Philip was in his high chair, resisting the apple sauce his mother was trying to spoon into him. The sheriff stood a moment watching the child, marveling at the normalcy which persists through any crisis when there is a baby about. Every blob of sauce spilled on the tray Philip tried to shove to the floor. What he couldn't get off the tray with his hands he went after with his tongue.

The sheriff grinned. "That's one way to get it into him."

"He's at that age now," his mother said, cleaning up the floor. She looked at Willets. "But I'm very grateful for him, especially now."

The sheriff nodded. "I know," he said. "Where's your father?"

"Up in his room."

"And the Thompson girl?"

"In the living room. Sheriff, you're not going to take them . . ."

"Not yet," he said, saving her the pain of finishing the sentence. He started for the inside door and paused. "I think Mrs. Lyons would be willing to have her there for a bit."

"I'll bet she would," Betty said. "I had to close the front windows, with people gaping in to see her. Some of them, and they weren't strangers either, kept asking . . . where her boy friend was."

"It won't be for long," Willets said; and then because he had not quite meant that, he added: "It won't be this way for long."

"Then let her stay. I think she feels better here, poor thing, just knowing Papa's in the house." She got up then and came to him. She was a pretty girl and, like her father's, her eyes seemed darker when they were troubled. "Mr. Willets, I was talking to Papa a while ago. He was trying to tell me about . . . him and Sue. He told her when he asked her to marry him that he was going to be as much a father to her . . . as a husband." Betty colored a bit. "As a lover," she corrected. "That's what he really said."

"And did he tell you what she had to say to that?"

"She said that's what she wanted because she'd never had either one."

The sheriff nodded at the obvious truth in that.

"I thought I'd tell you," Betty went on, "because I know what everybody says about Papa and her. They think he's peculiar. Almost like what I told you Matt Thompson said. And he's not. All the time mother was sick, until she died, he took care of her himself. He even sent me away to school. Most men would have said that was my job, and maybe it was, but I was terribly glad to go. Then when mother died, and I got married, it must have seemed as though . . . something ended for him. And fifty-nine isn't really very old."

"Not very," Willets said, being so much closer to it than she was.

"I'm beginning to understand what happened to him," Betty said. "I wish I'd thought about it sooner. There might have been something . . . somebody else."

The sheriff shook his head. "That's a man's own problem till he's dead."

"You're right," she said after a moment. "That's what really would have been indecent."

The sheriff nodded.

"I wish it was possible to separate the two things," Betty said as he was leaving, "him and Sue—and Mr. Thompson's murder. I wish to God it was."

"So do I," the sheriff said, thinking again of the pressures that would be put upon him because it was not possible to separate them, not only by the townspeople but by the state's attorney, who would find it so much more favorable to prosecute a murderer in a climate of moral indignation.

On the stairway, with its clear view of the living room, he paused to watch Sue Thompson for a moment, unobserved. She was sitting with a piece of crochet work in her lap at which she stitched with scarcely a glance. Whatever her feelings, the sheriff thought, she was not grieving. She had the attitude of waiting. All her life she had probably waited—but for what? Her father's death? A dream lover? A rescuer? Surely her girlish dreams had not conjured up Phil Canby in that role. The strange part of it was that it seemed unlikely to the sheriff she had dreamed of rescue at all. However she felt about her father, she did not fear him. Had she been afraid of him, she could not have announced to him that she intended to marry Phil Canby. And because she was not afraid of him, Willets decided, it was difficult to imagine that she might have killed him. She was a soft, plump girl, docile-eyed, and no match for her father physically. Yet she was the one alternate to Phil Canby in the deed, and he was the only one who knew her well enough to say if she was capable of it.

The sheriff went on and knocked at Canby's door. "I've got to talk to you some more, Phil."

Canby was lying on the bed staring at the ceiling. "I've told you all I know," he said, without moving.

The sheriff sat down in the rocker by the open window. The radio, which Canby claimed to have been listening to at 10 o'clock the night before, was on a table closer to the window; and across the way, no more than fifteen yards, the neighbors had not heard it.

"Mrs. Lyons says that little Philip was crying at 10:30 last night, Phil."

"Mrs. Lyons is a liar," Canby said, still without rising. His thin gray hair was plastered to his head with sweat and yet he lay on his back where no breeze could reach him. A pulse began to throb at his temple. The skin over it was tight and pale; it reminded Willets of a frog's throat.

"Betty admits you didn't change the baby. That wasn't like you, Phil, neglecting him."

"He was sleeping. I didn't want him to wake up. I had to think of my plans."

"What plans?"

"My marriage plans."

"What were they?"

Finally Canby rose and swung his slippered feet over the side of the bed. He looked at Willets. "We're going to be married in Beachwood." It was a village a few miles away. "I've got a house picked out on the highway and I'll open a shop in front of it."

It was fantastic, Willets thought: both Canby and the girl behaved as though they were not in any way suspected of Matt Thompson's death—as though nothing in the past should interfere with the future. This angered Willets as nothing save Mrs. Lyons's judgments had. "You're in trouble, Phil, and you're going to hang

higher than your fancy plans if you don't get out of it.
The whole damn town's against you.''

''I know that,'' Canby said. ''That's why I'm not
afraid.''

The sheriff looked at him.

''If I didn't know what everybody was saying,''
Canby went on, ''I wouldn't have run off home last night
when Matt Thompson said he was going to get me certified.''

''Phil,'' the sheriff said with great deliberateness,
''the state's attorney will maintain that's why you *didn't*
run home, why you *weren't* in this house to hear the baby
crying, you *weren't* home in time to change him, why
you *can't* admit Mrs. Lyons heard Philip crying! Because, he'll say, you were over in the Thompson kitchen,
doing murder and cleaning up after murder.''

Canby was shaking his head. ''That baby don't cry.
He don't ever cry with me around.''

The sheriff got up and walked the length of the room
and back, noting that Phil Canby was careful in his
things, their arrangement, their repair. He was a tidy
man. ''You're still planning to marry her, then?'' he said
when he reached Canby.

''Of course. Why shouldn't I?''

The sheriff leaned down until he was face to face with
the man. ''Phil, who do *you* think killed her father?''

Canby drew back from him, his eyes darkening. ''I
don't know,'' he said, ''and I guess I never rightly cared
. . . till now.''

Willets returned to the rocker and took a pipe from his
shirt pocket. He didn't light it; he merely held it in his
hand as though he might light it if they could talk together. ''When did you fall in love with Sue Thompson?''

Canby smoothed the crumpled spread. ''Sounds
funny, saying that about somebody my age, don't it?''
Willets didn't answer and Canby went on: ''I don't
know. Whatever it was, it happened last spring. She used

to stop by ever since she was a little girl, when I was out working in the yard, and watch me. Never said much. Just watched. Then when little Philip came, she used to like to see him. Sometimes I'd invite her in. If I was alone she'd come. Kind of shy of Betty, and whenever John'd speak to her she'd blush. John don't have a good opinion of her. He's like all the young fellows nowadays. They look at a girl's ankles, how she dances, what clothes she puts on. It's pure luck if they get a decent wife, what they look for in a girl . . ."

"You and Sue," the sheriff prompted, when Canby paused.

"Well. I was holding Philip one night and she was watching. He was puckering up to cry, so I rocked him to and fro and he just went off to sleep in my arms. I remember her saying, 'I wish I could do that,' so I offered her the baby. She was kind of scared of it." The man sank back on his elbows and squinted a bit, remembering. "It struck me then all of a sudden how doggone rotten a life Matt had given her as a kid."

"How, rotten?" the sheriff said.

"Nothing. No affection, no love at all. He bought her what she needed, but that was all. She was in high school before she knew people was different, what it was like to . . . to hold hands even."

"I wonder what got into him," Willets said. "Most men, losing a wife like he did, would put everything into the kid till they got another woman."

"He didn't want another woman. He liked his hurt till it got to mean more to him than anything el   "

The sheriff shook his head. It might be so, although he could not understand it. "Go on about you and Sue," he said.

Canby took a moment to bring himself back to the contemplation of it. He sat up so that he could illustrate with his hands, the strong, calloused, black-nailed hands. "I put Philip into his cradle and she was standing there and I just sort of put out my arms to her like she was maybe a little girl which'd lost something or was hurt, and she came to me." He paused, moistened his lips, and then plunged on. "While I was holding her . . . Oh, Jesus, what was it happened then?"

He sprang up from the bed and walked, his hands behind his back. "I thought that was all over for me. I hadn't felt nothing like it, not for years." He turned and looked down at Willets. "I was young again, that's all, and she wasn't a little girl. I was ashamed at first, and then I thought—what am I ashamed of? Being a man? I waited all summer thinking maybe it'd go away. But it didn't. It just got inside me deeper and quieter so's I wasn't afraid of it, and I wasn't ashamed. And when I asked her and she was willing to marry me, I explained to her that it couldn't be for long because I'm fifty-nine, but she didn't care." He opened his hands as if to show they were empty. "That's how it was, Andy. That's how. I can't explain it any more than that."

"That's how it was," the sheriff repeated, getting up, "but look how it is right now."

Willets went downstairs to Sue Thompson where she still sat, crochet work in hand, a bit back from the window yet with the people outside within her view.

"Know any of those folks, Miss Thompson?"

"No," she said, "I don't think I do."

He could believe that, although some of them had lived in the neighborhood all her lifetime. He sat down opposite her so that the light would be in her face. "Last night, Miss Thompson, why did you tell Mr. Canby your father said it would be all right to ask him to fix the drain?"

"Because I wanted him to come over. It was the only excuse I could think of."

"Your father didn't say it would be all right?"

"No."

"Didn't you expect trouble between them?"

"I didn't think my father would wake up."

"I see," the sheriff said. A pair, the two of them, he

thought, unless their guilt was black as night; one as naïve as the other. The marks of Canby's wrench were on the drainpipe where he had actually commenced to work. "When did you and Mr. Canby expect to be married?"

"Soon. Whenever he said."

"Were you making plans?"

"Oh, yes," she said, smiling then. "I've been doing a lot of work." She held up the crocheting by way of illustration.

"Didn't you expect your father to interfere—in fact, to prevent it?"

"No," she said.

The sheriff rested his chin upon his hand and looked at her. "Miss Thompson, I'm the sheriff of this county. Your father was murdered last night, and I'm going to find out why, and who murdered him. You'd better tell me the truth."

"I'm telling you the truth, Mr. Willets. I know who you are."

"And you didn't expect your father to interfere with your marriage?"

"He never interfered with anything I did," she said.

"Did you know he told Betty Murray that he would chain you up rather than see you marry her father?"

"I didn't know that. He never said it to me."

"Just what did he say when you told him?"

"He laughed. I think he said something like, 'Well, doesn't that beat everything.' "

The sheriff sat up. "He was treating you like a halfwit. You're an intelligent girl. Didn't you resent it?"

"Of course," she said, as though surprised that he should ask. "That's one reason why I'm so fond of Phil . . . Mr. Canby."

"You resented it," Willets repeated, "and yet you did nothing about it?"

"I was waiting," she said.

"For what? For him to die? To be murdered?"

"No," she said, "just waiting."

"Have you always got everything you wanted by wait-ing, Miss Thompson?"

She thought about that for a moment. "Yes, I think I have . . . or else I didn't want it any more."

Passive resistance, that's what it amounted to, the sheriff thought. If nations could be worn down by it, Matt Thompson was not invulnerable. But his murder was not passive resistance. "Last night you hid in the pantry during the quarrel?"

"Yes. Phil told me to go away, so I hid in there."

"Did you hear what they were saying?"

"Not much. I put my fingers in my ears."

"What did you hear exactly?"

She looked at him and then away. "I heard my father say 'insane asylum.' That's when I put my fingers to my ears."

"Why?"

"I was there once with him when I was a little girl."

"Can you tell me about it?" the sheriff said.

"Yes," she said thoughtfully. "There was a man working for him in the garden. I liked him, I remember. He would tickle me and laugh just wonderful. When I told my father that I liked him, he took me inside to see the other people. Some of them screamed at us and I was frightened."

"I see," the sheriff said, seeing something of Matt Thompson and his use of the afflicted to alarm the timid. "Last night, when did you come out of the pantry?"

"When my father told me to. He said it was all over and I could go up to bed."

"And you did? No words with him about the quarrel?"

"I went upstairs and went to bed, like I told you this morning."

"And you went to sleep right away because you felt so badly," he said, repeating her earlier account of it. He could see how sleep must have been her salvation many times. She had slept soundly through the night, by her account, and had wakened only to the persistent knocking of Phil Canby—who, when he was about to start his day's work, had remembered, so he said, the plumber's wrench. Going downstairs to answer Canby's knocking, she had discovered her father's body.

The sheriff took his hat. "You can have the funeral tomorrow, Miss Thompson," he said. "I'd arrange it quickly if I were you, and see to it there's a notice of it in the paper."

He went out the front door and across the yard, ignoring the questions pelted at him from the crowd. The technician in charge of the state crew was waiting. "I don't have much for you, Willets. Whoever did the job scrubbed up that kitchen afterwards. But good."

"Canby's clothes?"

"Nothing from that job on them. We'll run some more tests to be dead sure if you want us to."

"I want you to. What about hers?"

"Not even a spot to test. I put them back in her room, night clothes and day clothes."

The sheriff thought for a moment. "What was the kitchen cleaned up with?"

"A bundle of rags. Left in the sink. They came out of a bag hanging beside the stove."

"Handy," the sheriff said, and went upstairs.

After the male sparsity and drabness in the rest of the house—and that was how Willets thought of it, as though a woman's hand had not touched it in years—Sue's room screamed with color. Her whole life in the house was in this one room. There was crochet work and needlework of multi- and clashing colors, laces and linens, stacked piece on piece. She had fashioned herself a fancy lampshade that almost dripped with lace. At some time not too long before, she had tried her hand at painting, too. It was crude, primitive, and might very well be art for all he knew, but in his reckoning it was in contrast to the exact work of her needle. In a small rocker, left over from her childhood—perhaps even from her mother's childhood, by its shape and age—sat two dolls, faded and matted and one with an eye that would never close again. The dust of years was ground into them and he wondered if they had been sitting there while she grew into woman-hood, or if upon her recent courtship—if Phil Canby's at-tentions could be called that—she, a timid girl, and likely aware of her own ignorance, had taken them out to help her bridge the thoughts of marriage.

The bed was still unmade, Sue's pajamas lying on it. Not a button on the tops, he noticed, and the cloth torn out. The technician had put them back where he had found them. Her dress lay with its sleeves over the back of the chair, just as she had flung it on retiring. She had, no doubt, put on a fresh dress to go out to the fence and call Phil Canby. There was scarcely a crease in it. The sheriff trod upon her slippers, a button, a comb. The rug, as he looked at it, was dappled with colored thread from her sewing. Not the best of housekeepers, Sue Thomp-son, he thought, going downstairs and locking up the house; but small wonder, keeping house only for herself and in one room.

George Harris, the state's attorney, was in the sheriff's office when he returned to the county building. He didn't want to seem too eager, Willets thought, since obviously the sheriff had not yet made an arrest. He spoke of the murder as a tragedy and not a case, and thus no doubt he had spoken of it in town.

"I've had a lot of calls, Andy," he said, "a lot of calls."

The sheriff grunted. "Did you answer them?"

Harris ignored the flippancy. "Not enough evidence yet, eh?"

"I'm going to put it all together now," Willets said. "When I get it in a package I'll show it to you. Maybe in the morning."

"That's fine by me," Harris said. He started for the door and then turned back. "Andy, I'm not trying to tell you how to run your office, but if I were you, I'd call the

local radio station and give them a nice handout on it—
something good for the nerves.''

"Like what?"

"Oh, something to the effect that any suspect in the
matter is under police surveillance.''

He was right, of course, Willets thought. The very mention of such surveillance could temper would-be vigilantes.
He called the radio station and then worked through most of
the night. His last tour of duty took him past the two darkened houses where his deputies kept sullen vigil.

Fifty or so people attended the funeral service and as
many more were outside the chapel. Among them were
faces he had seen about the town most of his life. With
the murder they seemed to have become disembodied
from the people who clerked, drove delivery trucks, or
kept house. They watched him with the eyes of ghouls to
see how long it would take him to devour his prey.

The minister spoke more kindly of Matt Thompson
than his life deserved, but the clergyman had the whole
orbit of righteousness, frugality, and justice to explore
and, under the cricumstances and in the presence of those
attending, the word love to avoid.

Phil Canby stood beside the girl as tall as he could,
with the hard stoop of his trade upon his back. His head
was high, his face grim. Sue wept as did the other
women, one prompted by another's tears. Behind Canby
stood his daughter and his son-in-law, John Murray—
who, when the sheriff spoke to him at the chapel door,
said he had taken the day off to "see this thing finished."
It would be nice, Willets thought, if it could be finished
by John Murray's taking the day off.

When the final words were said, people shuffled about
uneasily. It was customary to take a last look at the deceased, but Matt Thompson's coffin remained unopened.
Then his daughter leaned forward and fumbled at a floral
wreath. Everyone watched. She caught one flower in her
hand and pulled it from the rest, nearly upsetting the

piece. She opened her hand and looked at the bloom. Willets glanced at Mrs. Lyons, who was on tiptoe watching the girl. She too was moved to tears by that. Then the girl looked up at the man beside her. If she did not smile, there was the promise of it in her round, blithe face. She offered him the flower. Phil Canby took it, but his face went as gray as the tie he wore. Mrs. Lyons let escape a hissing sound, as sure a condemnation as any words she might have cried aloud, and a murmur of wrathful shock went through the congregation. Willets stepped quickly to Canby's side and stayed beside him until they returned to the Murray house, outside which he then doubled the guard.

He went directly to the state's attorney's office, for George Harris had had the report on his investigation since 9 o'clock that morning.

"Everything go off all right?" Harris offered Willets a cigarette, shaking four or five out on the desk from the package. He was feeling expansive, the sheriff thought.

"Fine," he said, refusing the cigarette.

The attorney stacked the loose cigarettes. "I'll tell you the truth, Andy, I'm damned if I can see why you didn't bring him in last night." He patted the folder closest to him. It chanced to be the coroner's report. "You've done a fine job all the way. It's tight, neat."

"Maybe that's why I didn't bring him in," Willets said.

Harris cocked his head and smiled his inquisitiveness. At 45 he was still boyish, and he had the manner of always seeming to want to understand fully the other man's point of view. He would listen to it, weigh it, and change his tactics—but not his mind.

"Because," the sheriff said, "I haven't really gone outside their houses to look for a motive."

The attorney drummed his fingers on the file. "Tell me the God's truth, Andy, don't you think it's here?"

"Not all of it," the sheriff said doggedly.

"But the heart of it?"

"The heart of it's there," he admitted.

" 'All of it' to you means a confession. Some policemen might have got it. I don't blame you for that."

"Thanks," Willets said dryly. "I take it, Mr. Harris, you feel the case is strong against him?"

"I don't predict the outcome," the attorney said, his patience strained. "I prosecute and I take the verdict in good grace. I believe the state has a strong case, yes." He shrugged off his irritation. "Much hinges, I think, on whether Canby could feel secure from interruption while he did the job, and afterwards while he cleaned up."

Willets nodded.

Harris fingered through the folder and brought out a paper. "Here. The girl hid in the pantry when he told her to leave. She went upstairs to bed when her father told her to. Now I say that if she came downstairs again, all Canby had to do was tell her to go up again. She's the amenable type. Not bright, not stupid, just willing and obedient."

That from his documentation, Willets thought. If ever Harris had seen the girl it was by accident. "Then you think she was an accessory?" Certainly most people did now, having seen or heard of her conduct at the funeral.

The attorney pursed his lips. "I wouldn't pursue that right now. You haven't turned up anything to prove it. But he could feel secure about being able to send her upstairs again before she saw anything. That's what was important: that he could feel safe, secure. That's how I'd use it. Put that together with the Lyons woman's testimony and his own daughter's. No jury will take his word that he was home with his grandson between 10 and 11."

"Did he strip naked to do the job?" said Willets. "His clothes went through the lab."

"Old work clothes." The attorney looked him in the eyes. "There's been cleaner jobs than this before and I'll prove it. I don't expect to go in with the perfect case. There's no such thing."

"Then all I have to do," Willets said, "is get the warrant and bring him in."

"That's all. The rest is up to me." The sheriff had reached the door when Harris called after him. "Andy . . . I'm not the s.o.b. you seem to think I am. It's all in here." He indicated the file. "You'll see it yourself when you get to where you can have some perspective."

Harris might very well be right, the sheriff thought as he walked through the county court building. He had to accept it. Either Harris was right and he had done his job as sheriff to the best of his ability and without prejudice, making the facts stand out from sentiments . . . or he had to accept something that logic would not sanction: Sue Thompson as the murderer of her own father. That this amenable girl, as Harris called her, who by the very imperturbability of her disposition had managed a life for herself in the house of her father—that she, soft and slovenly, could do a neat and terrible job of murder, he could not believe. But even granting that she could have done it, could someone as emotionally untried as she withstand the strain of guilt? He doubted it. Such a strain would crack her, he thought, much as an overripe plum bursts while yet hanging on the tree.

But the motive, Canby's motive: it was there and it was not there, he thought. It was the thing which so far had restrained him from making the arrest—that, and his own stubborn refusal to be pressured by the followers of Mary Lyons.

The sheriff sat for some time at his desk, and then he telephoned Matt Thompson's friend, Alvin Rhodes. The appointment made, he drove out to see the former superintendent of the state hospital for the insane.

Rhodes, as affable as Thompson had been dour, told of Matt Thompson's visiting him the previous Wednesday, the day before his death. "We were not friends, Willets," the older man said, "although his visit implies that we were. He was seeking advice on his daughter's infatuation with a man three times her age."

As Thompson had grown more sullen with the years, the sheriff thought, Rhodes had mellowed into affability upon retirement. Such advice was not sought of someone uncongenial to the seeker. "And did you advise him, Mr. Rhodes?"

"I advised him to do nothing about it. I recounted my experience with men of Canby's age who were similarly afflicted. The closer they came to consummation, shall we say, the more they feared it. That's why the May and December affairs are rare indeed. I advised him to keep close watch on the girl, to forestall an elopement, and leave the rest to nature. In truth, Willets, although I did not say it to him, I felt that if they were determined, he could not prevent it."

"He cared so little for the girl," Willets said, "I wonder why he interfered at all. Why not let her go and good riddance?"

Rhodes drew his white brows together while he phrased the words carefully. "Because as long as he kept her in the house, he could atone for having begot her, and in those terms for having caused his wife's death." Willets shook his head. Rhodes added then: "I told him frankly that if anyone in the family should be examined, it was he and not the girl."

Willets felt the shock like a blow. "The girl?"

Rhodes nodded. "That's why he came to me, to explore the possibility of confining her—temporarily. In his distorted mind he calculated the stigma of such proceedings to be sufficient to discourage Canby."

And the threat of such proceedings, Willets thought, was sufficient to drive Canby to murder—as such threats against his own person were not. "I should think," he said, preparing to depart, "you might have taken steps against Matt Thompson yourself."

Rhodes rose with him. "I intended to," he said coldly. "If you consult the state's attorney, you will discover that I made an appointment with him for 2 o'clock yesterday afternoon. By then Thompson was dead. I shall give evidence when I am called upon.''

The sheriff returned to the courthouse and swore out the warrant before the county judge. At peace with his conscience at last, he drove again to the Murray house.

Betty Murray was staring out boldly at the watchers who had reconvened—as boldly as they were again staring in at her.

There would be a time now, Willets thought, when they could stare their fill and feel righteous in their pre-judgment of the man. Only then would they be willing to judge the full story, only then would they be merciful, vindicating their vindictiveness. He ordered his deputies to clear the street. John Murray opened the door when the sheriff reached the steps.

''Better take Betty upstairs,'' Willets said to her husband. He could see the others in the living room, Sue and Phil Canby sitting at either ends of the couch, their hands touching as he came.

''The old man?'' John whispered. Willets nodded and Murray called to his wife. Betty looked at him over her shoulder but did not move from the window.

''You too, Miss Thompson,'' Willets said quietly. ''You both better go upstairs with John.''

Betty lifted her chin. ''I shall stay,'' she said. ''This is my father's house and I'll stay where I want to in it.''

Nor did Sue Thompson make any move to rise. Willets strode across to Canby. ''Get up,'' he said. ''I'm arrest-ing you, Phil Canby, for the willful murder of Matt Thompson.''

''I don't believe it,'' Betty said from behind them, her voice high, tremulous. ''If God's own angel stood here now and said it, I still wouldn't believe it.''

''Betty, Betty,'' her husband soothed, murmuring something about good lawyers.

Canby's eyes were cold and dark upon the sheriff. ''What's to become of her?'' he said, with a slight indi-cation of his head toward Sue.

"I don't know," Willets said. No one did, he thought, for she looked completely bemused, her eyes wide upon him as she tried to understand.

"You're taking him away?" she said as Canby rose. Willets nodded.

"It won't be for long," John Murray said in hollow comfort, and more to his wife than to the girl.

"Don't lie to her," Canby said. "If they can arrest me for something I didn't do, they can hang me for it." He turned to Willets. "If you're taking me, do it now."

"You can get some things if you want."

"I don't want no things."

Willets started to the door with him. Betty looked to her husband. He shook his head. She whirled around then on Sue Thompson. "Don't you understand? They're taking him to jail. Because of you, Sue Thompson!"

Canby stiffened at the door. "You leave her alone, Betty. Just leave her alone."

"I won't leave her alone and I won't leave Sheriff Willets alone. What's the matter with everyone? My father's not a murderer." Again she turned on Sue. "He's not! He's a good man. You've got to say it, too. We've got to shout it out at everybody, do you hear me?"

"Betty, leave her alone," her father repeated.

"Then get her out of here," John Murray said, his own fury rising with his helplessness. "She sits like a bloody cat and you don't know what's going on in her mind . . ."

The sheriff cut him off. "That's enough, John. It's no good." He looked at the girl. Her face was puckered up almost like an infant's about to cry. "You can go over home now, Miss Thompson. I'll send a deputy in to help you."

She did not answer. Instead she seemed convulsed with the effort to cry, although there was no sound to her apparent agony. Little choking noises came then. She made no move to cover her face and, as Willets watched, the face purpled in its distortion. All of them stared at her, themselves feeling straitened with the ache of tears they could not shed. Sue's body quivered and her face crinkled up still more, like a baby's.

Then the sound of crying came—a high, gurgling noise—and it carried with the very timbre and rasp of an infant's. Willets felt Phil Canby clutch his arm and he felt terror icing its way up his own spine; he heard a sick, fainting moan from Betty Murray between the girl's spasms, but he could not take his eyes from the sight. Nor could he move to help her. Sue hammered her clenched fists on her knees helplessly. Then she tried to get up, rocking from side to side. Finally she rolled over on the couch and, her backside in the air, pushed herself up as a very small child must. Her first steps were like a toddle when she turned and tried to balance herself. Then, catching up an ashstand which chanced to stand in her way, she ran headlong at Willets with it, the infantile screams tearing from her throat . . .

In time it would be told that Sue Thompson reverted to the infancy she coveted at least once before her attack on Willets, rising from sleep as a child on the night of her father's quarrel with Canby, ripping off her night clothes when she could not manage the buttons, and in a rage with her father—when, perhaps, he berated her for nudity, immodesty, or some such thing a child's mind cannot comprehend—attacking him with a child's fury and a frenzied adult's strength . . . using the weapon at hand, Phil Canby's wrench.

Sheriff Willets could document much of it when the sad horror had been manifest before him: the crying Mrs. Lyons heard, even the cleaning up after murder, for he had watched Canby's grandson clean off the tray of his highchair. And he could believe she had then gone upstairs to fall asleep again and waken in the morning as Sue Thompson, nineteen years old and the happy betrothed of Phil Canby.

1954

The Muted Horn

These were the moments when it felt good to be a farmer, Jeb thought. From where he stood at the pump he could see the clean straight rows of young corn, unbroken in any direction he looked. A day's work.

He had cleared the field of thistle and he felt as though he had driven out a thousand devils.

The cat was watching him from the back porch while he filled the tub and lathered himself with soap. She smoothed the fur on her breast. "Stepping out tonight, Cindy?" Jeb said. His own mind was filled with thoughts of Ellen and the music shop, and their evening together after the shop was closed. He whipped a handful of suds to the ground and the cat leaped into it. She bristled with disappointment and stiff-legged it back to the porch.

"That was a dirty trick, Cindy. I'll give you the real stuff in a minute."

"She's had her milk," his father said from the doorway. "Supper's on the table and there's company waiting."

"I'll be right in. How does the corn look, Dad?"

The old man looked down at the field. "It'll be choked again in a week," he said, turning back into the house.

Jeb emptied the tub and hung it up. He wondered if, twenty years from then, he would be like his father. He was the sixth generation of Sayers farming this stubborn New England soil, and he was still washing at an outdoor pump. No, he decided, he would not be like his father.

The old man fought every improvement he tried to put into the place. He still distrusted electricity. Every time there was a thunder storm, the switch had to be thrown off before he would stay indoors. And he was not much worse than the majority of people in Tinton. Jeb tickled the cat's ear as he went up the steps. "It's a hell of a life, Cinderella. But we'll bring them round yet."

The company was Nathan Wilkinson, town moderator, deacon of the church, and publisher of the oldest weekly in the state. "I won't keep you from your supper," he said, shaking hands. "I've come to tell you I'm putting you up for elder in Tinton Church, Jeb."

"Oh," said Jeb, looking from Mr. Wilkinson who was examining the backs of his hands to his father.

"It's a great honor, my boy," the deacon continued. "There's no more than half a dozen men received it at your age in the whole history of Tinton. Your father should be mightily pleased."

"Oh, aye," his father said without looking up.

Jeb moistened his lips before speaking, "I feel I must decline the honor, Mr. Wilkinson . . . Will you have a bite with us?"

"I will not, thank you. May I ask your reason for declining? If you're afraid the board won't confirm it, in all humility, I can say my word is . . ."

Before he had selected the delicate word to complete his thought, Jeb said: "If it's not impertinent, sir, I'd rather know your reason for nominating me."

"It is impertinent, Jeb. Most impertinent."

"There's always been a Sayers on the church board, Jeb," his father murmured uneasily.

"Nominated for good and true service," Jeb said, "and upright citizenry. Would you credit me with those virtues, Mr. Wilkinson?"

"I think you're capable of them, Jeb—when you're through sowing your wild oats."

"I think I was done with them when I draped the parish

chains across the vicars' tombstones. That's a long time ago, sir.''

"But you're still proud of it, aren't you, Jeb?"

"Not exactly. It was a stupid thing to do. But I'm not ashamed of the reason I did it. It's a long past time that Tinton outgrew its chains.''

"The chains are nothing but a symbol, Jeb,'' Wilkinson said with paternal patience. "They're a symbol of sin and the bondage into which it sells a man. But I did not come to discuss either with you. Think over the honor I'm offering you. Give me your answer at services tomorrow. Good night, Martin.'' He nodded to Jeb's father and went out the back door.

"The meat's as hard as leather,'' the old man said, putting a portion on each of their plates.

"No harder than Wilkinson,'' said Jeb.

His father had nothing to say during the meal, but his face was tightened with pain. Finally Jeb could stand it no longer.

"Don't you see what he's trying to do, Dad? He wants me to get into line, into his line, and he figures if I'm an elder, I'll have to do it. I'm working for what I think is right for Tinton. There's nothing wrong in that. It used to be wrong to dance. Now there's even church dances. I want a town where people speak through their board members, instead of being spoken to or for.''

His father shook his head. "I know nothing of politics, Jeb, and I want to know less.''

"Damn it, Dad, you need to know more. We all do.''

"You'll not swear in this house, boy.''

Jeb got up from the table. "Then I'll swear out of it,'' he said, "if that's swearing.''

He went to his room and changed his clothes. It was the only place in the house where he felt at home, there and in the fields and woods. At times he thought that it would be better for him to leave Tinton. For five years he had put every spare moment into the town and the church. He had organized study groups and bought the books with his own money, money he should have laid away for the time Ellen would marry him. Despairing of bringing Tinton into the world, he tried to bring the world into Tinton. There was not even a high school in the town. Those who wanted it enough traveled eighteen miles morning and night.

"It's the chains," he said aloud, "the damned blasted chains."

There was a legend about the town that in the early days it had been a wicked place, so wicked that once the church elders had gone among the citizens in chains lest one of them fall into temptation. Thus bound together they had surrounded the maker of evil and captured him. Jeb could almost see them, so obsessed had he become with the story. He wondered what the poor devil had done. The chroniclers had left that out. Conveniently, he thought. But the chains still lay in the church belfry, and whenever a preacher was hard put for a subject, he was likely to stumble over the chains that day. It was after one such sermon, that Jeb, at eighteen, had hauled the chains to the cemetery and strung them over the tombstones of the vicars buried there in the seventeenth century.

Downstairs, he stopped at the kitchen door. His father was still sitting there, in the semi-darkness now. "I'll be home late," he said gently. "I'm sorry if I disappoint you, Dad. But I'm trying to do what I think right."

The old man looked up at him. For all his stubborn blindness, he knew how hard it was for Jeb to stay sometimes. His gratitude was in his eyes. "I'm glad to hear you say that, Jeb. Whenever you want to reform something, you do it from the inside if you're honest. It isn't the easiest way, ever. The easiest way is starting something new. But first you've got to try and fix up what you've got. If you're honest, that is. And I don't know a more honest person than you, Jeb."

"Thanks, Dad. I'll try."

He decided to walk the two miles to Tinton. When he reached the main road the sun had already set and a heavy blue mist hung close to the ground, reminding him of the thistle he had hoed that day. In a way, it was the same with all his work. Thistle was quicker than corn. But he could not abandon it any more than he could abandon Tinton itself. He tried to buoy his spirits with the thought of Ellen. But she, too, was part of Tinton. For all that she admitted her love of him, she had not consented to marriage. It was as though she were in some sort of bondage.

The full moon was rising. It would be overhead by his return. Far below him he could see the lights going on in the town, and he could see the smoke of the seven-fifty train. The mist lay like a long sheet over a hollow that ended at Hank's woods. He could hear a car grinding to a start somewhere, and the long whistle of the train. He watched it come into view between the hills and then vanish again. When its sound was gone, there was only the burble of frogs.

The usual Saturday night crowd had congregated along the main street, the men half-sitting on car fenders, waiting for their wives to finish shopping or the kids to get out of an early show. Jeb knew them all. He waved and said a word here and there. Outside Robbins' music store he stopped at the window. He had not seen Ellen for a week. She was showing a man and his two sons all the harmonicas in the place. As he watched her, Jeb's quarrel with Tinton fell away. There seemed to be an aura of goodness and happiness about her. A wisp of hair had strayed out of her braid. She kept brushing it away as she might a fly while she talked. By the time she noticed him, Jeb was pantomiming a hot harmonica player. Her eyes laughed at him. He went in, but Ellen did not leave her customers, not even for a moment to say a word to him. He was being over-sensitive, he told himself—hot and cold, like a kid with puppy love. He forced himself to watch her until she looked at him again. He winked. She came to him then.

"Silly Jeb. Where were you all evening?"

"Examining my conscience. Thinking of you."

"In that order?"

He nodded. "I still don't understand why you won't marry me."

"Sometimes I don't either," she said. There was a blast of sound from the counter. "Please boys, not unless you want to buy that one." She turned back to him. "Jeb, will you do me a favor? Mrs. Robbins bought some more relics. They're in back. Would you dust and put them in the case for me?"

As he walked to the rear of the store, he noticed other customers in the record booths. Ballet music and blues blended into each other as he passed. He was proud of the store. It was largely his idea. For years, Mrs. Robbins kept it as a curiosity shop to attract the tourists who came to Tinton because it was so "quaint." The relics, he found, were a mandolin without strings, a fife, and an ancient horn. All of them were clogged with dust, and the horn was tarnished black. He rummaged through a cupboard and found rags and silver polish. He was depressed again. Ellen was casual, and he had needed something strong, something warm. She came to the back room a few minutes later.

"I'll close up soon. How are you coming, Jeb?"

"Almost done. Where'd she get these things?" he asked, but not really caring.

"The Rutherford place. I'm afraid Miss Hannah is hard up. That fife's supposed to have been used in the Revolution."

"It looks it," he said.

"You're an angel, Jeb." She brushed his cheek with her lips as she left him to return to her customers. And for some reason that hurt him even more than her indifference. "Be a good boy," everyone seemed to say. He had to shake off this pettiness. He returned to work and tried to distract himself by thinking of the Rutherford place. It was the oldest house in Tinton. In fact, it had all but survived the family, for in his time there was only Hannah left. She was older than his father and unmarried. Perhaps when all the old families died out Tinton would change. He, himself, was the last of six generations in the town, and still not married at twenty-seven. There might be a reason beyond random for that. Surely something more than fancy held him waiting for Ellen all these years, and her from marrying him. He felt now that they would never marry.

The blackened horn was taking color in his hands, a deep gold that glowed like a core of fire. Indeed, it seemed very warm to his touch as though it were a thing he was tempering instead of cleaning. It was a simple instrument, not quite as long as his arm, and wonderfully fragile-looking. He pushed the rag gently through the bell end, and taking a coat-hanger and bending it, he worked the cloth up to the mouth, cleaning away, perhaps, the dust of centuries. When he had finished he spread a cloth on the table and laid the horn on it. Its simple beauty enchanted him. He was impelled to touch it, to run his fingers over its warm smoothness, around the notches which must have guided its tonal range. While he carried the fife and mandolin to the front of the store and made room in the case for them he felt an urgency to return to the horn.

"I'll be a few minutes more, Jeb," Ellen said.

He scarcely heard her. As he leaned down to lift the backboard of the case, he imagined he saw the horn glowing in the semi-darkness. He could close his eyes and see it, as one sees the sun long after having looked at it. Beside it again, he lost all sense of time and place, even of Ellen. He picked it up tenderly, with the feeling coming over him that he could take from it the music of heaven and earth, the stars, the sea, the grass, the birds, yesterday, tomorrow.

He moistened his lips and put them to the . uth of the horn. Against his lips the pressure was sweet and natural, as a kiss might be, and all the while the golden beauty of it enthralled him. He held it loosely for fear of injuring it, and then finally, like an impatient lover, he breathed into it his wish to give it life. The sound was no more than a whispered moan, the wind perhaps on a hushed night. But he could hear it still when he took the horn from his lips. Time being nothing to him, Ellen was beside him instantly.

"What are you doing, Jeb? That sound would raise the dead."

He showed her the horn but she saw nothing wondrous about it.

"You look flushed, Jeb. Do you feel well?"

"I'm all right," he said, running his fingers protectively over the horn. He was glad she had not commented on it, even on its beauty.

"If you must play that thing, please take it outside. I should be through soon. I think it's very inconsiderate of Mrs. Wells to buy records at this hour. She has all week . . . Really, Jeb. You don't look well."

He turned from her, the color driven higher in his face with anger at her words, "that thing." "I'm all right, I tell you."

"All right, Jeb. I must go back," she said quietly. "I'm near the end of my patience too."

He waited until he was sure that she had left the room before he moved. Then he unbolted the back door and went out, carrying the horn beneath his coat.

The closing of the door behind him released Jeb from every tie that had ever held him. In the moment or two that he stood in the shadows of the building, he seemed to see the climaxes of his life turning like reflections in the facets of a diamond, and then the reflections were gone, and only the crystal deepness of the unmarked facets passed before him, filling him with the urge to touch each one with his personality, his power. The sweet, buoyant air seemed part of him. He felt that he could bring a blessed warmth to wastelands, a coolness to the desert . . . this by nothing more than impulse. And all the while, the horn was warm next to his breast and becoming more and more a part of him.

He drew it out and looked at it, a thin line of fire in the darkness. He lifted it to his lips and once more breathed into it. The sound now was like a lonesome bird call. He paused and heard a rustle, as of animals stirring in the night. Again he touched the horn to his lips, this time covering a notch with his finger, changing the pitch. Presently he alternated the two notes. When he stopped to listen, the sound of rustling heightened. For a moment he thought the sea had climbed beyond its walls and driven in upon the town. He moved away from the building and the rustling followed him. As he went he heard his name called into the night at first behind him, and then to the left of him, and then to the right, starting as a familiar voice, and growing with each repetition more strange, more distant. He walked through the side streets stealthily, with catlike swiftness, and the rustling followed him, heightening all the while, and seeming at times to sweep above and past him. He could even feel it wafting about him the way the wind might, although not a leaf was stirring among the trees he passed.

At the edge of town he paused and sounded the golden horn more boldly, swelling the tones until they were true and strong. He played his fingers down the tonal openings, exciting a soft, rich trill of music. The rustling intensified. He was in the center of a whirlwind. He pushed through it, fashioning the rhythm of the music to the step he took along the road. Presently he was half-stepping, half-skipping, and the rustling took on his rhythm. Somewhere ahead of him two round lights came out of the darkness like two strange moons traveling side by side. Almost upon him, they turned with fierce abruptness and were gone. He took the horn from his lips. The light of the true moon was everywhere, and among the rustling sounds came the burble of the frogs, the frenzied scolding of birds disturbed in their nests, and the chatter of scurrying animals. Jeb laughed aloud, and the hills picked up his laughter, and swung it back into the fury of sounds about him. Again he played. He did not pause until he came to the edge of Hank's woods. There the fog still lay like spun linen and he felt that he might bounce upon it as a child bounces on a bed. It was a passing fancy, but it drew him from the road along the edge of the woods, where, as he went the birds awakened and followed him, joining their song with his. He sat down on a stump and rested. The birds carried along the melody, a translucent sort of music: little bells, reeds, the long thin tremolo of hair-like strings. In his hand the horn was vivid gold, giving a light that was reflected in the eyes of the little forest animals watching him. He realized the rustling sound was gone. He laid the horn across his lap and put his hand upon it, its velvety warmth answering his tenderness. His breathing quickened and the smell of earth came to him and a mustiness that was almost sweatlike. The rustling sounds were returning, at first quietly on one side of him and then surrounding him. He stood up and climbed onto the stump to breathe above the stifling air near the ground. The rustling swept away in front of him toward the meadow. The horn in his hand seemed to quicken to the movement of his fingers on it, and he drew his other hand affectionately about it as though he were alone for a moment with his beloved, suffering an exquisite anticipation.

The music when he once more tilted the horn into the night had a quiet sadness that soon grew into melancholy. It was a lament that might have been winded over the last fires of a dead hero's camp. The birds grew still. In the meadow the fog seemed to break, wisping upward in a hundred little pyramids, the slow movement of them suggesting prayer or mourning, and in the midst of them a larger core of whiteness writhed and vibrated. The shadows deepened as the moon passed further over the forest. Jeb played on, the melancholy in him growing deeper. Then the first fears of parting with the horn came to him when he saw a searchlight sweep the sky and was reminded of the dawn. His heart cried out against it, and his whole body shivered with the motion of the core of whiteness in the field. But, as becomes a lover who is still with his beloved, however immanent departure, he was moved to gayety.

The music changed, his fingers flying over the pitchkeys, provoking laughter in the throat of the horn. To this the birds responded, and soon the whole forest was merry. Even the frogs quickened their tympany. In the field the pyramids of mist were dissolving and gradually shaping into white swirls, churning, as if whirled about by many dancers. Inside himself, Jeb felt the growing of some struggle. It was his adolescence again, or more than that, it was a lifetime of adolescence, urging a definition or a freedom—a merging with the music. The field was vibrant. His mouth was burning with the heat of the horn against it, his whole body on fire with the wild white heat.

A sudden stillness came upon the creatures of the forest. Jeb was aware of it although he played on, feeling the climax of his music almost upon him, and feeling as he played that he must be stronger than some force that would try to stop him. Whatever was happening in the field was happening to him, and there was a logic to it, in the ways of his logic that night. There was a presence there, and it was a part of him and his beloved horn. The birds flew out of the trees and about him, almost touching him with their wings, and still he played. There was stirring somewhere behind him, as of the wind starting up suddenly among the leaves, and then came a rattle. It grew louder until he recognized it. The sound was the clanging of chains.

For a moment he stopped, but the horn clung to his lips, and while he listened to the clanging, almost upon him now, the horn grew cold to his touch, but clung still to his lips now like frosty metal in the winter. A terrible fear came on him. The birds were gone, and no small curious eyes stared up at him. In the field, the mist had taken the shapes of a hundred sheep tumbling out of the meadow, moving away from him faster and faster.

Watching them go, he felt a great surge of anger that drove the clanging noise from his ears. He stiffened every muscle in his body and forced himself to the greatest height he could reach. He strained his head upward and tightened his grip on the horn until it was cutting into his flesh. Then, poising the dying instrument high above him, he poured the full breath of his lungs into it, and through it—a great long cry that tore through the night like the anguish of the betrayed.

As he sounded the horn a second time he turned and emptied its last fierce tones into the woods, into the face of whatever evil crept upon him there. The chains were silent. His arms fell to his sides, and he heard a tinkling sound as the horn fell from his hand upon the stump. The swishing noise came upon him again, and he thought somehow of taffeta and buckskin trousers. With it came the musty smell of sweat and earth again. Something brushed him to the ground. His legs were too weak to hold him. He fell forward on his face, the ground sweet and steady beneath him. He rolled over, and for a moment saw the mists sweep into the woods above him. Then he slept.

When Jeb awoke the glisten of dawn was all about him. He knew where he was presently, but it seemed that he had come there a long time before. There was a lightness in his head as though he were coming out of ether. From somewhere near him he heard the plaintive lowing of a cow. He stood up and listened for the lowing again, and then followed it through the long, wet grass. "C'boss, c'boss," he called softly. The forlorn answer came to him, and after it, the weak bleating of a newborn calf. He found them in the shelter of a grove of trees that separated his land from Hank Trilling's, the cow licking her baby and trying to nudge it closer to the warmth of her body. Jeb took off his coat and wrapped it around the calf. He picked it up and carried it home, its weary mother following after them.

In the barn he scattered fresh straw and threw a blanket

over the cow. He prepared a hot mash which he was feed-
ing her when his father came in. The old man watched a
few moments without speaking. The calf had found its
mother's milk.

"Come early, didn't she?" the old man said.

"Some."

"Where'd you find her?"

"Near Hank's woods," Jeb said.

His father was thoughtful for a moment. "I wonder if
something could have frightened her?"

"Maybe," Jeb said.

"You ought to have changed your clothes before you
went out to look for her, Jeb." He said no more and was
gone about his chores when Jeb looked up.

The two men arrived early for church services that
morning as was their custom. Jeb was weary, but he felt a
contentment that he had not known before. The night was
no more than a dream to him, and Ellen was waiting at
the church gate, as lovely as the spring itself. He got out
of the truck and let his father park it.

"Are you all right, Jeb?" she asked, reaching out her
hand to him.

"Yes."

She clung to his hand a moment. "Will you ask me
again now to marry you?"

"I will, and I do ask you, Ellen. Will you marry me?"

"Yes, Jeb. Last night when you left me, and when I
called and you didn't answer, I thought that I had lost
you, and I knew then that if I had, I had lost my life."

He smiled at her and tightened her hand between his
arm and his side, but he didn't speak. Near them a group
of townsmen were talking.

". . . I tell you as sure as I'm standing here," one of
them said, "there was a tornado last night. I saw the spi-
ral on the road when I was going in town. I pulled off the
road just ahead of it and the motor died. I jumped out of
the car and lay in the ditch, and I heard the wind in it
screeching and howling."

"You dreamt it," somebody said. "You didn't hear of any damage this morning, did you?"

Ellen's hand was pressing into Jeb's arm as they listened.

Hank Trilling took off his hat and scratched his head. "Well, there was something queer going on last night. The dog kept barking, and I'd go to the door and listen. The birds were singing all night long."

Nathan Wilkinson was standing among them. He noticed Jeb and excused himself. "Jeb," he started, having tipped his hat to Ellen, "I'm afraid I was premature in my proposition to you last night. There's a peculiar revolt in the Board of Elders. I'd find it a bit awkward if they refused to confirm . . . Well, you see my position?"

"Yes, sir," Jeb said. "I appreciate your confidence in me anyway." Then he added with the same blandness: "Perhaps when I've proven myself worthy of the honor, you will propose me?"

"Of course, my boy. Of course I shall." He swept his hat off to Ellen.

Jeb and Ellen walked on toward the church. Among the women on the steps was old Hannah Rutherford. She caught Ellen by the arm and led her and Jeb apart. "Those things I gave Mrs. Robbins, Ellen, was there a horn among them?"

"Yes," Ellen said, the word scarcely getting out of her throat.

"I don't believe in superstitions, Ellen, but I think she ought to put that away where no one could try to play it."

"Why?" Jeb asked. "Why should no one play it, Miss Hannah?"

The old woman looked up at him. "Particularly you, young man. I remember your escapade with the chains. As I say, I put no store by it, but my grandfather found me with it in my hands once and he told me that a young man had brought it to the village in his grandfather's time when music wasn't allowed. They caught him playing the devil's tune on it, with the whole of Tinton dancing like the damned. He was executed as a witch, and he cursed them horribly. He wished them no rest until the chains were gone from Tinton. It's an old wives' tale, but I'd put the horn away just the same.''

''Ellen, wait here for me,'' Jeb whispered.

He went into the church and up through the choir loft. He pulled the ladder from under the dusty pews stored there and tilted it to the trap door of the belfry. There was nothing but the church bell, which began to toll the service then. The floor was thick with dust except where lately something had been moved from it. But there were no footprints, and the chains were gone.

1957

A Matter of Public Notice

". . . the victim, Mrs. Mary Philips, was the estranged wife of Clement Philips of this city who is now being sought by the police for questioning . . ."

Nancy Fox reread the sentence. It was from the Rockland, Minnesota *Gazette*, reporting the latest of three murders to occur in the city within a month. "Estranged wife" was the phrase that gave her pause. Common newspaper parlance it might be, but for her it held a special meaning: for all its commonplaceness, it most often signals the tragic story of a woman suddenly alone—a story that she, Nancy Fox, could tell. Oh, how very well she could tell it!—being now an estranged wife herself.

How, she wondered, had Mary Philips taken her estrangement from a husband she probably once adored? Did he drink? Gamble? Was he unfaithful? Reason enough—any one of them—for some women. Or was it a cruelty surprised in him that had started the falling away of love, piece by piece, like the petals from a wasting flower?

Had the making of the final decision consumed Mary Philips's every thought for months and had the moment of telling it been too terrible to remember? And did it recur, fragmenting the peace it was supposed to have brought? Did the sudden aloneness leave her with the feeling that part of her was missing, that she might never again be a whole person?

Idle questions, surely, to ask now of Mrs. Philips. Mary Philips, age 39, occupation beauty operator, was dead—strangled at the rear of her shop with an electric cord at the hands of an unknown assailant. And Clement Philips was being sought by the police—in point of fact, by Captain Edward Allan Fox of the Rockland force, which was why Nancy Fox had read the story so interestedly in the first place.

Clement Philips was sought, found, and dismissed, having been two thousand miles from Rockland at the time of Mary Philips's murder. Several others, picked up after each of the three murders, were also dismissed. It was only natural that these suspects were getting testy, talking about their rights.

The Chief of Police was getting testy also. His was a long history of political survival in Rockland. Only in recent years had his work appeared worthy of public confidence, and that was due to the addition, since the war, of Captain Fox to the force. Fox knew it. No one knew his own worth better than "the Fox" did. And he knew how many years past retirement the old chief had stretched his tenure.

The chief paced back and forth before Captain Fox's desk, grinding one hand into the other behind his back. "I never thought the day would come when we'd turn up such a maniac in this town! He doesn't belong here, Fox!"

"Ah, but he does—by right of conquest," Fox said with the quiet sort of provocation he knew grated on the old man.

The chief whirled on him. "You never had such a good time in your life, did you?"

Fox sighed. He was accustomed to the bombast, the show of wrath that made his superior seem almost a caricature. He did not have to take it: the last of the chief's whipping boys was the custodian now of the city morgue. "Once or twice before, sir," Fox said, his eyes unwavering before the chiefs.

The old man gave ground. He knew who was running the force, and he was not discontented. He had correctly estimated Fox's ambition: what Fox had of power, he had only with the old man's sanction. "In this morning's brief for me and the mayor, you made quite a thing of the fact that all three victims were separated from their husbands. Now I'm not very deep in this psychology business—and the missus and I haven't ever been separated more than the weekend it took to bury her sister—so you're going to have to explain what you meant. Does this separation from their husbands make 'em more—ah—attractive? Is that what you're getting at? More willing?"

Fox could feel a sudden pulse-throb at his temple. It was a lecher's picture the old man had conjured with his words and gestures, and his reference to Fox's own vulnerability—Nancy having left him—stirred him to a fury a weaker man would not have been able to control.

But he managed it, saying, "Only more available—and therefore more susceptible to the advances of their assailant."

The old man pulled at the loose skin of his throat. "It's interesting, Fox, how you got at it from the woman's point of view. The mayor says it makes damn good reading."

"Thank you, sir," Fox said for something that obviously was not intended as a compliment. "Do you remember Thomas Coyne?"

"Thomas Coyne," the chief repeated.

"The carpenter—the friend of Elsie Troy's husband," Fox prompted. Elsie Troy had been the first of the three victims. "We've picked him up again. No better alibi this time than last—this time, his landlady. I think he's too damned smug to have the conscience most men live

with, so I've set a little trap for him. I thought maybe
you'd like to be there."

"Think you can make a case against him?"

Fox rose and took the reports from where the old man
had put them. "Chief," he said then, "there are perhaps
a half dozen men in Rockland against whom a case could
be made . . . including myself."

The old man's jaw sagged. A lot of other people were
also unsure of Ed Fox—of the working mechanism they
suspected ran him instead of a heart. "Let's see this
Coyne fellow," the chief said. "I don't have much taste
for humor at a time like this."

"I was only pointing up, sir, that our killer's mania is
not apparent to either friends or victims—until it is too
late."

The old man grunted and thrust his bent shoulders as
far back as they would go—in subconscious imitation of
The Fox's military bearing. On the way to the "Sun
Room"—so called because of the brilliance of its
lighting—where Thomas Coyne was waiting, the chief
paused and asked, "Is it safe to say for sure now that
Elsie Troy was the first victim? That we don't have a
transient killer with Rockland just one stop on his itiner-
ary?"

There had been several indications of such a possibility.

"I think we may assume that Elsie Troy was the beginning," Fox said. "I think now that her murder was a random business, unpremeditated. She was killed at
night—in her bedroom, with the lights on and the window shades up. She was fully dressed, unmolested. It
wasn't a setup for murder. It was pure luck that someone
didn't see it happening.

"But having walked out of Elsie Troy's house a free
man, her assailant got a new sense of power—a thrill he'd
never had in his life. And then there began in him what
amounted to a craving for murder. How he chooses victims, I don't know. That's why I called attention to the

. . . the state of suspension in the marriages of the victims.'' Fox shrugged. ''At least, that's my reconstruction of the pattern.''

''You make it sound like you were there,'' the old man said.

''Yes,'' Fox said, ''I suppose I do.'' He watched the old man bull his neck and plow down the hall ahead of him, contemplating the bit of sadism in himself—in, he suspected, all policemen. It was their devil, as was avarice the plague of merchants, conceit the foe of actors, complacency the doctor's demon, pride the clergyman's. He believed firmly that man's worst enemy was within himself. His own, Fox thought grimly, had cost him a wife, and beyond that, God Almighty knew what else. There were times since Nancy's going when he felt the very structure of his being tremble. There was no joy without her, only the sometimes bitter pleasure of enduring pain.

Coyne sat in the bright light, as Fox had expected, with the serenity of a religious mendicant. His arms folded, he could wait out eternity by his manner. It was unnatural behavior for any man under police inquisition. Fox was himself very casual. ''Well, Tom, it's about time for us to start all over again. You know the chief?''

Coyne made a gesture of recognition. The chief merely glared down at him, his face a wrinkled mask of distaste.

''April twenty-ninth,'' Fox led. ''That was the night you decided finally that you had time to fix Mrs. Troy's back steps.''

''Afternoon,'' Coyne corrected. ''I was home at night.''

''What do you call the dividing line between afternoon and night?''

''Dark—at night it gets dark . . . sir.''

''And you want it understood that you were home *before* dark?''

''I was home before dark,'' Coyne said calmly.

There had never been reference in the newspaper to the

hour of Elsie Troy's death, partly because the medical examiner could put it no closer than between seven and nine. The month being April, darkness fell by seven.

"Suppose you tell the chief just what happened while you were there."

"Nothing happened. I went there on my way home from work. I fixed the steps. Then I called in to her that the job was done. She came out and said, 'That's fine, Tom. I'll pay you next week.' I never did get paid, but I guess that don't matter now."

Told by melancholy rote, Fox thought, having heard even the philosophic ending before. But then, most people repeated themselves under normal circumstances, especially about grievances they never expected to be righted.

"What I can't understand, Tom, is why you decided to fix the steps that day, and not, say, the week before?"

Coyne shrugged. "I just had the time then, I guess."

"She hadn't called you?"

"No, sir," he said with emphasis.

"You say that as though she would not have called you under any circumstances."

Coyne merely shrugged again.

"As a matter of fact, it was the husband—when they were still together—who asked you to repair the steps, wasn't it, Tom?"

"I guess it was."

"And you happened to remember it on the day she was about to be murdered."

"I didn't plan it that way," Coyne said, the words insolent, but his manner still serene. He tilted his chair back.

"It's a funny thing, Chief," Fox said. "Here's a man commissioned to do a job on a friend's house. He doesn't get around to it until the home has broken up. If it was me, I'd have forgotten all about the job under those circumstances—never done it at all."

"So would I," the chief said, "unless I was looking for an excuse to go there."

"Exactly," Fox said, still in a casual voice.

"It wouldn't be on account of you they broke up, would it, Coyne?" the chief suggested.

Coyne seemed to suppress a laugh. It was the first time his effort at control showed. "No, sir."

"Don't you like women?" the chief snapped.

"I'm living with one now," Coyne said.

"Mrs. Tuttle?" said Fox, naming Coyne's landlady.

"What's wrong with that? She's a widow."

Fox did not say what was wrong with it. But Mr. Thomas Coyne was not going to have it both ways: he had alibied himself with Mrs. Tuttle for the hours of all three murders. A paramour was not the most believable of witnesses. But then, from what Fox had seen of Mrs. Tuttle, he would not have called her the most believable of paramours, either.

With deliberate ease Fox then led Coyne through an account of his activities on the nights of the two subsequent murders. By the suspect's telling they brought Coyne nowhere near the scenes.

Finally Fox exchanged glances with the old man. He had had more than enough of Coyne by now and very little confidence that the carpenter had been worth bringing in again. "You can go now, Tom," Fox said, "but don't leave town." He nodded at the uniformed policeman by the door. And then, after a pause, "By the way, Tom, when was the last time you went swimming?"

"Oh, two or three weeks ago."

"Where?"

"Baker's Beach," Coyne said, naming the public park.

Fox nodded, held the door for the chief, and then closed it behind them.

"That guy should go on the radio," the old man said. "He knows all the answers."

"Seems like it," Fox said.

The second victim, Jane Mullins, had been strangled on the beach. But if Tom Coyne, as he said, had gone swimming two or three weeks ago, that would account for the sand found in Coyne's room.

Sand and a stack of newspapers—the only clues to Thomas Coyne's interests . . . and a clue also to the personality of his landlady; Mrs. Tuttle was a very careless housekeeper to leave sand and old newspapers lying around for weeks. She might be as careless with time—even with the truth.

Three strangulations—all of women who lived alone—within a month. It was enough to set the whole of a city the size of Rockland—population 110,000—on edge. As the *Gazette* editorialized: "When murder can match statistics with traffic deaths, it is time to investigate the investigators."

Knowing Ed Fox so well, Nancy wondered if he had not planted that line with the *Gazette;* it had The Fox's bite. It would be like him, if he was not getting all the cooperation he wanted from his superiors.

She looked at the clock and poured herself another cup of coffee. She was due at the radio station at eleven. Her broadcast time was noon: "The Woman's Way."

How cynical she had become about him, and through him about so many things. As much as anything, that cynicism had enabled her to make the break: the realization that she was turning into a bitter woman with a slant on the world that made her see first the propensity for evil in a man, and only incidentally his struggle against it. This philosophy might make Ed a good policeman, but it made her a poor educator. And she considered herself an educator despite his belittlement of her work. A radio commentator was responsible to her audience to teach them a little truth. Why just a little? Ed had always said to that.

She wondered if Ed thought about her at all these days, when she could scarcely think of anything except him. It was as though she bore his heelmark on her soul. A cruel image—oh, she had them. For a month she had lived apart from him, yet the morbid trauma of their life together still hung about her. If she could not banish the memories, she must find psychiatric help. That would greatly amuse Ed—one more useless occupation by his reckoning. Worse than useless, the enemy of justice: his hardest catch could escape the punishment that fit his crime by a psychiatrist's testimony.

Nancy folded the morning paper and rinsed her coffee cup.

Strange, the occupations of the three victims: Mary Philips had operated a beauty parlor, Elsie Troy had run a nursery school. She could hear Ed lecture on that: why have children if you pushed them out of the house in rompers? And poor Jane Mullins had written advertising copy—to Ed, perhaps the most useless nonsense of all. Well, that would give Ed something in common with the murderer—contempt for his victims. Ed always liked to have a little sympathy for the murderer: it made him easier to find. And no man ever suffered such anguish of soul as did Ed Fox at the hour of his man's execution.

There, surely, was the worst moment in all her five years of marriage to him: the night Mort Simmons was executed. Simmons had shot a man and Ed had made the arrest and got the confession. Nancy had known her husband was suffering, and she had ventured to console him with some not very original remarks about his having only done his duty, and that doubts were perfectly natural at such an hour.

"Doubts!" he had screamed at her. "I have no more doubt about his guilt than the devil waiting for him at the gates of hell!"

She had thought a long time about that. Slowly then the realization had come to her that Ed Fox suffered when such a man died because, in the pursuit and capture of him, Ed identified himself with the criminal. And fast upon that realization the thought had taken hold of her that never in their marriage had she been that close to him.

Nancy opened her hand and saw the marks of her nails in the palm. She looked at her nails. They needed polish. A beauty operator, Mary Philips. If Nancy had been in the habit of having her hair done by a professional, she might possibly have known Mrs. Philips. The shop was in the neighborhood where she and Ed had lived, where Ed still lived. . . .

She caught up her purse and briefcase and forced her thoughts onto a recipe for which she had no appetite. Ed was not troubled that way in his work. . . .

"Damn it, Fox, give them something! They're riding my back like a cartload of monkeys." This was the old man's complaint on the third day after Mary Philips's murder. Reporters were coming into Rockland from all over the country. The mayor had turned over the facilities of his own office to them.

So Captain Fox sat down and composed a description of a man who might have been the slayer. He did it aware of his cynicism.

The state police laboratory had been unable to bring out any really pertinent physical evidence in any of the cases. The murderer was a wily one—a maniac or a genius . . . except in the instance of Elsie Troy. Fox could not help but dwell on that random start to so successful a career.

The detective stood over the stenographer while she typed the description—twenty copies on the electric machine. He then dictated a few lines calculated to counteract the description, to placate the rising hysteria of all the lonely women in Rockland. So many lonely women, whether or not they lived alone . . . Did Nancy feel alarmed? he wondered. If she did, she had not called on him for reassurance. But then she would not. There was that streak of stubborn pride in her that made her

run like a wounded animal from the hand most willing
to help.

"Forty-eight complaints have already been investigated, twenty-one suspects questioned . . ." Give them
statistics, Fox thought. Nowadays they mean more to
people than words. Maybe figures didn't lie, but they
made a convincing camouflage for the truth.

He handed out the release over the chief of police's
name, and found himself free once more to do the proper
work of a detective, something unrelated to public relations. Suspect Number 22 had been waiting for over an
hour in the Sun Room.

It gave Fox a degree of satisfaction to know that he
was there—"Deacon" Alvin Rugg. Rugg with two g's.
G as in God, he thought. The young man was a religious
fanatic—either a fanatic or a charlatan, possibly both, in
Fox's mind. And he was The Fox's own special catch,
having been flushed out in the policeman's persistent
search for something the three women might have had in
common besides the shedding of their husbands. All
three—Elsie Troy, Jane Mullins, and Mary Philips—
were interested in a revivalist sect called "Church of the
Morning."

On his way to the Sun Room, Fox changed his mind
about tackling the suspect there. Why not treat him as if
he were only a witness?—the better to disarm him. He
had no police record, young Mr. Rugg, except for a vio-
lation of the peace ordinance in a nearby town: the complaint had been filed against his father and himself—their
zeal had simply begat too large a crowd.

Fox had the young man brought to the office, and there
he offered him the most comfortable chair in the room.
Rugg chose a straight one instead. Fox thought he might
prove rugged, Rugg.

The lithe youth wore his hair crested around his head a
little like a brushed-up halo, for it was almost the color of
gold. His eyes were large, blue, and vacuous, though no
doubt some would call them deep.

"Church of the Morning," Fox started, trying without much success to keep the cynicism from his voice. "When did you join up?"

"I was called at birth," Alvin replied with a rotish piety.

He was older than he looked, Fox realized, and a sure phony. "How old are you, Rugg?"

"Twenty."

"Let's see your draft registration. This is no newspaper interview."

"Thirty-two," Rugg amended, wistful as a woman.

"What do you do for a living?"

"Odd jobs. I'm a handyman when I'm not doing the Lord's work."

"How do you get these . . . these odd jobs?"

"My father recommends me."

"That would be the Reverend Rugg?"

The young man nodded—there was scarcely the shadow of a beard on his face. Fox was trying to calculate how the women to whom his father recommended him would feel about Alvin of the halo. Fox himself would have had more feeling for a goldfish, but then he was not a lonely woman. He must look up some of them, those still among the living. Fox had gone to the revival tent the night before—he and one-tenth the population of Rockland, almost 12,000 people. It did not seem so extraordinary then that all three victims had chanced to catch the fervor of the Church of the Morning.

"I suppose you talk religion with your employers?"

"That is why I am for hire, Captain."

The arrogance of an angel on its way to hell, Fox thought. "Who was your mother?" he snapped, on the chance that this was the young man's point of vulnerability.

"A Magdalen," Rugg said. "I have never asked further. My father is a holy man."

Fox muttered a vulgarity beneath his breath. He was a believer in orthodoxy, himself. Revivalists were not for him, especially one like Reverend Rugg whom he had heard last night speak of his boy, this golden lad, as sent to him like a pure spirit, a reward—this golden lad . . . of thirty-two.

"The reason I asked you to come in, Alvin," Fox said, forcing amiability upon himself, and quite as though he had not sent two officers to pick Rugg up, "I thought you might be able to help us on these murders. You've heard about them?"

"I . . . I had thought of coming in myself," Rugg said.

"When did that thought occur to you?"

"Well, two or three weeks ago at least—the first time, I mean. You see, I worked for that Mrs. Troy—cleaned her windows, things like that. Her husband was a bitter, vengeful man. He doesn't have the spiritual consolation his wife had."

A nice distinction of the present and past tenses, Fox thought. But what Troy did have was an unbreakable alibi: five witnesses to his continuous presence at a poker table on the night Elsie Troy was slain.

"She told you that about him?" Fox prompted cheerfully.

"Well, not exactly. She wanted to make a donation to the church but she couldn't. He had their bank account tied up . . . she said."

The hesitation before the last two words was marked by Fox. Either the Ruggs had investigated Elsie Troy's finances, he thought, or Alvin was covering up an intimacy he feared the detective suspected or had evidence of.

"But Mrs. Troy ran a nursery school," Fox said blandly. "I don't suppose she took the little ones in out of charity, do you?"

"Her husband had put up the money for the school. He insisted his investment should be paid back to him first."

"I wouldn't call that unreasonable, would you, Alvin? A trifle unchivalrous, perhaps, but not unreasonable?"

A vivid dislike came into the boy's, the man's, eyes. He had suddenly made an enemy of him, Fox thought with grim satisfaction. He would soon provoke the un- guarded word. "Didn't you and Mrs. Troy talk about anything besides money?"

"We talked about faith," Rugg said, and then clamped his lips tight.

"Did you also do chores for Mrs. Mullins?"

"No. But she offered once to get me a messenger's job at the advertising company where she worked. Said I could do a lot of good there."

"I'll bet," Fox said. "And how about Mary Philips? What was she going to do for you?" He resisted the temptation to refer to the beauty shop.

"Nothing. She was a very nice woman."

That, Fox thought, was a revelatory answer. It had peace of soul in it. The captain then proceeded to turn the heat on "Deacon" Rugg, and before half an hour was over he got from the golden boy the admission that both Elsie Troy and Jane Mullins had made amatory ad- vances. Seeking more than religion, the self- widowed starvelings! They kicked out husbands and then wel- comed any quack in trousers. Lady breadwinners! Fox could feel the explosion of his own anger; it spiced his powers of inquisition.

Alvin Rugg was then given such mental punishment as might have made a less vulnerable sinner threaten suit against the city. But while "The Deacon" lacked airtight alibis for the nights of the 29th of April, the 16th of May, and June 2nd, he had been seen about his father's tent by many people, and he maintained his innocence through sweat and tears, finally sobbing his protestations on his knees.

The extent of The Fox's mercy was to leave Rugg alone to compose himself and find his own way to the street.

* * *

"Until tomorrow then, this is Nancy Fox going 'The Woman's Way.' "

Nancy gathered her papers so as not to make a sound the microphone could pick up. The newscaster took over. The next instant Nancy was listening with all the concentration of her being.

". . . a man about forty, quick of movement, near six feet tall, a hundred and sixty pounds, extremely agile; he probably dresses conservatively and speaks softly. One of his victims is thought to have been describing him when she told a friend, 'You never know when he is going to smile or when he isn't—he changes moods so quickly . . .' "

Nancy pressed her lips together and leaned far away from the table. Her breathing was loud enough to carry into the mike. That was her own husband the newscaster was describing—Ed Fox himself right down to the unpredictable smile! Actually, it could be any of a dozen men, she tried to tell herself. Of course. Any of a hundred! What nonsense to put such a description over the air!

She had regained her composure by the time the reporter had finished his newscast. Then she had coffee with him, as she often did. But what a fantastic experience! Fantasy—that was the only word for it. The description had been part of a release from the office of the chief of police, which meant it had Ed's own approval.

"But now I'm going to tell you what it sounded like to me," the newsman said. "Like somebody—maybe on the inside—deliberately muddying up the tracks. I tell you somebody down there knows more than we're getting in these handouts."

"What a strange idea!" Nancy cried, and gave a deprecating laugh as hollow as the clink of her dime on the counter.

She spent the next couple of hours in the municipal library, trying to learn something about water rights. A bill on the water supply was before the city council. Two years of research would have been more adequate to the subject, she discovered. Once more she had dived into something only to crack her head in the shallows of her own ignorance. Then she drove out to the county fair-grounds to judge the cake contest of the Grange women. She fled the conversational suggestion that the murderer might be scouting there. Some women squealed with a sort of ecstatic terror.

A feeling of deepening urgency pursued her from one chore to the next: there was something she ought to do, something she must return to and attend to. And yet the specific identity of this duty did not reveal itself. Sometimes she seemed on the brink of comprehension . . . but she escaped. Oh, yes, that much of herself she knew: she was fleeing it, not it fleeing her.

With that admission she cornered herself beyond flight. There was a question hanging in the dark reaches of her mind, unasked now even as it was five years ago. Since the night Mort Simmons died in the electric chair, it clung like monstrous fungi at the end of every cavern through which she fled. And by leaving her husband's house she had not escaped it.

Ask it now, she demanded—ask it now!

She drove off the pavement and braked the car to a shrieking halt. "All right!" she cried aloud. "I ask it before God—is Ed Fox capable of . . ." But she could not finish the sentence. She bent her head over the wheel and sobbed, "Eddie, oh, Eddie dear, forgive me . . ."

Without food, without rest, she drove herself until the day was spent, and with it most of her energy. Only her nerves remained taut. She returned just before dark to the apartment she had subleased from a friend. It was in no way her home: she had changed nothing in it, not even the leaf on the calendar. And so the place gave her no message when she entered—neither warning nor welcome.

She left the hall door ajar while she groped her way to the table where the lamp stood, and at the moment of switching on the light she sensed that someone had followed her into the apartment. Before she could fully see him, he caught her into his arms.

"Don't, please don't!" she cried. Her struggling but made him tighten his grip.

"For God's sake, Nancy, it's me!"

"I know!" she said, and leaped away as Ed gave up his grasp of her. She could taste the retch of fear. She whirled and looked at him as if she were measuring the distance between them.

"You knew?" he said incredulously. "You knew that it was me and yet you acted like that?"

She could only stare at him and nod in giddy acknowledgment of the truth.

His hands fell limp to his sides. "My God," he murmured.

A world of revelation opened to her in that mute gesture, in the simple dropping of his hands.

Neither of them moved. She felt the ache that comes with unshed tears gathering in her throat as the bitter taste of fear now ran out. It was a long moment until the tears were loosed and welled into her eyes, a moment in which they measured each other in the other's understanding—or in the other's misunderstanding.

"I thought I might surprise an old love—if I surprised you," he said flatly. "And then when I realized you were afraid, it seemed so crazy—so inconsiderate a thing to do, with a maniac abroad." He stood, self-pilloried and miserable—immobile, lest one move of his start up the fear in her again.

At last she managed the words: "Eddie, I do love you."

Fox raised his arms and held them out to her and she ran to him with utter abandon.

Presently he asked, "How long have you been afraid of me?"

"I think since the night Mort Simmons was executed," she said, and then clinging to him again, "Oh, my dear, my beloved husband."

He nodded and lifted her fingers to his lips. "How did you conceal it? Fear kills love. They say like that." He snapped his fingers.

"I never called it fear," she said, lifting her chin—and that, she thought, that inward courage was what he mistook for pride—"not until . . ." She bit her lip against the confession of the final truth.

"Until the murder of one, two, three women," Fox said evenly, "with whose lives you knew I'd have no sympathy."

"I didn't know that exactly," she said. "I only knew your prejudices."

"Pride and Prejudice," he mused. He pushed her gently an arm's distance from him. "Take another look at my prejudices, Nancy, and see who suffers most by them."

"May I come home now, Eddie?"

"Soon, darling. Very soon." He picked up his hat from where it had fallen in their struggle. "But you must let me tell you when."

He should have known it, really, Fox thought, closing the apartment door behind him. He was so alert to it in others, he should have seen the fear grow in her since the night she caught him naked-souled, suffering the death of Mort Simmons. Suppose that night he had tried to explain what had happened to him? How could he have said that it was not Mort Simmons's guilt he doubted, but his own innocence? How tell her that at the hour of his death, Mort Simmons was in a very special way the victim of Ed Fox?

Fox drove to within a block of Thomas Coyne's boarding house. He parked the car and walked up the street to where the tail he had put on Coyne was sitting, a newspaper before him, in a nondescript Ford. Fox slipped in beside him.

"Coyne's in there," the other detective said. "Been there since he came home from work. Ten minutes ago he went down to the corner for a paper. Came right back."

Fox decided to talk first with Mrs. Tuttle. He approached her by way of the kitchen door, identified himself, and got a cup of warmed-over coffee at the table. A voluble, lusty, good-natured woman, she responded easily to his question—whether she was interested in the Church of the Morning. She shook her head. Fox described "Deacon" Alvin Rugg and his relationship to the murdered women.

Mrs. Tuttle clucked disapproval and admitted she had heard of him, but where she could not remember. To the captain's direct question as to whether she had ever seen the golden boy, she shook her head again. "I tell you, Mr. Fox, I like my men and my whiskey 100 proof, and my religion in a church with a stone foundation."

Fox laughed. "Anybody in the house here interested in the Revival?"

"What you want to know," she said, looking at him sidewise, "is if it was Tom Coyne who told me about him. Isn't that it?"

Fox admitted to the bush he had been beating around. "I'd like to know if Coyne has shown any interest in the sect."

"I don't know for sure. He takes sudden fancies, that one does."

"I understand he has a very deep fancy for you," Fox said bluntly.

Mrs. Tuttle frowned, the good nature fleeing her face. She took his cup and saucer to the sink and clattered it into the dish basin.

"I'm sorry to be clumsy about a delicate matter," Fox said, getting up from the table and following to where he could see her face. Shame or wrath? he wondered. Perhaps both. "It was very necessary to Coyne that he confide that information to the police," he elaborated, in subtle quest of further information.

"Was it?" she said. "Then maybe it was necessary for him to come to me in the first place. Can you tell me that, mister?"

"If you tell me when it was he first came to you—in that sense, I mean," Fox said.

"A couple of nights ago," she said. "Till then it was just . . . well, we were pals, that's all."

Fox examined his own fingernails. "He didn't take very long to tell about it, did he?"

"Now answer my question to you," she said. "Did he come just so he could tell you him and me were—like that?"

Fox ventured to lay his hand on her arm. She pulled away from his touch as though it were fire. Her shame was deep, her affair shallow, he thought. "Just stay in the kitchen," he said. She would have her answer soon enough.

He moved through the hall and alerted the detective on watch at the front. Then he went upstairs. Thomas Coyne was sitting in his room, the newspaper open on the table before him, a pencil in his hand. He had been caught in the obviously pleasurable act of marking an item in the paper, and he gathered himself up on seeing Fox—like a bather surprised in the nude.

It gave an ironic sequence to the pretense on which Fox had come. "I wanted to see your swim trunks," Captain Fox said.

Coyne was still gaping. Slowly he uncc d himself and then pointed to the dresser drawer.

"You get them," Fox said. "I don't like to invade your privacy." He turned partially away, in fact, to suggest that he was unaware of the newspaper over which he had surprised the man. He waited until Coyne reached the dresser, and then moved toward the table, but even there Fox pointed to the picture on the wall beyond it, and remarked that he remembered its like from his school days. A similar print, he said, had hung in the study hall. On and on he talked, and if Coyne was aware of the detective's quick scrutiny of his marked newspaper, it was less fearful for the man to pretend he had not seen it.

"My wife, Ellen, having left my bed and board, I am no longer responsible. . . ."

Fox had seen it. So, likely, had the husbands of Mary Philips and Jane Mullins and Elsie Troy given public notice sometime or other. The decision he needed to reach instantly was whether he had sufficient evidence to indict Tom Coyne: it was so tempting to let him now pursue the pattern once more—up to its dire culmination.

The detective stood, his arms folded, while Coyne brought the swim trunks. "Here you are, Captain," he said.

"Haven't worn them much," Fox said, not touching them.

"It's early," Coyne said.

"So it is," Fox said. "The fifth of June. Baker's Beach just opened Memorial Day, didn't it?"

There was no serenity in Coyne now. He realized the trap into which he had betrayed himself while under questioning by Fox and the chief of police. So many things he had made seem right—even an affair with Mrs. Tuttle; and now that one little thing, by Fox's prompting, was wrong. He would not have been allowed in the waters of Baker's beach before the thirtieth of May. In order to account for the sand in his room following the murder of Jane Mullins, he had said he had gone swimming at Baker's Beach two or three weeks before.

Before midnight Coyne confessed to the three homicides, the last two premeditated. He had not intended to kill Elsie Troy. But he had been watching her behavior with young Alvin Rugg, and as her husband's friend he had taken the excuse of fixing her steps to gain her company and reproach her. She had called him "a nasty little man," and where matters had gone from that, he said, he could not clearly remember . . . except that he killed her. He was sure because of the wonderful exhilaration it gave him after he had done it—so wonderful it had to be repeated.

The chief had pride in his eyes, commending Captain Fox for so fine a job. They went upstairs together to see the mayor, and there the chief took major credit as his due. He announced, however, that this would be his last case before retirement, and he put his arm about Captain Fox as the reporters were invited in. Fox asked to be excused.

"Damn, it, man, you've got to do the talking," the chief protested.

"Yes, sir, if you say so," Fox said. "But first I want to call my wife."

"By all means," the chief said. "Here, use the mayor's phone."

Nancy answered on the first ring.

"Will you pick me up tonight, my dear, on your way home?" Fox said.

1957

Mrs. Norris Observes

If there was anything in the world Mrs. Norris liked as well as a nice cup of tea, it was to dip now and then into what she called "a comfortable novel." She found it no problem getting one when she and Mr. James Jarvis, for whom she kept house, were in the country. The ladies at the Nyack library both knew and approved her tastes, and while they always lamented that such books were not written any more, nonetheless they always managed to find a new one for her.

But the New York Public Library at Fifth Avenue and Forty-second Street was a house of different entrance. How could a person like Mrs. Norris climb those wide marble steps, pass muster with the uniformed guard, and then ask for her particular kind of book?

She had not yet managed it, but sometimes she got as far as the library steps and thought about it. And if the sun were out long enough to have warmed the stone bench, she sometimes sat a few moments and observed the faces of the people going in and coming out. As her friend Mr. Tully, the detective, said of her, she was a marvelous woman for observing. "And you can take that the way you like, love."

It was a pleasant morning, this one, and having time to spare, Mrs. Norris contemplated the stone bench. She also noticed that one of her shoelaces had come untied; you could not find a plain cotton lace these days, even on

118

a blind man's tray. She locked her purse between her bosom and her arm and began to stoop.

"It's mine! I saw it first!"

A bunioned pump thumped down almost on her toe, and the woman who owned it slyly turned it over on her ankle so that she might retrieve whatever it was she had found. Mrs. Norris was of the distinct opinion that there had been nothing there at all.

"I was only about to tie my shoelace," Mrs. Norris said, pulling as much height as she could out of her dumpy shape.

A wizened, rouged face turned up at her. "Aw," the creature said, "you're a lady. I'll tie the lace for you."

As the woman fumbled at her foot, Mrs. Norris took time to observe the shaggy hair beneath a hat of many summers. Then she cried, "Get up from there! I'm perfectly able to tie my own shoelace."

The woman straightened, and she was no taller than Mrs. Norris. "Did I hear in your voice that you're Irish?"

"You did not! I'm Scots-born." Then remembering Mr. Tully, her detective friend, she added, "But I'm sometimes taken for North of Ireland."

"Isn't it strange, the places people will take you to be from! Where would you say I was born? Sit down for a moment. You're not in a hurry?"

Mrs. Norris thought the woman daft, but she spoke well and softly. "I haven't the faintest notion," she said, and allowed herself to be persuaded by a grubby hand.

"I was born right down there on Thirty-seventh Street, and not nearly as many years ago as you would think. But this town—oh, the things that have happened to it!" She sat a bit too close, and folded her hands over a beaded evening purse. "A friend of mine, an actress, gave this to me." She indicated the purse, having seen Mrs. Norris glance at it. "But there isn't much giving left in this city . . ."

Of course, Mrs. Norris thought. How foolish of her

not to have realized what was coming. "What a dreadful noise the buses make," she commented by way of changing the subject.

"And they're all driven by Irishmen," the woman said quite venomously. "They've ruined New York, those people!"

"I have a gentleman friend who is Irish," Mrs. Norris said sharply, and wondered why she didn't get up and out of there.

"Oh, my dear," the woman said, pulling a long face of shock. " 'The actress of whom I just spoke, you know? She used to be with the Abbey Theatre. She was the first Cathleen Ni Houlihan. Or perhaps it was the second. But she sends me two tickets for every opening night—and something to wear." The woman opened her hand on the beaded purse and stroked it lovingly. "She hasn't had a new play in such a long time."

Mrs. Norris was touched in spite of herself: it was a beautiful gesture. "Were you ever in the theater yourself?" she asked.

The old woman looked her full in the face. Tears came to her eyes. Then she said, "No." She tumbled out a whole series of no's as though to bury the matter. She's protesting too much, Mrs. Norris thought. "But I have done many things in my life," she continued in her easy made-up-as-you-go fashion. "I have a good mind for science. I can tell you the square feet of floor space in a building from counting the windows. On Broadway, that naked waterfall, you know . . ." Mrs. Norris nodded, remembering the display. "I have figured out how many times the same water goes over it every night. Oh-h-h, and I've written books—just lovely stories about the world when it was gracious, and people could talk to each other even if one of them wasn't one of those psychiatrists."

What an extraordinary woman!

"But who would read stories like that nowadays?" She cast a sidelong glance at Mrs. Norris.

"I would!" Mrs. Norris said.

"Bless you, my dear, I knew that the moment I looked into your face!" She cocked her head, as a bird does at a strange sound. "Do you happen to know what time it is?"

Mrs. Norris looked at her wrist watch. The woman leaned close to look also. "A Gruen is a lovely watch," she said. She could see like a mantis.

"It's time I was going," Mrs. Norris said. "It's eleven-thirty."

"Oh, and time for me, too. I've been promised a job today."

"Where?" asked Mrs. Norris, which was quite unlike her, but the word had spurted out in her surprise.

"It would degrade me to tell you," the stranger said, and her eyes fluttered.

Mrs. Norris could feel the flush in her face. She almost toppled her new, flowered hat, fanning herself. "I'm sorry," she said. "It was rude of me to ask."

"Would you like to buy me a little lunch?" the woman asked brazenly.

Mrs. Norris got to her feet. "All right," she said, having been caught fairly at a vulnerable moment. "There's a cafeteria across the street. I often go there myself for a bowl of soup. Come along."

The woman had risen with her, but her face had gone awry. Mrs. Norris supposed that at this point she was always bought off—she was not the most appetizing of sights to share a luncheon table with. But Mrs. Norris led the way down the steps at a good pace. She did not begrudge the meal, but she would begrudge the price of it if it were not spent on a meal.

"Wait, madam. I can't keep up with you," the woman wailed.

Mrs. Norris had to stop anyway to tie the blessed shoe-lace.

Her guest picked at the food, both her taste and her gab

dried up in captivity. "It's a bit rich for my stomach," she complained when Mrs. Norris chided her.

Mrs. Norris sipped her tea. Then something strange happened: the cup trembled in her hand. At the same instant there was a clatter of dishes, the crash of glass, the screams of women, and the sense almost, more than the sound, of an explosion. Mrs. Norris's eyes met those of the woman's across from her. They were aglow as a child's with excitement, and she grinned like a quarter moon.

Outside, people began to run across the street toward the library. Mrs. Norris could hear the blast of police whistles, and she stretched her neck, hoping to see better. "Eat up and we'll go," she urged.

"Oh, I couldn't eat now and with all this commotion."

"Then leave it."

Once in the street Mrs. Norris was instantly the prisoner of the crowd, running with it as if she were treading water, frighteningly, unable to turn aside or stem the tide. And lost at once her frail companion, cast apart either by weight or wisdom. Mrs. Norris took in enough breath for a scream which she let go with a piper's force. It made room for her where there had been none before, and from then on she screamed her way to the fore of the crowd.

"Stand back! There's nobody hurt but there will be!" a policeman shouted.

Sirens wailed the approach of police reinforcements. Meanwhile, two or three patrolmen were joined by a few able-bodied passers-by to make a human cordon across the library steps.

"It blew the stone bench fifty feet in the air," Mrs. Norris heard a man say.

"The stone bench?" she cried out. "Why, I was just sitting on it!"

"Then you've got a hard bottom, lady," a policeman

growled. He and a companion were trying to hold on to a young man.

Their prisoner gave a twist and came face to face with Mrs. Norris. "That's the woman," he shouted. "That's the one I'm trying to tell you about. Let go of me and ask *her!*"

A policeman looked at her. "This one with the flowers on her hat?"

"That's the one! She looked at her watch, got up and left the package, then ran down the steps, and the next thing . . ."

"Got up and left what, young man?" Mrs. Norris interrupted.

"The box under the bench," the young man said, but to one of the officers.

"A box under the bench?" Mrs. Norris repeated.

"How come you were watching her?" the officer said.

"I wasn't especially. I was smoking a cigarette . . ."

"Do you work in the library?"

No doubt he answered, but Mrs. Norris's attention was suddenly distracted, and by what seemed like half the police force of New York City.

"I have a friend, Jasper Tully, in the District Attorney's office," she declared sternly.

"That's fine, lady," a big sergeant said. "We'll take a ride down there right now." Then he bellowed at the top of his lungs, "Keep the steps clear till the Bomb Squad gets here."

In Jasper Tully's office, Mrs. Norris tried to tell her interrogators about the strange little woman. But she knew from the start that they were going to pay very little attention to her story. Their long experience with panhandlers had run so true to pattern that they would not admit to any exception.

And yet Mrs. Norris felt sure she had encountered the exception. For example, she had been cleverly diverted by the woman when she might have seen the package. The woman had put her foot down on nothing—Mrs.

Norris was sure of that. She remembered having looked down at her shoelace, and she would have seen a coin had there been one at her feet—Mrs. Norris was a woman who knew the color of money. Oh, it was a clever lass, that other one, and there was a fair amount of crazy hate in her. Mrs. Norris was unlikely to forget the venom she had been so ready to spew on the Irish.

She tried to tell them. But nobody had to button Annie Norris's lips twice. It was not long until they wished Jasper Tully a widower's luck with her, and went back themselves to the scene of the blast.

Mr. Tully offered to take her home.

"No, I think I'll walk and cogitate, thank you," she said.

"Jimmie gives you too much time off," Tully muttered. He was on close terms with her employer.

"He gives me the time I take."

"Is he in town now?"

"He is, or will be tonight. He'll be going full dress to the theater. It's an opening night."

"Aren't you going yourself?"

Mrs. Norris gave it a second's thought. "I might," she said.

The detective took a card from his pocket and wrote down a telephone number. "You can reach me through this at all hours," he said. "That's in case your cogitating gets you into any more trouble."

When he had taken her to the office door, Mrs. Norris looked up to his melancholy face. "Who was Cathleen Ni Houlihan?"

Tully rubbed his chin. "She wasn't a saint exactly, but I think she was a living person . . . How the hell would I know? I was born in the Bronx!" A second later he added, "There was a play about her, wasn't there?"

"There was," said Mrs. Norris. "I'm glad to see you're not as ignorant as you make yourself out to be."

"Just be sure you're as smart as you think you are,"

Tully said, "if you're off to tackle a policeman's job again."

He had no faith in her, Mrs. Norris thought, or he wouldn't let her do it.

All afternoon she went over the morning's incidents in her mind. As soon as Mr. Jarvis left the apartment for dinner and the theater, she went downtown herself. The evening papers were full of the bombing, calling it the work of a madman. The mechanism had been made up of clock parts, and the detonating device was something as simple as a pin. It was thought possibly to have been a hatpin.

Well!

And there was not a mention of her in any account. The police were obviously ashamed of themselves.

Mrs. Norris took as her place of departure Forty-sixth Street and Seventh Avenue. Turning her back on the waterfall atop the Broadway building, she walked toward Shubert Alley. Anyone who could even guess at the number of times the same water went over the dam must have looked at it at least as often. And Cathleen Ni Houlihan—no stranger to the theater had plucked that name out of the air.

The beggars were out in droves: the blind, the lame, and the halt. And there were those with tin cups who could read the date in a dead man's eye.

Mrs. Norris was early, and a good thing she was. Sightseers were already congesting the sidewalk in front of the theater. New York might be the biggest city in the world, but to lovers of the stage a few square feet of it was world enough on an opening night.

She watched from across the street for five minutes, then ten, with the crowd swelling and her own hopes dwindling. Then down the street from Eighth Avenue, with a sort of unperturbed haste, came the little beggar-woman. She wore the same hat, the same ragged coat and carried the same beaded purse.

And she also carried a box about six inches by six which she carefully set down on the steps of a fire exit.

Mrs. Norris plunged across the street and paused again, watching the beggar, fascinated in spite of herself. Round and round one woman she walked, looking her up and down, and then she scouted another. The women themselves were well-dressed out-of-towners by their looks, who had come to gape at the celebrated first-nighters now beginning to arrive. When the little pan-handler had made her choice of victims, she said, and distinctly enough for Mrs. Norris to hear:

"That's Mrs. Vanderhoff arriving now. Lovely isn't she? Oh, dear, that's not her husband with her. Why, that's Johnson Tree—the oil man! You're not from Texas, are you, dear?"

Mrs. Norris glanced at the arrivals. It was her own Mr. Jarvis and his friend. A Texas oil man indeed! The woman made up her stories to the fit of her victims! She was an artist at it.

Mrs. Norris edged close to the building and bent down to examine the box. She thought she could hear a rhythmic sound. She could, she realized—her own heartbeat.

"Leave that box alone!"

Mrs. Norris obeyed, but not before she had touched, had actually moved, the box. It was empty, or at least as light as a dream, and the woman had not recognized her. She was too busy spinning a tale. Mrs. Norris waited it out. The woman finally asked for money and got it. She actually got paper money! Then she came for the box.

"Remember me?" Mrs. Norris said.

The woman cocked her head and looked at her. "Should I?"

"This morning on the Public Library steps," Mrs. Norris prompted.

The wizened face brightened. "But of course! Oh, and there's something I wanted to talk to you about. I saw you speaking to my young gentleman friend—you know, in all that excitement?"

"Oh, yes," Mrs. Norris said, remembering the young man who had pointed her out to the police.

"Isn't he a lovely young man? And to have had such misfortune."

"Lovely," Mrs. Norris agreed.

"You know, he had a scholarship to study atomic science and *those* people did him out of it."

"*Those* people?"

"All day long you can see them going in and out, in and out, carting books by the armful. Some of them have beards. False, you know. And those thick glasses—I ask you, who would be fooled by them? Spies! Traitors! And *they* can get as many books as they want."

"Oh, *those* people," Mrs. Norris said understandingly.

"And my poor young friend. They won't even give him a library card, and after I wrote him such a nice reference."

"Do you know where he lives?" Mrs. Norris said as casually as she could.

"No. But I know where he works. He fixes watches for a jeweler on Forty-seventh Street. I walked by there once and saw him working in the window. If you wait here for me, I'll walk over and show you the place tonight. He's not there now, of course, but I'm sure he'll be there in the morning. I hope you can help him."

"I'll try," Mrs. Norris said. A watchmaker.

The warning buzzer sounded within the theater. The lights flickered.

"Excuse me for a moment," the woman said, and picked up the box. "I've brought some violets for the leading lady. I want to take them in before curtain. Wouldn't it be nice if she invited us to see the play? I shan't accept unless she invites both of us."

Mrs. Norris followed the woman down the alleyway and then hung back as she handed the box in at the stage door. The woman waited and, observing Mrs. Norris, nodded to her confidently. Mrs. Norris was only reasonably sure the box was empty. She was beset by doubts and fears. Was there such a thing as a featherweight bomb? The doorman returned and put something in the woman's hand. She bowed and scraped and came along, tucking whatever she'd got into her purse.

With Mr. Jarvis in the theater, Mrs. Norris was not going to take any chances. "Wait for me out front," she said. "I want to have a look in there myself."

"Too late, too late," the woman crowed.

Mrs. Norris hurried.

"No one's allowed backstage now, ma'am," the doorman said.

"That box the old woman gave you . . ." It was sitting on a desk almost within her reach. "It could be dangerous."

"Naw. She's harmless, that old fraud. There's nothing in it but tissue paper. She comes round every opening night. 'Flowers for Miss Hayes,' or Miss Tandy or whoever. The company manager gives her a dollar for luck. I'm sorry, ma'am, but you'll have to go now."

Mrs. Norris beat a dignified retreat. The old woman was nowhere to be seen. But a watchmaker on Forty-seventh Street . . . Forty-seventh Street was also the diamond center of New York. What a lovely place for a leisurely walk-through with Mr. Tully!

1959

Meeting at the Crossroad

It was a night of fitful winds, so quiet at times the fall of an acorn might have startled a listener. Then the wind would commence again, whispering at first, trembling the dead leaves; then it would rise to a wanton shriek that rattled the very stars, it seemed. And that fury spent, silence hung once more upon the mountainside. It was the sort of night that a man abroad in it was not likely to forget. It could make strangers of friends, and perhaps friends of strangers.

Two men surprised each other, meeting on the Upper Road well after midnight. One was walking south from the direction of Rossi's Tavern, although it was unlikely that he had come from there: Rossi was in the habit of closing at midnight sharp. The other man, Tom Sommers, was coming east, down Cemetery Road. They were only a few feet apart when both of them hesitated, and then, having recognized each other, came on to their inevitable meeting at the crossroad. There a great naked light bulb shone beneath a porcelain shield which resembled an upside-down spittoon.

Both men lived in the village below, Point True, and they rode the same commuters' bus into New York every day. Outside of that, and this chance meeting, they had little in common. Yet, about to pass each other with the merest of greetings, both men paused, and on an impulse each felt had come from the other's prompting, extended their hands.

The handshake was brief, but it was their only one in fifteen years of acquaintance.

"Going down?" Tom Sommers said.

"No, worse luck. Up again. My wife's still at the Shanleys'." Allan Ford jerked his head in the direction of Cemetery Road, the same road down which Sommers had just walked.

There were a few houses along the road—not many, because so few people could afford the search for water on the mountainside. Many a well-digging had had to be abandoned at that height, and with it the plans to build a house.

"Nice people though," Ford added, as though to amend what might have been taken as criticism. The Shanley house was the only one alight now, except for what seemed to be a night lamp burning at the Rossi window.

"Are they?" Sommers said. It was not a question. It was an avowal of his skepticism of the Shanleys as nice people, and of Ford himself, perhaps. By reputation Sommers was a sour man.

"Once in a while anyway," Ford said, rubbing the back of his neck. It was an old mannerism, always practised to the tune of a sly joke. "Here comes the wind again. Isn't it something?"

"You should hear it at the top of the mountain," Sommers said, and without so much as a gesture of farewell he strode off down the hill.

At the very end of Cemetery Road, in the long plateau atop the mountain, his wife was buried. She had died a good many years before, at the age of twenty-three . . .

Both men were on the eight o'clock bus in the morning. Sommers boarded it first because he lived farther north, and as was his habit, he sat beside the person least likely to attempt conversation. He was tight-lipped and somber-eyed, reportedly a fine engraver. He looked rather like an ascetic monk. But any comment about him among the commuters almost invariably centered about his daughter. Ellen was fifteen now, in her third year at the Township high school, an honor student, and a very sweet-dispositioned girl. She was quite popular despite her shyness. Nearly everyone considered it a miracle she had been so well brought-up without a woman's help.

Ford was not his usual hearty self that morning, but his explanation was familiar: "I wish to God we could get to bed nights." He and Sommers did not even greet each other, much less comment on their post-midnight encounter. There was nothing at all out of the way about the bus trip that morning.

By the time most of the same commuters met again on the 5:15 bus, northbound, an item in the afternoon newspapers—or in some cases, a call from home—provoked a fury of talk; Point True had been the scene of a brutal murder shortly after midnight the night before. Fred Rossi had been bludgeoned to death in the woods between his tavern on the Upper Road and his home on Cemetery Hill.

Tom Sommers looked up from his newspaper at precisely the moment Ford was moving past him. Their eyes met and held for an instant, and Ford thought about their handshake of the night before—after the murder had occurred. But not a word was exchanged between them.

Ford's wife was on the telephone when he got home. It gave him a moment he very much needed—a chance to be alone on familiar ground. He was aware of something shaky inside him. God knows, the sensation was common enough to an advertising man, this inner quaking. In his case, he thought, it usually portended a responsibility he did not want, a decision he did not want to make.

He wandered through the house and lingered a moment at the playroom door. Jeff was fond of cowboys again, judging by the television program that was on. He waved absently in response to Allan's "Hi, son."

Martha, off the phone, called out, "Allan?"

He returned to the kitchen. "Hi, honey."

"I suppose you've heard about Rossi?"

He nodded. "It's in the afternoon papers."

"Did you hear anything on the bus?"

"Gossip, you mean?"

"All right then—gossip."

Martha had a way of coaxing almost everything he knew out of him, and he resented it even while surrendering. The worst of it was that once she got hold of it, what he had to tell always seemed unimportant. She was a frighteningly digestive woman.

"Doc Rathensberger calls it the violent demise of one more blackguardly scoundrel," Allan said.

"It takes one to know one from what I've heard about Doc Rathensberger," Martha commented.

Allan shrugged. Doc's florid turn of phrase had rather appealed to him.

"Chief Kelley was here this afternoon, corroborating—is that the word?—Jack Shanley's statement."

"What did Jack say?"

"That we were guests there last night . . . who stayed until two thirty, and that we didn't hear anything unusual."

"I wish we hadn't stayed so late. I'll bet we wouldn't be asked to either if Jack had to ride the damned bus in every day." Shanley drove his own car into New York. "It's enough to kill a man." Allan was talking quickly. It had become a way of his—to cover with patter what he felt to be his slow process of reasoning. Apparently he had not been missed in the half hour or so he had been gone from the Shanley house.

"I don't think either Jack or I mentioned your having fallen asleep in the kitchen."

"Thanks," he said dryly. He could picture Martha lifting that proud chin of hers when Shanley observed: "Your husband's off again." He had tried not to fall asleep last night, though the practice was not uncommon to him. The Shanley's had an open kitchen grate, and a cat that lazed in a chair before it. Allan often retreated to its company when he'd had too much to drink and the talk got up to his ears. After midnight, Martha always seemed at her best, sharp, her humor brittle as ice. Listening to her and Jack—he was a criminal lawyer, and a brilliant one—was like following a tennis match by ear. Along about then, Allan's own humor had as much bounce as a wet rag.

"Does Kelley want my corroboration, too?" he asked.

"I don't suppose it's necessary," Martha said. She took a meat loaf from the oven to baste, but suddenly looked up from it. "Or *did* you hear something, Allan?"

"How could I when I was asleep?" he said, avoiding her eyes.

"So was Anna Rossi—at least, that's her story. She's supposed to have taken a sleeping pill, turned on some music, and gone to sleep by it. She didn't miss her husband until nine o'clock this morning."

Allan, walking past the Rossi house, had heard the music, and he had speculated all day, until he had heard of Rossi's murder, whether or not Tom Sommers might have been coming from there when they met at the crossroad. He had felt on their meeting that Sommers was not his usual dour self, that something had just given him one hell of a lift. And Allan had enjoyed this speculation. For one thing, he liked Anna Rossi. She was a big, affable woman who wore her sexual attractiveness like a cloak to warm a cold world. The vulgar talk around the village asked what Rossi expected: his own infidelities were common knowledge.

Strangely, Allan had met Anna Rossi at the Shanleys'. It was to Betty Shanley's credit, he thought, having Mrs. Rossi in their house. She was less their type than Allan himself. But then, Betty was a jabberer, and Allan supposed Anna Rossi made a good listener—and, he had thought since last night—perhaps a good mistress to Tom Sommers. Allan had worked it all out, the relationship between the widower and the attractive woman. It would account for Sommer's aloofness from village gossip; it might even explain his daughter Ellen's getting along so well without a mother.

With the news of Rossi's murder, however, he tried to suppress that whole line of speculation. After all, what would Sommers have been doing at the Rossi house at an hour when Fred Rossi ordinarily would have been coming home from work? Unless . . . Allan shook off the new surmise as unfair and unfounded, and a lot too dangerous to think about a man he didn't know any better than he did Sommers.

Martha eased the meat loaf back into the oven. "I'd say she was the last person in the world to need a sleeping pill, wouldn't you?"

"I don't know," Allan said, trying to catch up with his wife's thinking. "Some of the easiest talking people churn up inside."

"Men find her attractive, don't they?" Martha said.

Allan shrugged.

"Have you ever been in their house?" she persisted.

"What the hell would *I* be doing there?"

Martha laughed. "I don't know. I was just remembering that time you walked her home from the Shanleys'. It was you, wasn't it? Oh, Lord, Allan, I'm not accusing *you* of anything." She was on the verge of genuine mirth.

"I know you're not," he said irritably. He could not help feeling that there was something belittling in her taking him for granted so completely. "But you don't have to treat me like old dog Trey."

Martha sighed, her mirth vanished, and took the ice cubes from the refrigerator. "Will you make us a drink, dear?"

He got the ice bucket, and was gone from the room a few moments, getting the gin and vermouth.

"Allan, I've decided not to go to the Shanley's again for a while," she said when he returned.

"Oh?"

"You don't really enjoy it, do you?"

"Not much. That's the truth. It's pretty rough for a man to know he's accepted in a place only because his wife's so much brighter than he is. Jack makes no bones about his contempt. And sometimes, when we're there, you don't either."

"Now, that isn't true, Allan. That's just something in your own imagination that pops out when you've had a bad day. I know exactly when it happens—it comes out when your jokes go flat. Those silly wisecracks of yours—when they're bad, they're horrible, Allan. And even when they're good, they have a way of killing a conversation."

"They must be pretty rotten most of the time considering that the conversation doesn't usually begin to lag till two thirty in the morning."

"I didn't think it was that late," she said.

And so they were diverted from a growing quarrel. He twisted the lemon peels on top of their martinis, then touched his glass to hers.

"To us," Martha said. "I promise, no more late nights." She sipped her drink. "They say Kelley's volunteer police have messed things up again. Remember the drug store man last year?"

Allan nodded. It was closer to two years ago, but the Point True pharmacist had been murdered in his shop, a boxful of change had been taken by his attacker, and, it had been said, the murderer's tracks covered by the local investigators, presumably while investigating. The crime was still unsolved.

"They're saying the same thing's happened again—the temporary police threshing around the woods, looking for clues. As Jack said when he was trying to find him up there—and it seems to have caught on with everybody—'Has anybody here seen Kelley?' "

"When did you see Jack?"

"I didn't. I talked to Betty on the telephone. Allan, you don't think that Jack and I—that there's anything between us, do you?"

"No, I guess not," he said, and such a thought had never stayed very long in his mind, not really. "If there was, you wouldn't talk so much, the two of you."

"That's an interesting observation."

"My God, though, Martha—his own wife never shuts up. How does the man take it?"

"Very easily. Sometimes he listens, sometimes he doesn't." She went to the door and called out, "Jeff, five minutes. Wash up for dinner."

Tom Sommers, getting off the bus at his own gate, felt that his house was empty, and the cold fear got to him that never again would it hold Ellen and himself as it had, happily, for as much of the child's life as she could remember. Even if the Rossi business affected them no further . . .

They had had their breakfast in the usual manner, only a little of the strain between them showing, both seeming to pretend that nothing unusual had happened the evening before. It seemed best, by unspoken mutual consent, to carry this day on like all the others.

Only when he had been about to leave the house and paused to kiss her cheek, as was their custom, had the difference now between them been manifest: he sensed the little stiffening in her body as he came near her—and he had gone no nearer, saying his "Goodbye, my dear," to the back of her head, and getting a far too gay to be genuine, "Goodbye, papa." How ironic, he had thought then, if he were to become the principal object of her resentment.

But at breakfast time Ellen had not known that Rossi was dead. He was no longer as sure of it then himself as he had been the night before.

In the house he found a note from Ellen: she would soon be home, but in the meantime would he please set the oven at 350 degrees and put in the casserole which Sylvia had left? (Sylvia was the woman who worked for them by the day.) How like any other day's note this one

read, and how almighty unlike other days the day itself
had been!

And must continue to be. Sommers knew his own moment of decision was almost on him. There were at least
two people who would suggest his name to Chief of Police Kelley as a likely suspect for the murder of Rossi.

He lighted and set the stove . . . Allan Ford—who
was he, really? What kind of man was he beneath the
clown that he played as endlessly as a child at being a
grownup? What did he see when he shaved himself?
Someone, Sommers thought, he wasn't very fond of. Yet
out of all that heavy-drinking, loose-mouthed crowd who
chummed together on the bus, Ford was the only man
Sommers cared a second thought about. Ford might not
like what he was, but he didn't complain in public about
it, or of his job, his clients, or the squandering of his tal-
ents in the market place.

But how curious to have met him at the crossroad after
the murder! Ford had come down the road from the direction of the tavern, a tavern closed at least an hour by then,
as Sommers himself knew. What kind of mission had
sent Ford out on the desolate road at such an hour? Ford
was not a walker as Sommers himself was by nature.

His wife was at the Shanleys', he'd said—his pretty,
bauble-minded wife whom he must have thought he had
won by a miracle the day she consented to marry him.
That whole crowd, Sommers thought, like most American males, married from the neck down.

The phone rang, jangling every nerve in his body. But
it was Ellen. Would he mind terribly if she did not come
home for dinner? Cathie Rapp had asked her . . . He
minded; and also he did not mind because, he decided, it
indicated an answer to a question foremost in his dilemma: he would say now that Ellen did not know he had
gone out before last midnight and returned home well after one A.M.

But whether she knew it or not, the fact remained. He

had gone up to Rossi's; he had had motive to kill Rossi; and Rossi was dead.

Even Kelley could add that up to an indictment, and he would want to quickly, being still under fire for the drug store fiasco. This was the dilemma: if he confided in the police, might he not be merely sacrificing himself to them?

Somewhere in the hour during which he chopped wood, washed, and ate a meager supper, the idea took hold of him that it was a problem needful of a lawyer's advice.

Shanley?

It was hard not to think of him at such a moment, his reputation in criminal law being what it was. Sommers also knew Shanley's reputation as the man who threw the biggest parties in Point True—a boon to the village tradesmen, in fact to the whole village, where he was considered a sort of household god, their man of distinction. An advantage, especially considering Sommer's reputation as a recluse.

There was something elsc that entered into the rationalization of his calling on Shanley: his was the house where Ford had been last night, and where he might have mentioned meeting Tom Sommers at the crossroad at that most significant hour.

He telephoned, then walked up the hill to see the lawyer.

"A social call—or business?" Shanley asked, giving Sommers a hand as strong as a farmer's. He looked the outdoor man, robust, tanned, healthy.

"Let's call it social, anyway," Mrs. Shanley said, "and we can have a drink together before I go upstairs. I think I know your daughter, Mr. Sommers. A lovely child."

"A child, ha!" Shanley said.

A sudden lump rose to Sommer's throat, and with it a wariness of Shanley. His rationalizations for having come began to weaken.

The lawyer looked at him. "What do you drink?" It was scarcely more than a glance, but Sommers felt his soul to have been penetrated. He tried to tell himself that Shanley was more an actor than a seer.

"Scotch, please."

"I suppose you've heard all about the murder," Betty Shanley said. "That's one thing about living in a small town—you can't miss anything even if you try."

"Not easily," Sommers murmured.

"I suppose you want a stinger, Betty?" her husband said. "Damn fool woman's drink."

"That'd be just lovely, Jack." Mrs. Shanley winked at the visitor. "He always says that, pretending it's on my account he has to make it. But you just notice: he'll make one for himself at the same time."

Sommers managed a smile. Whatever he had expected in Shanley's wife, this woman did not fulfill it. She had probably once been as trim as Allan Ford's wife, but she had gone as soft as a warm chocolate cream, of which she reminded him. She spoke with a drawl, and endlessly, not seeming to require any answers.

Sommers felt himself recovering some inner composure in her dribbling sort of chatter. Shanley was at the other end of the big room, concocting the stinger, whatever that was, in an electric mixer. It was not so much what she was that restored him, Sommers thought, but that she was Shanley's wife. She made a least common denominator to which he could reduce Shanley himself, and in those terms the famous lawyer was not quite so formidable.

Mrs. Shanley was soon talking to Sommers as if he were an intimate. "We've got a friend who's awfully fond of Mrs. Rossi. I've often thought he might—well, kind of visit her on the sly sometimes. I wouldn't say anything more that that, him being a friend and all, and a married gentleman. That'd be gossip."

"Did she have visitors?" Sommers surprised himself, putting the question that way, or, indeed, at all.

"I'd say Anna accepted visitors sometimes, Jack wouldn't you?" Mrs. Shanley asked innocently, but of course understanding perfectly.

"I wouldn't say." Shanley passed the drinks. "Not your married gentleman, anyway. He doesn't have the guts to carry on an affair."

"Does it take guts?" Mrs. Shanley seemed to be musing aloud.

"It would take guts to kill her husband, at any rate," Shanley said, "and I don't think our Allan has 'em."

"Besides," Mrs. Shanley said, "he *was* here till two thirty."

Sommers kept his eyes on the glass while he thought about that. This, he told himself, was what he had really come to hear. He was inclined to agree that it would be hard to see Allan Ford as a murderer, although he disliked Shanley just a little more for the way he had said it. And nobody here seemed to have known Ford was out of the house at the crucial time! It must make a man feel strange—to make so inconspicuous an absence! No wonder Ford's hand had come out of the darkness in search of a friend.

Shanley sat down opposite him. "Did you know Rossi?"

"No." The word seemed to crack in Sommer's throat.

The lawyer's eyes were probing. "But you must have heard certain things about him?"

"There was gossip, you know," Mrs. Shanley put in.

"I keep pretty much to myself," Sommers said, retreating even further. "Because of Ellen, and by choice."

"Ellen, of course," Betty Shanley said. "I was trying to remember your daughter's name."

"Rossi was several kinds of scum," Shanley said. "For my part I don't believe he was clobbered to death over a satchel of money."

"They found the satchel in one of the abandoned well-diggings,'' his wife said, ''and the money too—the change was scattered all over the woods.''

''A killer with a hole in his pocket and a police chief with a hole in his head,'' said the lawyer.

'' 'Has anybody here seen Kelley?','' Mrs. Shanley drawled chidingly, and looked at her husband. ''Oh, Jack, what a thing to say about a man!''

''Poor fool—he deserves it.'' Shanley shook with silent laughter.

Sommers took a mouthful of his drink. He was afraid to drink it, and afraid not to, so precarious was his position. He did not know what the joke was about, but he was sure he would not like it. This was the house of a despoiler. Shanley would defend the devil no more cynically than he would the innocent. And he was a leech; he seemed to suck at the very substance of a man's soul while bantering him with words.

''Now you didn't come to see me about the Rossi affair, Sommers, did you?'' the lawyer said blandly. He turned to his wife. ''Why don't you take the shaker, Betty, and go along upstairs now?''

Mrs. Shanley got up while she spoke. ''Where I come from, the gentleman waits for the lady to retire. The trouble with you, Jack . . .''

''I'm not a gentleman,'' Shanley finished her sentence.

''No need to go, Mrs. Shanley.'' Sommers got clumsily to his feet. ''On my account, at least. It was only about—Kelley that I came to see you.'' He hoped fervently that this sudden lie would serve to get him out of here. And poor Kelley would scarcely feel another kick. ''If this murder goes unsolved, I think we should abolish the Point True police force and consolidate with the township.''

''You think so?'' Shanley sat where he was for a moment, smiling, scrutinizing his visitor. Then he got up and without another word strode across to the adjoining room, a library or study.

Mrs. Shanley lingered, a little look of apprehension on her face. When the lawyer returned, she said, "Now, Jack, it's just coincidence."

"Go upstairs," he said. And to Sommers, "Here's something you may want to sign, if that's the way you feel."

Sommers glanced at the petition thrust into his hands. It outlined the same idea he had just proposed. "Yes," he said. "I shall certainly want to sign it." He could feel the pulse throbbing at his right temple.

"I drew this up after the last meeting of the Village Board," Shanley said, "two weeks ago."

"You can see how far out of touch I am then. I thought I'd come up with a new idea." He supposed now he must have overheard talk on the bus which his subconscious dredged up when he needed an excuse to get away. "I'm sorry to have troubled you."

"Good night, Mr. Sommers," Shanley's wife said from the stairway. "I hope you'll come again and bring your charming daughter. I adore teenaged girls. And I'm sure Jack does, don't you, honey?"

Shanley did not answer. He stood smiling, aloof and tolerant, until she was out of sight. Then he said, imitating his wife's drawl: "Teenaged girls *can* be very enticing."

Sommers went, almost blindly to the door. He suspected now that Shanley was deliberately provoking him. Or was it all his imagination, the nightmare inside a nightmare? Shanley might only be mocking his own wife.

"Sommers," Shanley said when they were both outdoors. "It's not necessary that you like your lawyer, you know. You just have to hold his advocacy in some regard."

"I'll remember that," Sommers murmured.

"And something else—I don't like being played for a sucker, but I won't ever turn down a Point True man who comes to me for counsel."

* * *

Chief Phil Kelley knew most of the things being said about him in the village. He knew how shaky his job was, and he also knew he had five kids to support, the oldest one in high school, the youngest—and last, please God—in rompers.

He knew the parallel the villagers were drawing between Rossi's murder and the druggist's, and he knew that some of the loudest talkers were aware that the comparison was neither fair nor accurate. But who ever worried about being fair to a policeman? In the case of the druggist, somebody in the police service had deliberately messed up the clues, somebody who had hated the druggist's guts; Kelley knew it, he even knew who the deputy was, but he had no proof. And in the end he could not even fire the deputy: the Village Board had turned down his recommendation on the basis of insufficient grounds.

In the Rossi case, his deputies were not plowing under any possible clues. The little black money satchel had turned up in an abandoned well-drilling. It was not unreasonable to hope the weapon might also turn up in an old well. That meant a difficult search: the abandoned diggings were not all dry.

One of the favorite jokes about Kelley—and he knew this one, too—was on the way he had of sitting in the patrol car outside Rossi's Tavern and clocking speeders on the Upper Road. How else was a cop to make a living in Point True, they grinned. But the fact of the situation was that too many kids from the township high school used Rossi's as a rendezvous, and Kelley felt that the presence of the patrol car there would turn some of the youngsters away.

Now and then, too, he was in the habit of walking into the place—to get a cup of coffee, or more often, to call his wife. Thus, without making an issue of it, he watched for licensing violations. And it was in this unostentatious fashion that he had learned of Rossi and his clientele, a knowledge that he hoped fervently would serve him now.

He knew, for example, that Rossi was fond, far too fond, of young girls—though never could a complaint be got against him.

But that evening, when it was reported to him by a deputy that Tom Sommers had just paid a visit to the lawyer, Shanley, Kelley thought about Ellen Sommers. He had never seen her at the tavern. But that did not prove anything.

Kelley went into his dining room after getting the report. It seemed a shame to disturb so perfect a picture: four of his children doing homework at once. He asked his daughter to come into the kitchen for a minute.

"Do you know if Ellen Sommers has a boy friend?"

"No, I don't," she said—in a way Kelley understood to mean she did know but wasn't telling.

"I don't think her father would know it if she had one," the policeman said, "him being as strict a man as he is."

"He isn't as fierce as he looks," his daughter said. "That's just his way. I think he's handsome."

"Mr. Sommers?" Kelley said, no longer understanding.

The girl said, "Now, don't be jealous, daddy!"

"Oh, for heaven's sake! Go back to your homework."

He was putting on his coat, however, when she came out to the hall. "Daddy, I'll tell you, only you mustn't say where you heard it. Ellen's just mad about Ted Green. It's awful really, because Ted makes fun of her. I mean, about how she was brought up, so strict, and she won't drink or anything. But Ellen's so mad in love, she doesn't care what he says."

"Thanks. I won't say anything. Good night, my dear." Kelley kissed her forehead. "Tell mother not to wait up for me."

Ted Green was a regular customer at Rossi's Tavern.

Sommers, coming down into the village after his nerve-wracking half hour at the Shanley house, wanted more than anything else to see his daughter. It was after nine o'clock, so he called at the Rapps' and asked Ellen if she would like to walk home with him.

They walked block after block in painful silence. Ellen, he noticed, stayed carefully apart from him.

"I wish to God your mother were alive now," he blurted out finally, as helpless as a child himself.

"I wish I was dead," the girl said, the morning's pretense of high spirits vanishing.

"Why?"

Ellen did not answer.

"Something like your experience happens to most people, Ellen, at one time or other. It's the sad truth about human beings. And you know he's dead, don't you?"

"It isn't him. It's you. I don't want to talk about it even."

"But I do, Ellen. Whatever it is you're accusing me of, I must know what it is."

"I wish I hadn't told you what happened! Oh, how I wish I hadn't." The child began to cry. She was a wraith of a girl, all the more a child for crowding a womanhood she did not understand. "You made me feel so filthy."

"Child dearest, I meant just the opposite, whatever I may have said. I was talking about Rossi . . ."

"Stop talking about him, papa! He's dead and I don't care. I'm not even glad. Only I don't want to talk about him—not ever!"

After a few long seconds Sommers said quietly, "Do you want to talk about Ted Green?"

"Oh, no—no!" she said, even more in agony.

"What did I say, Ellen? What did I do? I tried to tell you that all men were not like him—not like Rossi."

"I know that's what you said. And you proved it! You said you hadn't seen a woman since my mother."

"Is that what it is—my saying that?"

The girl didn't answer. She averted her face and began to weep softly. Sometimes her feet stumbled, but she caught herself and still stayed apart from him.

Yes, Sommers thought, he could remember saying that: so righteous, so wrongly righteous, and after she had brought the whole agonizing story to him, even confessing her humiliation in waiting for a boy . . . He cleared his throat. "I wish I could explain something that happened to me last night after you had gone to bed. I wanted to kill him . . ."

"He doesn't matter, papa."

"I know that, I believe it, too." He wanted desperately now to communicate the good thing that had happened to him. But he knew even while he spoke that the telling of it was merely a diversion. Nevertheless he plunged ahead. "Let me try to tell you this, Ellen. I won't go into where or how, and I don't believe in ghosts, but there was an instant last night when I felt your mother as close to me as she ever was alive."

In the light of an approaching car he glimpsed the girl's face. What he was trying to say was not getting through to her at all. "Ellen!"

When she looked at him he forced himself, flatly, simply, to tell a very personal truth—a truth which related to her agony, not to his mystical experience. "It's not that I haven't wanted to see another woman. Sometimes I've wanted to very much."

Her tears welled abundantly, along with little choking sobs. He had touched the very core of her misery. "Oh, papa, isn't it awful, what happens inside us?"

He dared then to take her hand in his and squeeze it gently. Her response was quick and fierce, a clutch of his hand and then the freeing of it. She was too diffident for anything demonstrative.

"It isn't awful at all," he said. "Sometimes it's wonderful. What is awful is not being able to understand it or talk about it."

Chief Kelley did not conceal his car. But he parked it around the corner from the Sommers' house, not wanting to call the neighbors' attention to it. Then he waited on the porch. It was such a clear night he could see the lights across the river doubled by their reflection in the water. He spoke as soon as father and daughter turned in the gate.

Sommers hesitated, then came on. "Good evening, Kelley. Ellen, I think it would be better if you go up to your room."

"I'd like to talk to Ellen too, Mr. Sommers."

He came as quickly to the point as he could, accepting only the hospitality of a chair in the living room. "I want to ask you, Ellen, when was the last time you were in Rossi's Tavern?"

It was an unfair approach, but both father and daughter responded.

"I was only . . ."

"Ellen does not patronize taverns," Sommers said over the girl's words.

Kelley was not turned aside. "My daughter isn't allowed to either, Mr. Sommers, but I got the feeling that if there was somebody in one she wanted very much to be with, she might just make an exception to the rules I lay down. Ellen, speak for yourself."

"Yes, sir."

"When?"

"Yesterday evening. Only the person I wanted to see wasn't there."

"Who was there?"

The girl's voice was very low, and her face flushed. Sommers sat, pale and tense, working his hands.

"Just Mr. Rossi, sir—at first. I asked him if he'd seen this person I was looking for, and he said no, but that I could wait. He expected him."

"You may as well tell me the whole story," Kelley said.

"The man got her in a corner and made advances to her," Sommers interrupted. The veins were standing out on his forehead.

"Nothing else happened, Mr. Kelley," Ellen said. "I

tried to run away but he'd locked the door. You see, he'd got me to go into the back room to wait so that I wouldn't actually be in the tavern. And then—I don't quite know how it happened. But Mrs. Rossi came in through the rear door. She had a key, I think. But I just ran. She was shouting at him in Italian. But I ran all the way down through the woods home.''

"And told your father?"

She nodded.

"I don't suppose there's much point now in asking why you didn't come to me about it, Mr. Sommers?"

"If you can't keep youngsters like Green out of places like that, what could I expect? This isn't the first time something like this has happened.''

"I know it's not, but I need a signed complaint before I can do anything." The policeman paused, thinking about it. "Can you tell me another time something like this happened?''

"No, but I'd suggest you talk to Shanley on the hill about it.''

"I just might," Kelley said. There was no one he cared less to talk to. Shanley had the arrogance of Satan. "Is that what you went to see him about?''

"No—it was on a private matter.''

"I see." Kelley turned to Ellen who was making pellets in her lap out of damp kleenex. "Who else did you talk to besides your father? ''

"Nobody. I swear it, Mr. Kelley.''

"Didn't Ted Green want to know why you didn't meet him?''

The girl spoke almost in a whisper. "He didn't know I was going to be there, Mr. Kelley. It wasn't actually a date, you see.''

"Isn't that enough, Kelley?" Sommers demanded.

"From Ellen? I think so, Mr. Sommers, and I guess if it's all right with you, the two of us could do our talking down in the village.''

He purposely avoided mentioning the stationhouse,

and Sommers threw him a grateful look. Outdoors, the policeman said, "Just what did you do about it, Sommers?"

"Nothing in the end. But I'm not sure I can prove it."

The policeman opened the car door. "Do you have such little confidence in the Point True police that you feel you've got to prove your innocence?"

"I don't have much confidence, that's the truth," Sommers admitted. He seemed to be examining his hands by the light of the dashboard. "And maybe I'm a little ashamed of my innocence."

They drove in silence to the station, and there waiting at the desk was Allan Ford.

Sommers smiled faintly. "Another crossroad?"

"The light's a lot better down here. You can tell a friend from a stranger. Have you told him about meeting me?"

"No. I assumed you had."

Ford shook his head.

"Sometimes I'm just lucky," the policeman said with a trace of bitterness. "Now you can both tell me." He took a cluster of messages from the desk officer and motioned Ford and Sommers to sit down while he glanced through them.

"About one o'clock this morning," Ford started, "Sommers and I met at where Cemetery Road crosses the Upper Road."

"You were not at Shanley's?" Kelley said, looking up.

"I was, but sometimes when I can't keep awake, I go out for a walk. If Rossi's Tavern is open, I have a quick beer. I've done it before and never been missed."

"Shanley wouldn't miss his own wife, he's that self-centered," the policeman said.

"Especially his wife," Sommers said.

Ford looked at him. "You know them?"

"Only from a half-hour's observation tonight."

"Let's take care of last night first," Kelley said. "Go on, Ford."

"The tavern was closed when I got there, so I turned around and started back to the Shanley house. That's when I met Sommers coming down Cemetery Road."

"And where were you coming from, Mr. Sommers?" Kelley asked quietly.

Sommers drew a deep breath. "The cemetery. I'll tell you the truth, Kelley, and you'll have to make out of it what you will. I did go to Rossi's Tavern. I waited until Ellen went to bed, and it must have been just before twelve when I got there, but the place was already closed. I had a .32 revolver in my pocket and I intended to kill him. At least, that's what I thought I intended to do." He glanced at Ford. "He had—molested my daughter."

Ford did not say anything.

"I ran most of the way to Rossi's house then, down the Upper Road and up Cemetery Hill. There was a light on, and music playing. I hammered on the door, but no one came. I went round to the back and did the same thing. Still no one answered. Then, just standing there . . ." He shrugged. "A little mad, perhaps—I realized how close I was to the cemetery, to Ellen's mother's grave."

Sommers entwined, then freed his long, thin fingers—too delicate by far, Kelley thought, for the brutal bludgeoning that had killed Rossi.

"I was coming down from there when I met Allan Ford. Well, first I had gone into the cemetery. I can't tell you what happened to me. It was a wild night . . . an extraordinary experience." He got up and moved about like someone long pent up, a prisoner. "I don't know how to tell it. It was like being in communication with the spirit world. Maybe its just—that I didn't want to kill. But I tell you now, I think I had the feeling that Rossi was dead. Something, somehow, made that known to me."

There was silence for a few seconds, except for the police radio rumbling indistinct alarms behind them.

"I can believe that," Ford said. "I saw him, Chief. I shook hands with him, just passing, and I tell you there was something different about him, something electric."

"It was a spooky night, I know that myself," the policeman said.

"I heard the music at Rossi's, too," Ford said.

"But neither of you heard anything you'd connect with the murder?"

"Not unless it was the music playing at the Rossi house," Ford said.

"I'll say this," Sommers offered. "I would swear Shanley knew tonight what had happened to my daughter. And there were only two people from whom he could have found it out—Rossi or Rossi's wife. Unless she told you today and you passed it on to him?"

Kelley shook his head. "Did he *say* he knew it?"

Disappointingly, Sommers admitted that he had not said it in so many words.

"But look," Ford said, "unless my wife and Betty Shanley can back him up—doesn't Shanley's alibi for last night disappear when he's no longer alibi-ing me?"

"It does," the policeman said.

"But Shanley and Anna Rossi," Ford said tentatively. "It just doesn't seem right."

"His devotion to his wife is no deterrent," Sommers said.

"Maybe not," Ford said, weakening a little, "and by God, Betty Shanley hints at something like it every once in a while. But why would Shanley kill Rossi? If Rossi did know about him and his wife, I don't think he'd have made much fuss over it, considering his own infidelities. He might even have bragged about it."

"Isn't that just possibly your answer?" Sommers said quietly. "Do you think Shanley would tolerate gossip in the village about him and—and someone he'd consider a peasant woman?"

"Why not?" Ford said after a moment. 'I'll tell you the truth, I don't see why not."

"You think it would please his ego," Sommers said, "for the village to know that he had so—sexy—a mistress?"

His hesitation on the word made both Kelley and Ford turn suddenly to look at him. "You know her too, then?" Kelley said.

"Only from observation," Sommers said, "though I've sometimes wished it otherwise." He lifted his head. "I'm a walker in the hills, and I've watched her work in the garden, among the vineyards she's coaxing to grow up there. I've even heard her singing, and I've felt she would be a wonderful woman to—to know."

"Me, too," Ford said. "She's a pleasure to hear and to look at, and I've always liked her, the times I've met her."

Kelley drew his legs slowly beneath him, dreading to get up. "I guess that's how we all feel about Anna Rossi. You gentlemen have made me sure that I'm right. I'm not even going to say thank you. It's a funny thing: I think I'm going to prove to all you people now that I'm a pretty good cop, and in the end it'll probably lose me my job. Nobody's going to pin a medal on me for arresting Anna Rossi for the murder of her husband."

Anna Rossi did not even have a second sleeping pill to indicate there might have been a first one; she did not have a prescription, or a box or bottle, to show the policeman. Music had been her best friend for years, she said, like somebody in the house worth having there. It was her natural accessory in a crude plot that night. The weapon was a stone hammer—the peculiar shape of which had been clearly indicated in the photographs of the victim's skull. She said she would try to remember in which old well she had dropped it. Only vaguely had she planned to have the murder seem like an older one in the village below. The comparison had been drawn by the villagers. Actually she was not concerned whether she was discovered or not.

"I had to kill a pig," she said with terrifying matter-of-factness. " After all, it was my pig."

Sommers and Ford exchanged the briefest of greetings the morning after Mrs. Rossi's arraignment. They would both be witnesses for the defense. And both agreed: she had a good lawyer in Shanley.

1959

By the Scruff of the Soul

Most people, when they go down from the Ragapoo Hills, never come back; or if they do, for a funeral maybe—weddings don't count for so much around here any more either—you can see them fidgeting to get away again. As for me, I'm one of those rare birds they didn't have any trouble keeping down on the farm after he'd seen Paree.

It's forty years since I've seen the bright lights, but I don't figure I've missed an awful lot. Hell, I can remember the Ku Klux Klan marching right out in the open. My first case had to do with a revenue agent—I won it, too, and we haven't had a government man up here since. And take the League of Nations—I felt awful sorry in those days for Mr. Wilson though I didn't hold with his ideas.

Maybe things have changed, but sometimes I wonder just how much. This bomb I don't understand, fallout and all, but I've seen what a plague of locusts can do to a wheat field and I don't think man's ever going to beat nature when it comes to pure, ornery destruction. I could be wrong about that. Our new parson says I am and he's a mighty knowing man. Too knowing, maybe. I figure that's why the Synod shipped him up to us in Webbtown.

As I said, I don't figure I'm missing much. There's a couple of television sets in town and sometimes of an evening I'll sit for an hour or so in front of whichever one of them's working best. One of them gets the shimmies

154

every time the wind blows and the other don't bring in anything except by way of Canada. Same shows but different commercials. That kind of tickles me, all them companies advertising stuff you couldn't buy if you wanted to instead of stuff you wouldn't want if you could buy it.

But, as you've probably guessed by now, I'd rather talk than most anything, and since you asked about The Red Lantern, I'll tell you about the McCracken sisters who used to run it—and poor old Matt Sawyer.

I'm a lawyer, by the way. I don't get much practice out here. I'm also Justice of the Peace. I don't get much practice out of that either, but between the two I make a living. For pleasure I fish for trout and play the violin, and at this point in my life I think I can say from experience that practice ain't everything.

I did the fiddling at Clara McCracken's christening party, I remember, just after coming home from the first World War. Maudie was about my age then, so's that'd make a difference of maybe twenty years between the sisters, and neither chit nor chizzler in between, and after them, the whole family suddenly dies out. That's how it happens up here in the hills: one generation and there'll be aunts and uncles galore, and the next, you got two maiden ladies and a bobtailed cat.

The Red Lantern Inn's boarded up now, as you saw, but it was in the McCracken family since just after the American Revolution. It was burned down once—in a reprisal raid during the War of 1812, and two of the McCrackens were taken hostage. Did you know Washington, D.C. was also burned in reprisal? It was. At least that's how they tell it over in Canada—for the way our boys tore up the town they call Toronto now. You know, history's like a story in a way: it depends on who's telling it.

Anyways, Maudie ran the inn after the old folks died, and she raised Clara the best she could, but Clara was a wild one from the start. We used to call her a changeling:

one minute she'd be sitting at the stove and the next she'd
be off somewhere in the hills. She wasn't a pretty girl—
the jutting McCracken jaw spoiled that—but there were
times she was mighty feminine, and many a lad got
thorny feet chasing after the will-o'-the-wisp.

As Clara was coming to age, Maudie used to keep a
birch stick behind the bar, and now and then I dare say
she'd use it, though I never saw it happen but once myself. But that birch stick and Old Faithful, her father's
shotgun, stood in the corner side by side, and I guess we
made some pretty rude jokes about them in those days.
Anyways, Maudie swore to tame the girl and marry her
to what she called a "settled" man.

By the time Clara was of a marrying age, The Red
Lantern was getting pretty well rundown. And so was
Maudie. She wasn't an easy woman by any calculation.
She had a tongue you'd think was sharpened on the grind-
stone and a store of sayings that'd shock you if you didn't
know your Bible. The inn was peeling paint and wanting
shutters to the northeast, which is where they're needed
most. But inside, Maudie kept the rooms as clean and
plain as a glass egg. And most times they were about as
empty.

It was the taproom kept the sisters going. They drew
the best beer this side of Cornwall, England. If they knew
you, that is. If they didn't know you, they served you a
labeled bottle, stuff you'd recognize by the signboard
pictures. About once a month, Maudie had to buy a case
of that—which gives you an idea of how many strangers
stopped over in Webbtown. We had more stores then and
the flour mill was working, so the farmers'd come in regular. But none of them were strangers. You see, even to
go to Ragapoo City, the county seat, you've got to go
twenty miles around—unless you're like Clara was,
skipping over the mountain.

Matt Sawyer came through every week or two in those
days and he always stopped at Prouty's Hardware Store.
Matt was a paint salesman. I suppose he sold Prouty a

few gallons over the year. Who bought it from Prouty, I couldn't say. But Prouty liked Matt. I did myself when I got to know him. Or maybe I just felt sorry for him.

It was during the spring storms, this particular day. The rain was popping blisters on Main Street. Most everyone in Webbtown seems to have been inside looking out that day. Half the town claimed afterwards to have seen Matt come out of Prouty's raising his black umbrella over Maudie's head and walking her home. I saw them myself, Maudie pulling herself in and Matt half in and half out. I know for a fact she'd never been under an umbrella before in her life.

Prouty told me afterwards he'd forgot she was in the store when he was talking to Matt: Maudie took a mighty long time making up her mind before buying anything. Like he always did, Prouty was joshing Matt about having enough money to find himself a nice little woman and give up the road. Maudie wasn't backward. She took a direct line: she just up and asked Matt since he had an umbrella, would he mind walking her home. Matt was more of a gentleman than anybody I ever knew. He said it would be a pleasure. Maybe it was, but that was the beginning of the doggonedest three-cornered courtship in the county history. And it's all documented today in the county court records over in Ragapoo City. But I'm getting ahead of myself.

I've got my office in my hat, you might say, and I hang that in rooms over Kincaid's Drug Store. I was standing at the window when Matt and Maudie came out of Prouty's. I remember I was trying to tune my violin. You can't keep a fiddle in tune weather like that. I played kind of ex tempore for a while, drifting from one thing to another—sad songs mostly, like "The Vacant Chair." *We shall meet but we shall miss him . . . there will be one vacant chair.* I got myself so depressed I hung up the fiddle and went down to The Red Lantern for a glass of Maudie's Own.

Well, sure enough, there was Matt Sawyer sitting at the bar advising Maudie on the costs of paint and trimming and how to estimate the amount of paint a place the size of The Red Lantern would need. Now I knew Maudie couldn't afford whitewash, much less the high-class line of stuff Matt represented. But there she was, leaning on the bar, chin in hand and her rump in the air like a swaybacked mule. She drew me a beer and put a head on Matt's. Then she went back to listening to him.

I don't know how long it took me to notice what was really going on: I'm slow sometimes, but all this while Clara was standing on a stool polishing a row of fancy mugs Maudie kept on a ledge over the back mirror. The whole row of lights was on under the ledge and shining double in the mirror. Hell, Matt Sawyer wasn't actually making sense at all, what he was saying in facts and figures. He was just making up words to keep old Maudie distracted—he thought—and all the while gazing up at Clara every chance he'd get. I might as well be honest with you: it was looking at Clara myself I realized what was going on in that room. The way she was reaching up and down in front of that mirror and with a silk petticoat kind of dress on, you'd have sworn she was stark naked.

Well, sir, just think about that. Matt, being a gentleman, was blushing and yearning—I guess you'd call it that—but making conversation all the time; and Maudie was conniving a match for Clara with a man who could talk a thousand dollars' worth of paint without jumping his Adam's apple. I'll say this about Maudie: for an unmarried lady she was mighty knowing in the fundamentals. Clara was the only innocent one in the room, I got to thinking.

All of a sudden Maudie says to me, "Hank, how's your fiddle these days?"

"It's got four strings," I said.

"You bring it up after supper, hear?" It was Maudie's way never to ask for something. She told you what you were going to do and most often you did it. Clara looked round at me from that perch of hers and clapped her hands.

Maudie laid a bony finger on Matt's hand. "You'll stay to supper with us, Mr. Sawyer. Our Clara's got a leg of lamb in the oven like you never tasted. It's home hung and roasted with garden herbs."

Now I knew for a fact the only thing Clara ever put in the oven was maybe a pair of shoes to warm them of a winter's morning. And it was just about then Clara caught on, too, to what Maudie was maneuvering. Her eyes got a real wild look in them, like a fox cornered in a chicken coop. She bounded down and across that room . . .

I've often wondered what would've happened if I hadn't spoken then. It gives me a cold chill thinking about it—words said with the best intentions in the world. I called out just as she got to the door: "Clara, I'll be bringing up my fiddle."

I don't suppose there ever was a party in Webbtown like Maudie put on that night. Word got around. Even the young folks came that mightn't have if it was spooning weather. Maudie wore her best dress—the one she was saving, we used to say, for Clara's wedding and her own funeral. It was black, but on happier occasions she'd liven it up with a piece of red silk at the collar. I remember Prouty saying once that patch of red turned Maudie from a Holstein into a Guernsey. Prouty, by the way, runs the undertaking parlor as well as the hardware store.

I near split my fingers that night fiddling. Maudie tapped a special keg. Everybody paid for his first glass, but after that she put the cash box away and you might say she drew by heart.

Matt was having a grand time just watching mostly. Matt was one of those creamy-looking fellows, with cheeks as pink as winter apples. He must've been fifty but there wasn't a line or wrinkle in his face. And I never seen him without his collar and tie on. Like I said, a gentleman.

Clara took to music like a bird to wing. I always got the feeling no matter who was taking her in or out she was actually dancing alone; she could do two steps to everybody else's one. Matt never took his eyes off her, and once he danced with her when Maudie pushed him into it.

That was trouble's start—although we didn't know it at the time. Prouty said afterwards he did, but Prouty's a man who knows everything after the fact. That's being an undertaker, I dare say. Anyway, Matt was hesitating after Clara—and it was like that, her sort of skipping ahead and leading him on, when all of a sudden, young Reuben White leaped in between them and danced with Clara the way she needed to be danced with.

Now Reuben didn't have much to recommend him, especially to Maudie. He did an odd job now and then—in fact, he hauled water for Maudie from the well she had up by the brewhouse back of Maple Tree Ridge. And this you ought to know about Maudie if you don't by now—anybody she could boss around, she had no use for.

Anyways, watching that boy dance with Clara that night should've set us all to thinking, him whirling her and tossing her up in the air, them spinning round together like an August twister. My fiddle's got a devil in it at a time like that. Faster and faster I was bowing, till plunk I broke a string, but I went right on playing.

Matt fell back with the other folks, clapping and cheering, but Maudie I could see going after her stick. I bowed even faster, seeing her. It was like a race we were all in together. Then all of a sudden, like something dying high up in the sky and falling mute, my E string broke and I wasn't playing any more. In the center of the tavern floor Clara and Reuben just folded up together and slumped down into a heap.

Everybody was real still for about a half a minute. Then Maudie came charging out, slashing the air with that switch of hers. She grabbed Clara by the hair—I swear she lifted the girl to her feet that way and flung her towards the bar. Then she turned on Reuben. That boy slithered clear across the barroom floor, every time just getting out of the way of a slash from Maudie's stick. People by then were cheering in a kind of rhythm—for him or Maudie, you couldn't just be sure, and maybe they weren't for either. "Now!" they'd shout at every whistle of the switch. "Now! Now! *Now!*"

Prouty opened the door just when Reuben got there, and when the boy was out Prouty closed it against Maudie. I thought for a minute she was going to turn on him. But she just stood looking and then burst out laughing. Everybody started clouting her on the back and having a hell of a time.

I was at the bar by then and so was Matt. I heard him, leaning close to Clara, say, "Miss Clara, I never saw anything as beautiful as you in all my life."

Clara's eyes snapped back at him but she didn't say a word.

Well, it was noon the next day before Matt pulled out of town, and sure enough, he forgot his umbrella and came back that night. I went up to The Red Lantern for my five o'clock usual, and him and Maudie were tête-à-tête, as they say, across the bar. Maudie was spouting the praises of her Clara—how she could sew and cook and bake a cherry pie, Billy Boy. The only attention she paid me was as a collaborating witness.

I'll say this for Clara: when she did appear, she looked almost civilized, her hair in a ribbon, and her wearing a new striped skirt and a grandmother blouse clear up to her chin. That night, by glory, she went to the movie with Matt. We had movies every night except Sundays in those days. A year or so ago, they closed up the Bellevue altogether. Why did she go with him? My guess is she wanted to get away from Maudie, or maybe for Reuben to see her dressed up that way.

The next time I saw all of them together was Decoration Day. Matt was back in town, arranging his route so's he'd have to stop over the holiday in Webbtown. One of them carnival outfits had set up on the grounds back of the schoolhouse. Like I said before, we don't have any population to speak of in Webbtown, but we're central for the whole valley, and in the old days traveling entertainers could do all right if they didn't come too often.

There was all sorts of raffle booths—Indian blankets and kewpie dolls, a shooting gallery and one of those things where you throw baseballs at wooden bottles and get a cane if you knock 'em off. And there was an apparatus for testing a man's muscle: you know, you hit the target on the stand with a sledgehammer and then a little ball runs up a track that looks like a big thermometer and registers your strength in pounds.

I knew there was a trick to it no matter what the barker said about it being fair and square. Besides, nobody cares how strong a lawyer is as long as he can whisper in the judge's ear. I could see old Maudie itching herself to have a swing at it, but she wasn't taking any chance at giving Matt the wrong impression about either of the McCracken girls.

Matt took off his coat, folded it, and gave it to Clara to hold. It was a warm day for that time of year and you could see where Matt had been sweating under the coat, but like I said, he was all gentleman. He even turned his back to the ladies before spitting on his hands. It took Matt three swings—twenty-five cents worth—but on the last one that little ball crawled the last few inches up the track and just sort of tinkled the bell at the top. The womenfolk clapped, and Matt put on his coat again, blushing and pleased with himself.

I suppose you've guessed that Reuben showed up then. He did, wearing a cotton shirt open halfway down to his belly.

"Now, my boy," the barker says, "show the ladies, show the world that you're a man! How many?"

Reuben sniggled a coin out of his watch pocket, and mighty cocky for him, he said, "Keep the change."

Well, you've guessed the next part, too: Reuben took one swing and you could hear that gong ring out clear across the valley. It brought a lot of people running and the carnival man was so pleased he took out a big cigar and gave it to Reuben. "That, young fellow, wins you a fifty-cent Havana. But I'll send you the bill if you broke the machine, ha! ha!"

Reuben grinned and took the cigar, and strutting across to Clara, he made her a present of it. Now in Matt's book, you didn't give a lady a cigar, no, sir. Not saying a word, Matt brought his fist up with everything he had dead to center under Reuben's chin. We were all of us plain stunned, but nobody more than Reuben. He lay on the ground with his eyes rolling round in his head like marbles.

You'd say that was the blow struck for romance, wouldn't you? Not if you knew our Clara. She plopped down beside Reuben like he was the dying gladiator, or maybe just something she'd come on helpless in the woods. It was Maudie who clucked and crowed over Matt. All of a sudden Clara leaped up—Reuben was coming round by then—and she gave a whisk of that fancy skirt and took off for the hills, Maudie bawling after her like a hogcaller. And at that point, Reuben scrambled to his feet and galloped after Clara. It wasn't long till all you could see of where they'd gone was a little whiff of dust at the edge of the dogwood grove. I picked up the cigar and tried to smoke it afterwards. I'd have been better off on a mixture of oak leaf and poison ivy.

Everything changed for the worse at The Red Lantern after that. Clara found her tongue and sassed her sister, giving Maudie back word for word, like a common scold. One was getting mean and the other meaner. And short of chaining her, Maudie couldn't keep Clara at home any more, not when Clara wanted to go.

Matt kept calling at The Red Lantern regularly, and Maudie kept making excuses for Clara's not being there. The only times I'd go to the inn those days was when I'd see Matt's car outside. The place would brighten up then, Maudie putting on a show for him. Otherwise, I'd have as soon sat in Prouty's cool room. It was about as cheer-ful. Even Maudie's beer was turning sour.

Matt was a patient man if anything, and I guess being smitten for the first time at his age he got it worse than most of us would: he'd sit all evening just waiting a sight of that girl. When we saw he wasn't going to get over it, Prouty and I undertook one day in late summer to give him some advice. What made us think we were authori-ties, I don't know. I've been living with my fiddle for years and I've already told you what Prouty'd been living with. Anyways, we advised Matt to get himself some hunting clothes—the season was coming round—and to put away that doggone collar and tie of his and get out in the open country where the game was.

Matt tried. Next time he came to Webbtown, as soon as he put in at The Red Lantern, he changed into a plaid wool shirt, brand-new khaki britches, and boots laced up to his knees, and with Prouty and me cheering him on, he headed for the hills. But like Cox's army, or whoever it was, he marched up the hill and marched down again.

But he kept at it. Every week-end he'd show up, change, and set out, going farther and farther every time. One day, when the wind was coming sharp from the northeast, I heard him calling out up there: "Clara . . . Clara . . ."

I'll tell you, that gave me a cold chill, and I wished to the Almighty that Prouty and I had minded our own busi-ness. Maudie would stand at the tavern door and watch him off, and I wondered how long it was going to take for her to go with him. By then, I'd lost whatever feeling I ever had for Maudie and I didn't have much left for Clara either. But what made me plain sick one day was Maudie confiding in me that she was thinking of locking Clara in her room and giving Matt the key. I said something mighty close to obscene such as I'd never said to a woman before in my life and walked out of the tavern.

It was one of those October days, you know, when the clouds keep building up like suds and then just seem to wash away. You could hear the school bell echo, and way off the hawking of the wild geese, and you'd know the only sound of birds till spring would be the lonesome cawing of the crows. I was working on a couple of things I had coming up in Quarter Sessions Court when Prouty pounded up my stairs. Prouty's a pretty dignified man who seldom runs.

"Hank," he said, "I just seen Matt Sawyer going up the hill. He's carrying old man McCracken's shotgun."

I laughed kind of, seeing the picture in my mind. "What do you think he aims to do with it?"

"If he was to fire it, Hank, he'd be likely to blow himself to eternity."

"Maybe the poor buzzard'd be as well off," I said.

"And something else, Hank—Maudie just closed up the tavern. She's stalking him into the hills."

"That's something else," I said, and reached for my pipe.

"What are we going to do?" Prouty fumbled through his pockets for some matches for me. He couldn't keep his hands still.

"Nothing," I said. "The less people in them hills right now the better."

Prouty came to see it my way, but neither one of us could do much work that afternoon. I'd go to the window every few minutes and see Prouty standing in the doorway. He'd look down toward The Red Lantern and shake his head, and I'd know Maudie hadn't come back yet.

Funny, how things go on just the same in a town at a time like that. Tom Kincaid, the druggist, came out and swept the sidewalk clean, passed the time of day with Prouty, and went inside again. The kids were coming home from school. Pretty soon they were all indoors doing their homework before chore time. Doc Sissler stopped at Kincaid's—he liked to supervise the making up of his prescriptions. It was Miss Dorman, the schoolteacher, who gave the first alarm. She always did her next day's lessons before going home, so it was maybe an hour after school let out. I heard her scream and ran to the window.

There was Matt coming down the street on Prouty's side, trailing the gun behind him. You could see he was saying something to himself or just out loud. I opened my window and shouted down to him. He came on then across the street. His step on the stair was like the drum in a death march. When he got to my doorway he just stood there, saying, "I killed her, Hank. I killed her dead."

I got him into a chair and splashed some whiskey out for him. He dropped the gun on the floor beside him and I let it lie there, stepping over it. By then Prouty had come upstairs, and by the time we got the whiskey inside Matt, Luke Weber, the constable, was there.

"He says he killed somebody," I told Weber. "I don't know who."

Matt rolled his eyes towards me like I'd betrayed him just saying what he told me. His face was hanging limp and white as a strung goose. "I know Matt Sawyer," I added then, "and if there was any killing, I'd swear before Jehovah it must've been an accident."

That put a little life back in him. "It was," he said, "it was truly." And bit by piece we got the story out of him.

"I got to say in fairness to myself, taking the gun up there wasn't my own idea," he started. "Look at me, duded up like this—I had no business from the start pretending I was something I wasn' t."

"That was me and Hank's fault," Prouty said, mostly to the constable, "advising him on how to court Miss Clara."

He didn't have to explain that to Weber. Everybody in town knew it.

"I'm not blaming either one of you," Matt said. "It should've been enough for me, chasing an echo every time I thought I'd found her. And both of them once sitting up in a tree laughing at me fit to bust and pelting me with acorns . . ."

We knew he was talking about Reuben and Clara. It

was pathetic listening to a man tell that kind of story on himself, and I couldn't help but think what kind of an impression it was going to make on a jury. I had to be realistic about it: there's some people up here would hang a man for making a fool of himself where they'd let him go for murder. I put the jury business straight out of my mind and kept hoping it was clear-cut accident. He hadn't said yet who was dead, but I thought I knew by then.

"Well, I found them for myself today," he made himself go on, "Clara and Reuben, that is. They were cosied in together in the sheepcote back of Maudie's well. It made me feel ashamed just being there and I was set to sneak away and give the whole thing up for good. But Maudie came up on me and took me by surprise. She held me there—by the scruff of the soul, you might say—and made me listen with her to them giggling and carrying on. I was plain sick with jealousy, I'll admit that.

"Then Maudie gave a shout: 'Come out, you two! Or else we'll blow you out!' Something like that.

"It was a minute or two: nothing happened. Then we saw Reuben going full speed the other way, off towards the woods.

" 'Shoot, Matt, now!' That's what Maudie shouted at me. 'You got him clear to sight.' But just then Clara sauntered out of the shelter towards us—just as innocent and sweet, like the first time I ever laid eyes on her."

I'm going to tell you, Prouty and me looked at each other when he said that.

The constable interrupted him and asked his question straight: "Did she have her clothes on?"

"All but her shoes. She was barefoot and I don't consider that unbecoming in a country girl."

"Go on," Weber told him.

Matt took a long drag of air and then plunged ahead. "Maudie kept hollering at the boy—insults, I guess—I know I'd have been insulted. Then he stopped running and turned around and started coming back. I forget what it was she said to me then—something about my manhood. But she kept saying, 'Shoot, Matt! Shoot, shoot!' I was getting desperate, her hounding me that way. I slammed the gun down between us, butt-end on the ground. The muzzle of it, I guess, was looking her way. And it went off.

"It was like the ground exploding underneath us. Hell smoke and brimstone—that's what went through my mind. I don't know whether it was in my imagination—my ears weren't hearing proper after all that noise—but like ringing in my head I could hear Clara laughing, just laughing like hysterics . . . And then when I could see, there was Maudie lying on the ground. I couldn't even find her face for all that was left of her head."

We stood all of us for a while after that. Listening to the tick of my alarm clock on the shelf over the washstand, I was. Weber picked up the gun then and took it over to the window where he examined the breech.

Then he said, "What did you think you were going to do with this when you took it from the tavern?"

Matt shook his head. "I don't know. When Maudie gave it to me, I thought it looked pretty good on me in the mirror."

I couldn't wait to hear the prosecutor try that one on the jury.

Weber said, "We better get on up there before dark and you show us how it happened."

We stopped by at Prouty's on the way and picked up his wicker basket. There wasn't any way of driving beyond the dogwood grove. People were following us by then. Weber sent them back to town and deputized two or three among them to be sure they kept the peace.

We hadn't got very far beyond the grove, the four of us, just walking, climbing up, and saying nothing. Hearing the crows a-screaming not far ahead gave me a crawling stomach. They're scavengers, you know.

Well, sir, down the hill fair-to-flying, her hair streaming out in the wind, came Clara to meet us. She never hesitated, throwing herself straight at Matt. It was instinct made him put his arms out to catch her and she dove into them and flung her own arms around his neck, hugging him and holding him, and saying things like, "Darling Matt . . . wonderful Matt. I love Matt." I heard her say that.

You'd have thought to see Matt, he'd turned to stone. Weber was staring at them, a mighty puzzled look on his face.

"Miss Clara," I said, "behave yourself."

She looked at me—I swear she was smiling—and said, "You hush, old Hank, or we won't let you play the fiddle at our wedding."

It was Prouty said, hoisting his basket up on his shoulder, "Let's take one thing at a time."

That got us started on our way again. Clara skipping along at Matt's side, trying to catch his hand. Luke Weber didn't say a word.

I'm not going into the details now of what we saw. It was just about like Matt had told it in my office. I was sick a couple of times. I don't think Matt had anything left in him to be sick with. When it came to telling what had happened first, Clara was called on to corroborate. And Weber asked her, "Where's Reuben now, Miss Clara?"

"Gone," she said, "and I don't care."

"Didn't care much about your sister either, did you?" Weber drawled, and I began to see how really bad a spot old Matt was in. There was no accounting Clara's change of heart about him—except he'd killed her sister. The corroborating witness we needed right then was Reuben White.

Prouty got Weber's go-ahead on the job he had to do. I couldn't help him though I tried. What I did when he asked it, was go up to Maudie's well to draw him a pail of water so's he could wash his hands when he was done. Well, sir, I'd have been better off helping him direct. I couldn't get the bucket down to where it would draw the water.

After trying a couple of times, I called out to Weber asking if he had a flashlight. He brought it and threw the beam of light down into the well. Just about the water level a pair of size-twelve shoes were staring up at us—the soles of them like Orphan Annie's eyes.

There wasn't any doubt in our minds that what was holding them up like that was Reuben White, headfirst in the well.

The constable called Clara to him and took a short-cut in his questioning.

"How'd it happen, girl?"

"I guess I pushed him," Clara said, almost casual.

"It took a heap of pushing," Weber said.

"No, it didn't. I just got him to look down and then I tumbled him in."

"Why?"

"Matt," she said, and smiled like a Christmas cherub.

Matt groaned, and I did too inside.

"Leastways, it come to that," Clara explained. Then in that quick-changing way of hers, she turned deep serious. "Mr. Weber, you wouldn't believe me if I told you what Reuben White wanted me to do with him—in the sheepcote this afternoon."

"I might," Luke Weber said.

I looked at Prouty and drew my first half-easy breath. I could see he felt the same. We're both old-fashioned enough to take warmly to a girl's defending her virtue.

But Weber didn't bat an eye. "And where does Matt here come in on it?" he said.

"I figure he won't ever want me to do a thing like that," Clara said, and gazed up at old stoneface with a look of pure adoration.

"Where was Matt when you . . . tumbled Reuben in?" Weber asked, and I could tell he was well on his way to believing her.

"He'd gone down the hill to tell you what'd happened to Sister Maudie."

"And when was it Reuben made this—this proposal to you?" Weber said. I could see he was getting at the question of premeditation. Luke Weber's a pretty fair policeman.

"It was Matt proposed to me," Clara said. "That's why I'm going to marry him. Reuben just wanted . . ."

Weber interrupted. "Why, if he wasn't molesting you just then, and if you'd decided to marry Matt Sawyer, why did you have to kill him? You must've known a well's no place for diving."

Clara shrugged her pretty shoulders. "By then I was feeling kind of sorry for him. He'd have been mighty lonesome after I went to live with Matt."

Well, there isn't much more to tell. We sort of disengaged Matt, you might say. His story of how Maudie died stood up with the coroner, Prouty and I vouching for the kind of man he was. I haven't seen him since.

Clara—she'll be getting out soon, coming home to the hills, and maybe opening up The Red Lantern again. I defended her at the trial, pleading temporary insanity. Nobody was willing to say she was insane exactly. We don't like saying such things about one another up here. But the jury agreed she was a temporary sort of woman. Twenty years to life, she got, with time off for good behavior.

You come around some time next spring. I'll introduce you.

1963

The Purple is Everything

You are likely to say, reading about Mary Gardner, that you knew her, or that you once knew someone like her. And well you may have, for while her kind is not legion it endures and sometimes against great popular odds.

You will see Mary Gardner—or someone like her—at the symphony, in the art galleries, at the theater, always well-dressed if not quite fashionable, sometimes alone, sometimes in the company of other women all of whom have an aura, not of sameness, but of mutuality. Each of them has made—well, if not a good life for herself, at least the best possible life it was in her power to make.

Mary Gardner was living at the time in a large East Coast city. In her late thirties, she was a tall lean woman, unmarried, quietly feminine, gentle, even a little hesitant in manner but definite in her tastes. Mary was a designer in a well-known wallpaper house. Her salary allowed her to buy good clothes, to live alone in a pleasant apartment within walking distance of her work, and to go regularly to the theater and the Philharmonic. As often as she went to the successful plays, she attended little theater and the experimental stage. She was not among those who believed that a play had to say something. She was interested in "the submerged values." This taste prevailed also in her approach to the visual arts—a boon surely in the wallpaper business whose customers for the most part prefer their walls to be seen but not heard.

In those days Mary was in the habit of going during her

lunch hour—or sometimes when she needed to get away from the drawing board—to the Institute of Modern Art which was less than a city block from her office. She had fallen in love with a small, early Monet titled "Trees Near Le Havre," and when in love Mary was a person of searching devotion. Almost daily she discovered new voices in the woodland scene, trees and sky reflected in a shimmering pool—with more depths in the sky, she felt, than in the water.

The more she thought about this observation the more convinced she became that the gallery had hung the picture upside down. She evolved a theory about the signature: it was hastily done by the artist, she decided, long after he had finished the painting and perhaps at a time when the light of day was fading. She would have spoken to a museum authority about it—if she had known a museum authority.

Mary received permission from the Institute to sketch within its halls and often stood before the Monet for an hour, sketchbook in hand. By putting a few strokes on paper she felt herself conspicuously inconspicuous among the transient viewers and the guards. She would not for anything have persumed to copy the painting and she was fiercely resentful of the occasional art student who did.

So deep was Mary in her contemplation of Claude Monet's wooded scene that on the morning of the famous museum fire, when she first smelled the smoke, she thought it came from inside the picture itself. She was instantly furious, and by an old association she indicted a whole genre of people—the careless American tourist in a foreign land. She was not so far away from reality, however, that she did not realize almost at once there was actually a fire in the building.

Voices cried out alarms in the corridors and men suddenly were running. Guards dragged limp hoses along the floor and dropped them—where they lay like great withered snakes over which people leaped as in some tribal rite. Blue smoke layered the ceiling and then began to fall in angled swatches—like theatrical scrims gone awry. In the far distance fire sirens wailed.

Mary Gardner watched, rooted and muted, as men and women, visitors like herself, hastened past bearing framed pictures in their arms; and in one case two men carried between them a huge Chagall night scene in which the little creatures seemed to be jumping on and off the canvas, having an uproarious time in transit. A woman took the Rouault from the wall beside the Monet and hurried with it after the bearers of the Chagall.

Still Mary hesitated. That duty should compel her to touch where conscience had so long forbidden it—this conflict increased her confusion. Another thrust of smoke into the room made the issue plainly the picture's survival, if not indeed her own. In desperate haste she tried to lift the Monet from the wall, but it would not yield.

She strove, pulling with her full strength—such strength that when the wire broke, she was catapulted backward and fell over the viewer's bench, crashing her head into the painting. Since the canvas was mounted on board, the only misfortune—aside from her bruised head which mattered not at all—was that the picture had jarred loose from its frame. By then Mary cared little for the frame. She caught up the painting, hugged it to her, and groped her way to the gallery door.

She reached the smoke-bogged corridor at the instant the water pressure brought the hoses violently to life. Jets of water spurted from every connection. Mary shielded the picture with her body until she could edge it within the raincoat she had worn against the morning drizzle.

She hurried along the corridor, the last apparently of the volunteer rescuers. The guards were sealing off the wing of the building, closing the fire prevention door. They showed little patience with her protests, shunting her down the stairs. By the time she reached the lobby the police had cordoned off civilians. Imperious as well as impervious, a policeman escorted her into the crowd, and in the crowd, having no use of her arms—they were still locked around the picture—she was shoved and jostled toward the door and there pitilessly jettisoned into the street. On the sidewalk she had no hope at all of finding anyone in that surging, gaping mob on whom she could safely bestow her art treasure.

People screamed and shouted that they could see the flames. Mary did not look back. She hastened home-ward, walking proud and fierce, thinking that the city was after all a jungle. She hugged the picture to her, her raincoat its only shield but her life a ready forfeit for its safety.

It has been in her mind to telephone the Institute office at once. But in her own apartment, the painting propped up against cushions on the sofa, she reasoned that until the fire was extinguished she had no hope of talking with anyone there. She called her own office and pleaded a sudden illness—something she had eaten at lunch though she had not had a bite since breakfast.

The walls of her apartment were hung with what she called her "potpourri": costume prints and color lithographs—all, she had been proud to say, limited editions or artists' prints. She had sometimes thought of buying paintings, but plainly she could not afford her own tastes. On impulse now, she took down an Italian litho-graph and removed the glass and mat from the wooden frame. The Monet fit quite well. And to her particular de-light she could now hang it right side up. As though with a will of its own, the painting claimed the place on her wall most favored by the light of day.

There is no way of describing Mary's pleasure in the company she kept that afternoon. She would not have taken her eyes from the picture at all except for the joy that was renewed at each returning. Reluctantly she turned on the radio at five o'clock so that she might learn more of the fire at the Institute. It had been extensive and destructive—an entire wing of the building was gutted.

She listened with the remote and somewhat smug so-licitude that one bestows on other people's tragedies to the enumeraton of the paintings which had been de-stroyed. The mention of "Trees Near Le Havre" startled her. A full moment later she realized the explicit meaning of the announcer's words. She turned off the radio and sat a long time in the flood of silence.

Then she said aloud tentatively, "You are a thief, Mary Gardner," and after a bit repeated, "Oh, yes. You are a thief." But she did not mind at all. Nothing so por-tentous had ever been said about her before, even by her-self.

She ate her dinner from a tray before the painting, hav-ing with it a bottle of French wine. Many times that night she went from her bed to the living-room door until she seemed to have slept between so many wakenings. At last she did sleep.

But the first light of morning fell on Mary's conscience as early as upon the painting. After one brief visit to the living room she made her plans with the care of a reli-gious novice well aware of the devil's constancy. She dressed more severely than was her fashion, needing her-ringbone for backbone—the ridiculous phrase kept run-ning through her mind at breakfast. In final appraisal of herself in the hall mirror she thought she looked like the headmistress of an English girls' school, which she sup-posed satisfactory to the task before her.

Just before she left the apartment, she spent one last moment alone with the Monet. Afterward, wherever, however the Institute chose to hang it, she might hope to feel that a little part of it was forever hers.

On the street she bought a newspaper and confirmed the listing of "Trees Near Le Havre." Although that wing of the Institute had been destroyed, many of its paintings had been carried to safety by way of the second-floor corridor.

Part of the street in front of the Institute was still cor-doned off when she reached it, congesting the flow of morning traffic. The police on duty were no less brusque than those whom Mary had encountered the day before. She was seized by the impulse to postpone her mission— an almost irresistible temptation, especially when she was barred from entering the museum unless she could show a pass such as had been issued to all authorized personnel.

"Of course I'm not authorized." she exclaimed. "If I were I shouldn't be out here."

The policeman directed her to the sergeant in charge. He was at the moment disputing with the fire insurance representative how much of the street could be used for the salvage operation. "The business of this street is business," the sergeant said, "and that's my business."

Mary waited until the insurance man stalked into the building. He did not need a pass, she noticed. "Excuse me, officer, I have a painting—"

"Lady . . ." He drew the long breath of patience. "Yes, ma'am?"

"Yesterday during the fire a painting was supposedly destroyed—a lovely, small Monet called—"

"Was there now?" the sergeant interrupted. Lovely small Monets really touched him.

Mary was becoming flustered in spite of herself. "It's listed in this morning's paper as having been destroyed. But it wasn't. I have it at home."

The policeman looked at her for the first time with a certain compassion. "On your living-room wall, no doubt," he said with deep knowingness.

"Yes, as a matter of fact."

He took her gently but firmly by the arm. "I tell you what you do. You go along to police headquarters on Fifty-seventh Street. You know where that is, don't you? Just tell them all about it like a good girl." He propelled her into the crowd and there released her. Then he raised his voice: "Keep moving! You'll see it all on the television."

Mary had no intention of going to police headquarters

where, she presumed, men concerned with armed robbery, mayhem, and worse were even less likely to understand the subtlety of her problem. She went to her office
and throughout the morning tried periodically to reach
the museum curator's office by telephone. On each of her
calls either the switchboard was tied up or his line was
busy for longer than she could wait.

Finally she hit on the idea of asking for the Institute's
Public Relations Department, and to someone there, obviously distracted—Mary could hear parts of three con-
versations going on at the same time—she explained how
during the fire she had saved Monet's "Trees Near Le
Havre."

"Near where, madam?" the voice asked.

"Le Havre." Mary spelled it. "By Monet," she
added.

"Is that two words or one?" the voice asked.

"Please transfer me to the curator's office," Mary
said and ran her fingers up and down the lapel of her her-
ringbone suit.

Mary thought it a wise precaution to meet the Institute's
representative in the apartment lobby where she first
asked to see his credentials. He identified himself as the
man to whom she had given her name and address on the
phone. Mary signaled for the elevator and thought about
his identification: Robert Attlebury III. She had seen his
name on the museum roster: Curator of . . . she could
not remember.

He looked every inch the curator, standing erect and
remote while the elevator bore them slowly upward. A
curator perhaps, but she would not have called him a connoisseur. One with his face and disposition would always
taste and spit out, she thought. She could imagine his
scorn of things he found distasteful, and instinctively she
knew herself to be distasteful to him.

Not that it really mattered what he felt about her. She
was nobody. But how must the young unknown artist feel

standing with his work before such superciliousness? Or had he a different mien and manner for people of his own kind? In that case she would have given a great deal for the commonest of courtesies.

"Everything seems so extraordinary—in retrospect," Mary said to brook the silence of their seemingly endless ascent.

"How fortunate for you," he said, and Mary thought, perhaps it was.

When they reached the door of her apartment, she paused before turning the key. "Shouldn't you have brought a guard—or someone?"

He looked down on her as from Olympus. "I am someone."

Mary resolved to say nothing more. She opened the door and left it open. He preceded her and moved across the foyer into the living room and stood before the Monet. His rude directness oddly comforted her: he did, after all, care about painting. She ought not to judge men, she thought, from her limited experience of them.

He gazed at the Monet for a few moments, then he tilted his head ever so slightly from one side to the other. Mary's heart began to beat erratically. For months she had wanted to discuss with someone who really knew about such things her theory of what was reflection and what was reality in "Trees Near Le Havre." But now that her chance was at hand she could not find the words.

Still, she had to say something—something . . . casual. "The frame is mine," she said, "but for the picture's protection you may take it. I can get it the next time I'm at the museum."

Surprisingly, he laughed. "It may be the better part at that," he said.

"I beg your pardon?"

He actually looked at her. "Your story is ingenious, madam, but then it was warranted by the occasion."

"I simply do not understand what you are saying," Mary said.

"I have seen better copies than this one," he said. "It's too bad your ingenuity isn't matched by a better imitation."

Mary was too stunned to speak. He was about to go. "But . . . it's signed," Mary blurted out, and feebly tried to direct his attention to the name in the upper corner.

"Which makes it forgery, doesn't it?" he said almost solicitously.

His preciseness, his imperturbability in the light of the horrendous thing he was saying, etched detail into the nightmare.

"That's not my problem!" Mary cried, giving voice to words she did not mean, saying what amounted to a betrayal of the painting she so loved.

"Oh, but it is. Indeed it is, and I may say a serious problem if I were to pursue it."

"Please do pursue it!" Mary cried.

Again he smiled, just a little. "That is not the Institute's way of dealing with these things."

"You do not *like* Monet," Mary challenged desperately, for he had started toward the door.

"That's rather beside the point, isn't it?"

"You don't *know* Monet. You can't! Not possibly!"

"How could I dislike him if I didn't know him? Let me tell you something about Monet." He turned back to the picture and trailed a finger over one vivid area. "In Monet the purple is everything."

"The purple?" Mary said.

"You're beginning to see it yourself now, aren't you?" His tone verged on the pedagogic.

Mary closed her eyes and said, "I only know how this painting came to be here."

"I infinitely prefer not to be made your confidant in that matter," he said. "Now I have rather more important matters to take care of." And again he started toward the door.

Mary hastened to block his escape. "It doesn't matter

what you think of Monet, or of me, or of anything. You've got to take that painting back to the museum.''

''And be made a laughingstock when the hoax is discovered?'' He set an arm as stiff as a brass rail between them and moved out of the apartment.

Mary followed him to the elevator, now quite beside herself. ''I shall go to the newspapers!'' she cried.

''I think you might regret it.''

''Now I know, I understand!'' Mary saw the elevator door open. ''You were glad to think the Monet had been destroyed in the fire.''

''Savage!'' he said.

Then the door closed between them.

In time Mary persuaded—and it wasn't easy—certain experts, even an art critic, to come and examine ''her'' Monet. It was a more expensive undertaking than she could afford—all of them seemed to expect refreshments, including expensive liquors. Her friends fell in with ''Mary's hoax,'' as they came to call her story, and she was much admired in an ever-widening and increasingly esoteric circle for her unwavering account of how she had come into possession of a ''genuine Monet.'' Despite the virtue of simplicity, a trait since childhood, she found herself using words in symbolic combinations—the language of the company she now kept—and people far wiser than she would say of her: ''How perceptive!'' or ''What insight!''—and then pour themselves another drink.

One day her employer, the great man himself, who prior to her ''acquisition'' had not known whether she lived in propriety or in sin, arrived at her cocktail time bringing with him a famous art historian.

The expert smiled happily over his second Scotch while Mary told again the story of the fire at the Institute and how she had simply walked home with the painting because she could not find anyone to whom to give it. While she talked, his knowing eyes wandered from her face to the painting, to his glass, to the painting, and back to her face again.

"Oh, I could believe it," he said when she had finished. "It's the sort of mad adventure that actually could happen." He set his glass down carefully where she could see that it was empty. "I suppose you know that there has never been an officially complete catalogue of Monet's work?"

"No," she said, and refilled his glass.

"It's so, unfortunately. And the sad truth is that quite a number of museums today are hanging paintings under his name that are really unauthenticated."

"And mine?" Mary said, lifting a chin she tried vainly to keep from quivering.

Her guest smiled. "*Must* you know?"

For a time after that Mary tried to avoid looking at the Monet. It was not that she liked it less, but that now she somehow liked herself less in its company. What had happened, she realized, was that, like the experts, she now saw not the painting, but herself.

This was an extraordinary bit of self-discovery for one who had never had to deal severely with her own psyche. Till now, so far as Mary was concerned, the chief function of a mirror had been to determine the angle of a hat. But the discovery of the flaw does not in itself effect a cure; often it aggravates the condition. So with Mary.

She spent less and less time at home, and it was to be said for some of her new-found friends that they thought it only fair to reciprocate for having enjoyed the hospitality of so enigmatically clever a hostess. How often had she as a girl been counseled by parent and teacher to get out more, to see more people. Well, Mary was at last getting out more. And in the homes of people who had felt free to comment on her home and its possessions, she too felt free to comment. The more odd her comment—the nastier, she would once have said of it—the more popular she became. Oh, yes. Mary was seeing more people, lots more people.

In fact, her insurance agent—who was in the habit of just dropping in to make his quarterly collection—had to get up early one Saturday morning to make sure he caught her at home.

It was a clear sharp day, and the hour at which the Monet was most luminous. The man sat staring at it, fascinated. Mary was amused, remembering how hurt he always was that his clients failed to hang his company calendar in prominence. While she was gone from the room to get her checkbook, he got up and touched the surface of the painting.

"Ever think of taking out insurance on that picture?" he asked when she returned. "Do you mind if I ask how much it's worth?"

"It cost me . . . a great deal," Mary said, and was at once annoyed with both him and herself.

"I tell you what," the agent said. "I have a friend who appraises these objects of art for some of the big galleries, you know? Do you mind if I bring him round and see what he thinks it's worth?"

"No, I don't mind," Mary said in utter resignation.

And so the appraiser came and looked carefully at the painting. He hedged about putting a value on it. He wasn't the last word on the Nineteenth Century impressionists and he wanted to think it over. But that afternoon he returned just as Mary was about to go out, and with him came a bearded gentleman who spoke not once to Mary or to the appraiser, but chatted constantly with himself while he scruntinized the painting. Then with a "tsk, tsk, tsk," he took the painting from the wall, examined the back, and rehung it—but reversing it, top to bottom.

Mary felt the old flutter interrupt her heartbeat, but it passed quickly.

Even walking out of her house the bearded gentleman did not speak to her; she might have been invisible. It was the appraiser who murmured his thanks but not a word of explanation. Since the expert had not drunk her whiskey Mary supposed the amenities were not required of him.

She was prepared to forget him as she had the others—it was easy now to forget them all; but when she came home to change between matinee and cocktails, another visitor was waiting. She noticed him in the lobby and realized, seeing the doorman say a word to him just as the elevator door closed off her view, that his business was with her. The next trip of the elevator brought him to her door.

"I've come about the painting, Miss Gardner," he said, and offered his card. She had opened the door only as far as the latch chain permitted. He was representative of the Continental Assurance Company, Limited.

She slipped off the latch chain.

Courteous and formal behind his double-breasted suit, he waited for Mary to seat herself. He sat down neatly opposite her, facing the painting, for she sat beneath it, erect, and she hoped formidable.

"Lovely," he said, gazing at the Monet. Then he wrenched his eyes from it. "But I'm not an expert," he added and gently cleared his throat. He was chagrined, she thought, to have allowed himself even so brief a luxury of the heart.

"But is it authenticated?" She said it much as she would once have thought but not said, Fie on you!

"Sufficient to my company's requirements," he said. "But don't misunderstand—we are not proposing to make any inquiries. We are always satisfied in such delicate negotiations just to have the painting back."

Mary did not misunderstand, but she certainly did not understand either.

He took from his inside pocket a piece of paper which he placed on the coffee table and with the tapering fingers of an artist—or a banker—or a pickpocket—he gently maneuvered it to where Mary could see that he was proffering a certified check.

He did not look at her and therefore missed the spasm

she felt contorting her mouth. "The day of the fire," she thought, but the words never passed her lips.

She took the check in her hand: $20,000.

"May I use your phone, Miss Gardner?"

Mary nodded and went into the kitchen where she again looked at the check. It was a great deal of money, she thought wryly, to be offered in compensation for a few months' care of a friend.

She heard her visitor's voice as he spoke into the telephone—an expert now, to judge by his tone. A few minutes later she heard the front door close. When she went back into the living room both her visitor and the Monet were gone . . .

Some time later Mary attended the opening of the new wing of the Institute. She recognized a number of people she had not known before and whom, she supposed, she was not likely to know much longer.

They had hung the Monet upside down again.

Mary thought of it after she got home, and as though two rights must surely right a possible wrong, she turned the check upside down while she burned it over the kitchen sink.

1963

Lost Generation . . .

Lost Generation

The school board had sustained the teacher. The vote was
four to three, but the majority made it clear they were not
voting for the man. They voted the way they had because
otherwise the state would have stepped in and settled the
appeal, ruling against the town . . .

Tom and Andy, coming from the west of town, waited
for the others at the War Memorial. The October frost
had silvered the cannon, and the moonlight was so clear
you could read the words FOR GOD AND COUNTRY on the
monument. The slack in the flagpole cord allowed the
metal clips to clank against the pole. That and the wind
made the only sounds.

Then Andy said, "His wife's all right. She came up to
Mary after it was over and said she wished he'd teach like
other teachers and leave politics alone."

"Politics," Tom said. "Is that what she calls it?"

"She's okay just the same. I don't want anything happening to her—or to their kid."

"Nothing's going to happen to them," Tom said.

"The kid's a funny little guy. He don't say much, but
then he don't miss much either," Andy said.

Tom said nothing. He knocked one foot against the
other.

"It's funny, ain't it, how one man—you know?"
Andy said.

"One rotten apple in the barrel," Tom said. "Damn,

186

it's getting cold. I put anti-freeze in half the cars in town today, but not my own. In his even.''

"The kid—he's just a kid, you know," Andy said.

Tom wiped the moisture from beneath his nose. "I told you nothing's going to happen to him."

"I know, I know, but sometimes things go wrong."

The others came, Frankie and Murph, walking along the railroad tracks that weren't used any more except by the children taking a short cut on their way to and from school. You could smell the creosote in the smoke from the chimneys of the houses alongside the tracks. One by one the railroad ties were coming loose and disappearing.

The four men climbed the road in back of what had once been the Schroeders' chicken coops. The Schroeders had sold their chickens and moved down the hill when the new people took over, house by house, that part of town. One of the men remarked you could still smell the chicken droppings.

"That ain't what you smell," Tom said. "That coop's been integrated."

Frankie gave a bark of laughter that ricocheted along the empty street.

"Watch it, will you?" Tom said.

"What's the matter? They ain't coming out this time of night."

"They can look out windows, can't they? It's full moon."

"I'd like to see it. I'd like to see just one head pop out a window." Frankie whistled the sound of speed and patted the pocket of his jacket.

"I should've picked the men I wanted," Tom said, meaning only Andy to hear. "This drawing lots is for the birds."

"You could've said so on the range." The town's ten policemen met for target practice once a week. They had met that afternoon. After practice they had talked about the school-board meeting they expected to attend that night. They joked about it, only Andy among them having ever attended such a meeting before.

"I'd still've picked you, Andy," Tom said.

"Thanks."

Frankie said, "I heard what you said, Tom. I'm going to remember it too."

Andy said, "You might know he'd live in this part of town. It all adds up, don't it?"

No one answered him. No one spoke until at the top of the street Murph said, "There's a light on in the hallway. What does that mean?"

"It means we're lucky. We can see him coming to the door."

Tom gave the signal and they broke formation, each man moving into the shadow of a tree, except Tom who went up to the house.

The child was looking out the window. It was what his father made him do when he'd wake up from having a bad dream. The trouble was, he sometimes dreamed awake and couldn't go back to sleep because there were a lot of people in his room, all whispering. What kind of people, his father wanted to know. Men or women? Old people or young? And was there anyone he knew?

Funny-looking people. They didn't have any faces. Only eyes—which of course was why they whispered.

His father told him: Next time you tell them if they don't go away you'll call your dad. Or better still, look out the window for a while and think of all the things you did outdoors today. Then see if the funny people aren't gone when you look around the room again.

So at night he often did get up. The window was near his bed and the people never tried to stop him. Looking out, he would think about the places he could hide and how easy it would be to climb out from the bottom of his bed. He had a dugout under the mock-orange bushes, and under the old cellar doors propped together like a pup tent in the back of the garage; down the street were the sewer pipes they hadn't used yet, and what used to be the pumphouse next to Mrs. Malcolm's well, which was the best hiding place of all; the big boys sometimes played there.

Tom passed so close that the boy could have reached out and touched him.

The doorbell rang once, twice, three times.

The man, awakened from his sleep, came pulling on his bathrobe. He flung open the door at the same time he switched on the porch light.

A fusillade of shots rang out. The man seemed frozen like a picture of himself, his hand stretched out and so much light around him. Then he crumpled up and fell.

Twenty minutes later Andy was sitting on his bed at home when the ambulance siren sounded somewhere up the hill. His wife put out her hand to see if he was there. "Andy?"

"Yes?"

She went back to sleep until the town alarm sounded, four long blasts for a police emergency.

Andy dressed again and once more took his revolver from the bureau drawer.

"What time is it?" His wife turned over at the clicking sound as he refilled the chamber of the gun.

"Almost half-past three."

"It isn't right, a man your age."

"Someone has to go." In the hall he phoned the police station for instructions.

This time Andy drove, as did the other deputies. Cars clogged the street where lights were on in all the houses, and people stood outdoors, their coats over their nightclothes, and watched the ambulance drive off. They told one another of the shots they took for granted to have been the backfires of a car.

Doc Harrington drove up. Black bag in hand, he went into the house. Andy followed on his heels. Both men stepped carefully around the bloodstains in the front hall.

The woman was hysterical. "They took our little boy. They killed his father and they took our little boy." She kept crying out for someone to help her; anyone. The Chief of Police and Tom, who was in the room with them, tried to calm her down. She couldn't say who "they" were.

When Doc appeared and commanded that someone get a neighbor woman in to help him, Tom started to leave. Andy caught his arm.

"I don't know what she's talking about," Tom said. "She says the boy's been kidnapped. More like a neighbor's got him, but I'm going to organize a search. If we don't find him it'll be the State Police, and after that the F.B.I."

"The kid's not here?"

"Maybe you can find him. I've been from basement to roof."

Room by room Andy searched the house. The child's bed had not been slept in much that night. You couldn't really tell, the things a youngster took in bed with him. The window was open just a little and it was hard to raise it higher. The back door to the house was open and Andy would have said the kid had gone that way because on the back steps was a woolen monkey, its ears still frosty damp with spittle.

Andy got a flashlight from the car and joined the other deputies, Tom, Murph, and Frankie among them. They went from house to house to ask if anyone had seen the child. No one had and the mother's cry of kidnapping had gone the rounds.

They searched till dawn. By then the State Police were in the town; the Chief cordoned off the house and set a guard. The house was quite empty. Doc Harrington had given the woman an injection and driven her himself the eight miles to the hospital.

The men, chilled to the bone, were having coffee at the station house when old Mrs. Malcolm, on her way to early Mass, stopped by to say she'd heard a noise that sounded like a kitten's mew at the bottom of her well. The well had long been dry and she'd had it boarded up after the Russo dog had fallen in and died there. But the kids kept coming back. They pried loose the boards and played at flushing "Charlie" from his underground hideout.

Tom and Andy were already in the Malcolm yard when the fire truck arrived. With their own hands they tore away the boards that weren't already loose at the well's mouth. The shaft was dark, but there were steps at least halfway down the shoring. It was decided, however, to put a ladder down.

Tom, again making himself the boss, said *he* was going down. The others linked themselves together, a human chain, to keep the ladder from striking bottom. The depth was about thirty feet. Andy was the signalman. He reported every step Tom took, and he cried out the moment Tom's flashlight discovered the child on the rocks heaped at the bottom of the dry well.

"He's sleeping," Tom shouted up. "He's sleeping like a little baby."

"He can't be, falling that far down. Be careful how you lift him," Andy said.

Tom steadied the ladder among the rocks, draped the limp child over his shoulder, and started up. The firemen went back to the truck for their emergency equipment. Andy kept up a singsong cautioning: a kid was just a little thing, it got hurt real easy. Tom was too large a man for such a job, and he ought to have more patience.

"Will you shut your damned mouth up there?" Tom shouted. "I'm coming up the best I can."

He'd got past halfway when the boy recovered consciousness. At first he squirmed and cried. The men crowded in to watch. Andy begged them not to block the light.

"Just keep coming easy," Andy crooned, and to the child, "There's nothing you should be a-scared of, little fella. You're going to come out fine."

Then—it was at the moment Tom's face moved into the light—the child began to scream and beat at him with fists and feet, and a rhythm of words came out of him, over and over again, until no one who wasn't deaf could mistake what he was saying: "My dad, my dad, you shot my dad!"

Tom tried to get a better hold of him, or so he claimed when he got up, but the child fought out of his grasp. Tom caught him by the leg; then the ladder jolted—a rock displaced below. The child slipped away and plummeted silently out of sight. That was what was so strange, the way he fell, not making any cry at all.

Tom lumbered down again. He brought the child up and laid him on the ground. Everyone could see that he was dead, the skull crushed in on top.

Andy searched the wrists anyway and then the chest where the pajamas had been ripped, but he found no hearbeat, and the mouth was full of blood. He looked up at Tom who stood, dirty and sullen, watching him.

"I didn't want to let go of him. I swear it, Andy."

Andy's eyes never left his face. "You killed him. You killed this baby boy."

"I didn't, Andy."

"I saw it with my own eyes." Andy drew his gun.

"For God's sake, man. Murph, Frankie, you saw what happened!"

They too had drawn their guns. The Chief of Police and the State Troopers were coming up the hill, a minute or two away. The two firemen coming with the resuscitator were unarmed.

Tom backed off a step, but when he saw Andy release the safety catch he turned and ran. That's when they brought him down, making sure he was immediately dead.

1971

Old Friends

The two women had been friends since childhood, their mothers friends before them. Both were in their late twenties; neither had married. Amy intended not to, although she was beginning to lose some of the vehemence with which she declared that purpose. Virginia was still saying she was waiting for the right man to come along. She admitted herself to be an old-fashioned girl. One of the sadnesses in her life was that the men she liked most were already married. It made her furious when Amy would say, "Happily?"

"I suppose you think I should have an affair," Virginia said.

"Yes, as a matter of fact, it would be good for you."

"How do you know?"

"Well, let me put it this way," Amy would say, and the same conversation had occurred in some form or other a number of times, "it would be better than a bad marriage just for the sake of being married."

"According to you," Virginia would say, "there are no good marriages."

"Not many, and I don't know of a single one that came with a guarantee."

One might have thought that it was Amy who had grown up in the broken home. Her parents had only recently celebrated their thirty-fifth wedding anniversary. Whereas Virginia's mother had divorced her third husband, each of whom had left her better off financially than had his predecessor. She and Virginia were often taken for sisters. But so were Virginia and Amy. Or, to make Virginia's own distinction, she was always being taken for Amy's sister.

At one time they had worked for the same New York publishing house, Virginia as an assistant art director, Amy as an assistant to the senior editor. Amy's father, a retired executive of the firm, had arranged interviews for both girls after they finished college. The jobs, he insisted, they had got for themselves. Virginia stayed with hers. More than anything in the world, except possibly a husband who loved and respected her, she wanted her independence of her mother. Amy, to cap the interminable subject, once suggested that was why Virginia wanted a husband, to protect her from her mother.

"I am perfectly capable of protecting myself."

And that of course, Amy realized in time, was her friend's trouble. Nobody could do anything for her. She resented anyone's attempting it. Which made her yearning for a husband suspect: what Virginia really wanted, Amy decided, was a baby. This insight, as well as others just as profound if true, had slipped beyond Amy's conscious reckoning of her friend's character long before the weekend Amy reneged on the invitation to the country.

Sometimes months went by when they did not see each other. Amy, on inheriting an ancient cottage from an aunt, gave up her regular job for freelance writing, copy editing, and restoring the cottage. While not far from the city and not actually isolated, the cottage retained a rare privacy. It had settled deeper and deeper into the ground with the decades, and the mountain laurel that surrounded it was as snug as a shawl.

Knowing Virginia to be a Sunday painter, Amy thought of her whenever there was a change in nature. Such a change had come that week with the sudden November stripping of the leaves. The light took on a special quality and the long grass in the meadow quivered glossily golden in the sun and turned silver under the moon. She called Virginia on Thursday.

"Well, now, I would like to," Virginia said, mulling over the invitation aloud. "I half promised Allan—I don't know if I've told you about him, the architect?—I didn't actually commit myself. Thank you, Amy. I'd love to come."

Amy was on the point of saying she could bring Allan, the architect, and then it occurred to her that he might be an invention of Virginia's, part of that same old face-saving syndrome which, when they saw too much of one another, made their friendship dreary. She almost wished she had not called. However, they discussed the bus schedule and settled on a time for Virginia's arrival.

"If I miss that one, I'll take the next," Virginia said. There was always a little hitch to allow room for independence.

That very afternoon Amy received a call from Mike Trilling, one of the few men with whom she had ever been deeply in love. A newspaper correspondent, Mike had been sent overseas just when they had become very happy together. If he had asked it, she would have followed him, but he had not asked it, and she had been a long time getting over the separation. Except that she was not over it. She knew that the moment she heard his voice.

Her end of the conversation was filled with pauses.

Finally Mike said, "Are you still hung up on me?"

"What humility! Yes, damn you."

"You don't have to swear at me. I've got the same problem—once in love with Amy, here I am again. I'd come out for the weekend if you'd ask me."

"All right, you're invited."

"I'll rent a car and be there early tomorrow evening. We can have dinner at The Tavern. Is the food as good as it used to be?"

"I'll fix us something. It's not that good. You can bring the wine." She refrained from saying that he could take the bus, an hour's trip. There was no better way to put a man off than to try to save his money for him.

She postponed the decision on what to say to Virginia, and while she cleaned house she let her memory of the times she and Mike had been together run full flood. She washed her hair and dried it before the blaze in the fireplace. Mike loved to bury his face in her hair, to discover in it the faint fragrance of wood smoke; he loved to run his fingers through it on the pillow and give it a not altogether gentle tug, pulling her face to his.

She could not tell Ginny that Mike was the reason she was asking her to postpone until the following weekend. It would be unkind. Anyone else might understand, but Ginny would understand even more than was intended: she would reexamine the whole of her life in terms of that rejection. Amy did not call her until morning.

"Ginny, I've had the most tremendous idea for a story. I was up half the night thinking about it, afraid to lose it, or that it wouldn't be any good in the morning. But it's a good one and I want to dash it off fresh. Will you come next week instead? I know you understand . . ." She made herself stop. She was saying too much.

"Of course," Virginia said, and her voice had that dead air of self-abnegation. "I envy you."

"Bless you for understanding," Amy said. "The same time next weekend. I'll be watching for you."

Once off the phone she gave herself up to the pleasure of anticipation. Almost a year had passed since she and Mike were last together. She had had a couple of brief encounters since, but no one had taken his place. She had worked. She had done a lot more work with Mike away than when he was around. They had not corresponded. He had called her on New Year's Eve. Collect, because he was at a friend's house and the British would not accept his credit-card charge. She had not asked him about the friend. She did not propose to ask any questions now.

At first it seemed like old times, their sitting before the

fire with martinis, Mike on the floor at her feet, his head resting on his arm where it lay across her knees. His hair had begun to thin on the very top of his head. She put her finger to the spot, a cold finger, for she had just put down her glass.

Mike got up and sat in the chair opposite hers, brushing back his hair, something almost tender in the way he stroked the spot.

"I'm wicked, aren't I?" she said, carrying off as best she could what she knew to have been a mistake.

"Tell me about that," he said, purposely obtuse.

"Naughty, I mean."

"Oh, nuts. With the British, every other word is 'naughty.' Aren't I the naughty one?" He mimicked someone's accent. "It's such a faggoty word."

"I guess it is," Amy said.

He fidgeted a moment, as though trying to get comfortable in the chair, then got up and gave one of the logs a kick. "It's not easy—getting reacquainted when so much has happened in between."

"Oh?" In spite of herself.

He looked around at her. "I've been working bloody hard. Five months in Cyprus."

"I know."

"Does nobody in America read history?"

"I suspect the trouble is that nobody listens to those who read history."

"Did you follow my dispatches?"

"Every word, my darling."

Things went a little better. He looked at his glass. "I can't drink martinis like I used to. What kind of vermouth did you use?"

The phone rang and Amy, on her way to answer it, said, "Try putting in more gin."

It was Virginia, of all people. "I won't disturb you except for a minute."

"It's all right. I'm taking a break." She was afraid Mike might put on a record.

"I want to ask a favor of you, Amy. I got myself into a predicament. When Allan called a while ago, I decided I didn't want to talk to him, so I said I was on my way to spend the weekend with you. I don't think he'll call, but in case he does, would you tell him I've gone on a long walk or something like that?"

Amy drew a deep breath and tried to think of something to say that would not expose the extent of her exasperation. The most natural thing in the world would have been: Ginny, the reason I asked you not to come—

"I don't think he will call."

"Okay, Ginny. I'll tell him."

"Get his number and say I'll call him back."

"I'll tell him that," Amy said. It was all a fantasy, and in some way or other Virginia thought she was getting even. If there was an Allan and if these little exchanges did occur, she would then have to call Virginia back and tell her that Allan had telephoned her.

"Was that Virginia?" Mike said.

"Yes."

"Hasn't she hooked herself a man yet?"

"You damn smug—" Amy exploded, possibly because she was annoyed with both Virginia and him. But Virginia, being the more vulnerable and absent, got such loyal defense in the argument that ensued, she would have been stunned. Indeed, it might have changed her whole picture of herself.

Mike and Amy did reach a rapprochement. After all, it was his remembering Amy's complaints about her friend in the old days that had provoked his comment: she should blame herself, not him. After the second martini they were laughing and talking about old intimacies, and how they had used to put the third martini on ice for afterward. Such good memories and the kisses which, if they weren't the same, were better than most, sufficed to get them into the bedroom. There, alas, nothing went the same as it had used to.

"Damn it," Mike kept saying, "this never happens to me."

"It's all right," Amy said over and over again, although well aware he had used the present tense.

Later, watching him stoop to see himself in her dressing-table mirror while he knotted his tie, she said, "Bed isn't everything."

"That's right."

"But it's a lot," she said and threw off the blankets.

By the time she finished in the bathroom, he had gone back to the living room where he stood before the fire and stared into it. A fresh log was catching on, the flames like little tongues darting up the sides. He had not brought the martini pitcher from the kitchen.

"You can't go home again," she said.

"I guess not." He could at least have said that it was fun trying. But what he said was, "Amy, let's not spoil a beautiful memory."

"Oh, boy. I don't believe you said it. Not Mike Trilling."

"All right. 'You can't go home again' wasn't exactly original either. We aren't going to make it, Amy, so why don't I just take off before we start bickering again? No recriminations, no goodbyes, no tears."

Her throat tight as a corked bottle, she went up the stairs and got his coat and overnight bag.

On the porch they did not even shake hands—a turn and a quickly averted glance lest their eyes get caught, and a little wave before he opened the car door. When he was gone, she remembered the wine. It was as well she had forgotten it. A "thank you" for anything would have humiliated them both.

Returning to the house she felt as sober as the moon and as lonely. There was a whispery sound to the fire, and her aunt's Seth Thomas floor clock ticked with the slow heavy rhythm of a tired heart. Most things break: the phrase from somewhere she could not remember kept running through her mind. The old clock rasped and struck once. Hard though it was to believe, the hour was only half-past eight.

She called Virginia.

Her friend took her time picking up the phone. "I wasn't going to answer. I thought it might be Allan. Did he call me there?"

"Not so far, dear. Ginny, you could make the nine-thirty bus and come on out. The story isn't ready yet. I always start too soon. I'm botching it terribly."

"Thank you, but I don't think I will, Amy. I want to stay home by myself now where I can think things out comfortably. I'm a mess, but since I know it, I ought to be able to do something about it."

"You sound awfully down. Do come and see me."

"Actually, I'm up. Have a nice weekend, Amy."

Have a nice weekend: that was the *coup de grace*. Amy went to the kitchen and got out the martini jug. She closed the refrigerator door on an eight-dollar steak. The cat, her paws tucked out of sight where she sat on the table, opened her eyes and then closed them again at once.

Amy returned to the living room by way of the dining-room door. As she entered, she discovered a man also coming into the room, he by the door to the vestibule. She had not locked up after Mike's departure.

"Hello. I did knock," he said, "but not very loudly. I thought I'd surprise you."

"You have, and now that I'm surprised, get the hell out of here before I call my husband."

"Funny. Ginny didn't tell me about him. In fact, she said you didn't want one."

"You're Allan."

He had stopped. They both had, in their tracks, on see-ing one another. They now moved tentatively forward. He was handsome in an odd way: his quick smile and his eyes did not seem to go together. The eyes, she would have sworn, took in everything in the room while not seeming to look directly at anything, even at her when they came face to face.

"Yes, I'm Allan. So Ginny's told you about me? I'm surprised, though come to think of it, I shouldn't be. She's told me a lot about you, too. Where is she?"

Damn Ginny. "She's gone for a walk." She regretted at once having said that. Now it was reasonable for him to expect to wait for her return. "Don't you think, Mr.—" She stopped and waited.

"Just Allan," he said, which she did not like either, the familiarity of it. No. The anonymity: it was more like that.

"Mr. Allan, don't you think if Ginny wanted to see you, she would have arranged it?"

"It takes two to make an arrangement, Amy." His eyes, not really on hers anyway, slipped away to the glass where Mike had left it. Her glass was on the side table near which she stood, the martini pitcher in her hand. He might well have arrived in time to have seen Mike leave.

He then said, "Should I confess something to you, Miss Amy—I guess that's what you'd like me to call you, but it certainly rings strange against the picture Ginny gave me of you—let me tell you the reason I crashed this party. I wanted to see the cottage, and I wasn't sure I'd ever get an invitation, leaving it to Ginny. It's pre-Revolutionary, isn't it?"

"Yes."

"Don't you need an architect?"

That disarmed her—he was a man with humor at least. "Will you have a drink?" She swirled the contents of the pitcher. "A martini?"

"Thank you."

"I'll get a glass."

A few steps took him to the table where Mike's glass sat. "If this was Ginny's glass, I don't mind using it."

No more lies. She hardly knew now which were hers

and which were Ginny's. "It wasn't Ginny's glass," she said.

He brought it to her anyway. "Whose ever it was, it won't poison me."

All the same, those eyes that just missed hers saw everything that passed through her mind. She wanted to escape them, however briefly, in the time it would take to get a glass from the other room. "That's ridiculous," she said. "Sit down, Allan. That chair is better for your long legs than this one."

His movements were such that she thought him about to take the far chair as she had suggested, but she had no more than stepped into the dining room than he was behind her.

"What a marvelous old room!"

Of all six rooms this was the plainest, with nothing to recommend it except the view of the garden and that was not available at night. One end of it had been chopped off in the nineteen-twenties to provide space for a bathroom. She took a glass from the cupboard.

"May I see the kitchen?" he asked, throwing her a quick, persuasive smile.

"Why not?" This time she stepped aside and let him go on by himself. The kitchen was straight ahead, not to be missed. He had an athlete's build as well as one's lightness of step, she observed as he passed her.

"Puss, puss, puss," he said, seeing the cat. She came wide-awake, stood up, and preened herself for him.

Amy kept trying to tell herself that it was she who was behaving oddly, letting her imagination run wild. She tried to think what he and Ginny would be like together. They were similar in a way she could not put her finger on. Then she had it: Ginny never seemed quite able to hit the nail on the head. God knows, he was direct enough, but his eyes slipped past what he was presumably looking at.

Well, he had made it to the kitchen and if there was something there he wanted—a knife or a hammer—there was no preventing his getting it. She turned into the vestibule, that entrance to it opposite the bathroom, with the purpose of making sure the shotgun was in its place alongside the porch door, more or less concealed by her old Burberry coat and the umbrella stand. She could not see it where she stood, but that did not mean it was not there. For just an instant she thought of making a dash to the front door.

"Amy?"

They very nearly collided, him coming in as she turned back.

"Is the kitchen fireplace a replica of the old one?"

"Probably."

"Afterwards I'll show you where I think the old one was." He caught her hand as though he were an old friend and led her back to the living room. When she tried to remove her hand he gave it a little squeeze before letting go.

She poured the drinks shakily. "I should have got more ice."

"Are you afraid of me?"

"Certainly not," she said.

"I'm harmless enough. You'd have to know that for a fact from Ginny's having anything to do with me."

She laughed, thinking how obviously so that was. If she knew Ginny. Sometimes she felt that she knew Ginny so well she could not possibly know her at all. Maybe there were two Ginnies. "Cheers."

The drink was strong enough, but it was going tepid.

"Would you allow me to get more ice and give these another stir?" he asked.

"I would allow it." She poked up the embers under the half-burned log. The sparks exploded and vanished. Ginny ought to have come even if she didn't believe the story about the story. It was funny how sure she had been that Allan was imaginary. Nor could she remember anything Ginny had ever told her about him. Had she told her anything? Or had Amy simply turned it off, doubting that there was a real live Allan?

He returned with the pitcher and the glasses, having taken them also to the kitchen. They now were white with frost. He poured the drinks, touched her glass with his, and said, "What else would you allow?"

Harmless? She said, trying to strike a pose of propriety without overdoing it: "I'd allow as how—I wouldn't allow much."

He shrugged. "No offense."

"None taken."

He started to shuffle across to the chair she had appointed his, then turned back. "What's much?" Having again amused her, he bent down and kissed her as she was reasonably sure he had never kissed Ginny. "Perfectly harmless," he said and trotted over to the chair while neatly balancing the glass so that he did not spill a drop. "Does she often take long walks at this time of night?"

"As a matter of fact she does."

"And if I'm not mistaken, we're at the full moon." He helped make the lie more credible. Knowingly? "Has Ginny talked about me?"

"Well now," Amy said, avoiding a direct answer, "I almost suggested that she bring you out for the weekend."

"How intuitive of me then to be here."

"I suppose Ginny has given you a complete dossier on me?"

"We do talk a lot," he said in a sly, wistful, almost hopeless way that again amused her. "Have you anything to suggest I do about it?"

She knew exactly what he meant. "A marriage proposal?"

"That's a bit drastic."

"It sounds archaic when you set it off and listen to it by itself—a marriage proposal."

"Or the title to a poem by Amy Lowell," he said. "You weren't by any chance named after her?"

"Good God, no."

"She did like a good cigar, didn't she?" he said, deadpan.

Amy sipped her drink and gave a fleeting thought to Mike, to the steak in the refrigerator, to the Haut Brion '61. And to the rumpled bed in the room back of the fireplace.

He put his glass on the table and got up with a sudden show of exuberance. "Shall I bring in more wood? I saw the pile of it outside."

"Not yet." Amy put the one log left in the basket onto the fire. While she swept in the bits of bark and ash, he came and stood beside her, bent, studying the fire, but stealing glimpses of her face. He touched his fingers lightly to a wisp of hair that had escaped one of the braids she wore in a circle round her head. "Your hair must be very long and beautiful."

"I've been told so."

"Ginny said it was."

"I wasn't thinking of Ginny."

"I wasn't either. Except in the way you hang onto somebody in the dark."

When they had both straightened up, he waited for her to face him, and then he lifted her chin, touching it only with the backs of his fingers as though to take hold of it might seem too bold. He kissed her. It was a long kiss which, nonetheless, didn't seem to be going anywhere until she herself thrust meaning into it. She had not intended to, but then the situation was not one open to precise calculations. He tasted of licorice as well as gin.

He drew back and looked at her. At that proximity his eyes did not seem to have the disconcerting vagary. He was, despite these little overtures, agonizingly shy: the realization came in a flash. Someone had prescribed—possibly a psychiatrist—certain boldnesses by which he might overcome the affliction. *Miss* Amy: that was closer to his true self.

He said, averting his eyes once more, "Ginny said we'd like one another . . . even though you don't like men."

"What?"

"She thinks you don't care much for men."

"What kind of woman does she think I am then? The kind who gets paid?"

Color rushed to his face. He backed off and turned, starting back to his chair in that shuffling way—a clown's way, really, the "don't look at me but at what I'm doing" routine which reinforced her belief in his shyness.

"I don't want another drink," she said, "but if you do, help yourself. I say what's on my mind, Allan. People who know me get used to it. By the sound of things, Ginny speaks hers too on occasion. I'd never got that picture of her."

"I shouldn't have blabbed that."

"No, you shouldn't." She started from the room, thinking: God save me from middle-aged adolescents.

"Where are you going?"

"To the bathroom for now. Then I'll decide where else."

She had not reached the door when he caught her from behind and lifted her from her feet, holding her close against him, her arms pinned to her sides. He kissed the back of her neck and then with his teeth he removed, one by one, her plastic hairpins and let them drop to the floor. "Please don't be so fierce," he said, his mouth at her ear. She felt the dart of his tongue there, but so tentative, as though he were following a book of instructions.

"Put me down. Your belt buckle's hurting me."

Her feet on the floor, she faced him. "I don't have to be fierce at all," she said and loosened the braids, after which she shook out that abundance of rich brown hair.

He ran his tongue round his lips. "It's just too bad that Ginny's going to be walking in."

"She's not."

"She's not?" he repeated. Something changed in his face, which was certainly natural with that bit of news. "I don't believe you," he said, the smile coming and going.

She motioned to him with one finger as much as to say, wait, and going to the phone, she dialed Virginia's number. With each ring Amy felt less sure of herself, less sure of Ginny. Then, after the fourth ring, came the gentle slow-voiced, "Hello."

Amy held the phone out toward Allan. He simply stared, his head slightly to the side. I could not have been more than a second, but it did seem longer before Ginny repeated more clearly, "Hello?"

He was about to take the phone. Amy broke the connection, pressing her finger on the signal, then returning the phone to its cradle.

"I don't get it," he said.

"It was a change of plan. That's all."

"And not anything to do with me?"

"My dear man, I wasn't even sure you were real."

"Maybe I'm not," he said, and smiled tentatively. It seemed flirtatious.

Amy threw her head back. "There's one way to find out."

He gave a funny little shudder, as though a chill had run through him. Or better, something interestingly erotic. He wet a finger and held it up as to the wind. Unerringly he then pointed to the closed door of the bedroom back of the fireplace. He motioned her to move on ahead of him. Had he looked in through, say, a part of the drapes at her and Mike? Or had Virginia told him that Amy slept downstairs? There did not seem to be much Ginny had not told him. With interpretations.

"Don't turn on the lights," he said.

Amy was not surprised. "We can always turn them off again."

"No." And then: "I'm able to see you i~ the dark."

A good trick. She said nothing. It was beginning to irritate her that Ginny had said she did not like men. Liking sex and liking men deserved a distinction, true. But she did not think it one Ginny was likely to make. And she had loved Mike. She had. Now it was over, ended. Nothing was beginning; nothing was about to be born. Except that you couldn't really tell. That was what was so marvelous about an encouter such as this: you couldn't really tell.

She bent down to remove her slippers. She felt his hand running lightly over her bare shoulder, sweeping the hair before it. A jolting pain struck at the base of her skull. Then came nothingness.

She awoke to the sound of voices and with a headache worse than any she had ever suffered. A woman's voice said that she was coming to. Like hell, she wanted to say; not if she could help it, not with all this pain. There was other pain besides that of her head, and with the awareness of it she began to realize what had happened. She tried to put her hand between her thighs. Someone gently pulled it away.

"Amy?"

She opened her eyes to the familiar ceiling beam with its ancient knot, the eye of the house. She turned her head far enough to see Virginia's round and worried face. "What are you doing here?"

A woman in a white uniform hovered alongside Ginny. She was filling a hypodermic needle from a medicine bottle. When Ginny glanced up at her, she moved away.

"On the phone," Ginny said, "I couldn't hear anything except the clock, but I'd know its tick anywhere. Remember when we were kids: 'take a *bath*, take a bath, take a *bath*, take a bath . . .' I decided I'd better catch the next bus out."

Amy gave her hand a weak squeeze. At the door of the room were two uniformed policemen, one of whom she thought she remembered having once talked out of giving her a speeding ticket. "How did *they* get in on the act?"

"I called the ambulance," Ginny said, and leaning close, she murmured, "You were"—she couldn't bring herself to say the exact word—"molested."

"I guess," Amy said.

One of the policemen said, "When you're strong enough we need the full story, miss. Did you recognize the intruder?"

The intruder. In a way he was, of course. She took a

long time in answering. "Is there any way I can be sure he'll get psychiatric attention?"

The cops exchanged glances. "The first thing is to identify him so we can bring him in."

"And then I have to swear out a complaint against him?"

"If you don't, ma'am, some other woman may not get the chance to do it."

"To some extent it was my own fault," she said, not much above a whisper.

The cop made a noise of assent. Neither he nor his partner seemed surprised. "All the same, we better get him in and let the shrinks decide what happens to him. Okay?"

She thought of telling them of the point at which she had been knocked out and decided against it for the time being. "Okay," she said.

"Can you give us a description? Race, age, height, color of his eyes—"

"Ginny, I'm sorry. It was your friend Allan."

"Oh."

It was a little cry, scarcely more than a whimper.

"Would you give them his name and address? You won't have to do anything else."

"But, Amy, I can't. I mean, actually I've never seen Allan. He calls me and we just talk on the telephone.

1975

The Last Party

The Winthrops had a tremendous collection of Big Band records—Miller, Lombardo, Harry James . . . But then, the Winthrops had a tremendous collection of almost everything, and when they gave a party, Tom Winthrop's measure of its success was the variety of his possessions to which his guests found their way. His hospitality was excessive: champagne, the best of liquors: the dining-room buffet—replenished throughout the evening, with monster prawns, half-lobsters, mounds of succulent beef, crisp vegetables, mousses, and soufflés, melons, cheeses, and the most delicate of pastries.

The trouble with the Winthrops' parties was that nothing ever happened at them; paradoxically, too much was going on. There was a billiard room in the basement for those not drawn to the dance. Next to the billiard room was the gun room, with its trophies of ancestral hunts. Tom liked to tell that it was part of Sally's inheritance. Her great-grandfather was supposed to have gone big-game hunting with Teddy Roosevelt. The younger residents of Maiden's End had a modest reverence for *that* Roosevelt, but their politics, for the most part, were in the tradition of his cousin Franklin. Nor did they have much taste for guns or the hunt. It was generally by accident that a guest found himself—or herself—in the gun room. Or he might pass through it on his way to a room Winthrop called "The Double Entendre," where he housed his collection of pornographic art.

It remains to be said of Winthrop—or perhaps of Maiden's End—that since he had built Woodside, a neo-Tudor mansion that dwarfed the sedate, more modest houses, some of which were historically significant, no one in the community had ever asked him if he was related to other Winthrops of their acquaintance.

On the afternoon of what became known as the last Winthrop party, Jan Swift stopped by the Adams house to see what Nancy was going to wear. Jan, a plump, self-conscious woman, didn't like parties, but she went to them. She'd have liked it less not to be asked, and if you didn't go to one, you might not be asked to the next. Or so Jan feared. What it amounted to was that when the invitation came she was so relieved to have been asked—for Fred's sake mostly, she told herself—that there was never any doubt of their accepting.

"Hello?" she called up the stairs. The Adamses still left their door unlocked in the daytime. "Nancy, it's me."

"Hello, you," Nancy called down, a greeting that always gave Jan pleasure, something about the intimacy of it. Jan had never heard her say it to anyone else. "Come up if you like. Or I'll be down in a minute. I'm doing a bed in the guest room."

Jan climbed the stairs, a little aware of her weight, and wondered what she could wear and be comfortable to dance in that wouldn't look like a tent. She loved to dance when she got high enough and someone besides Fred asked her. Fred danced much as he did most things, determined to succeed. She stood at the guest-room door and watched Nancy turn down one of the twin beds.

"A comforter should do him," Nancy said. It was going to be one of those warm summer nights when people would want to go swimming after the party. Or sailing on the river.

Jan thought about the word *comforter,* the coziness of it. "Who's coming?"

"Eddie Dorfman. He was Dick's roommate in college. He shows up now and then on his way somewhere—generally broke, but with great expectations. Is it hot in here? I was going to put him in Ellen's room, but I don't like to do that." Ellen was the oldest of the Adamses' three daughters.

"It'll cool off by bedtime," Jan said. She was thinking how nice it was for Nancy, the girls of an age to take care of themselves. Her own two had to be picked up at the Swim Club anytime now. Nancy was ten years older than Jan, well up in her forties, but with a finely boned face and dark, deepset eyes that made her look more striking the older she got. She played tennis and swam and wrote poetry that Jan did her best to understand. Jan nodded at the open bed. "Is he a bachelor?"

"To all intents and purposes. He's a charming rogue, if you want to know."

"I don't particularly. What are you going to wear tonight?"

"Oh, God. Something I won't have to hang up afterward. She gave a last look around the room. Following her eyes, Jan noticed the published volume of Nancy's poems on the bedside table. Nancy gave Jan a nudge into the hall ahead of her. "Eddie tried to seduce me the night Dick and I announced our engagement. Whenever I see him, he pretends regrets at not having succeeded." She hooked her arm through Jan's. "Don't hold it against him, you puritan. He thinks he's being *trés galant.*"

Eddie was still at it, Jan judged, by the way he danced with Nancy, cheek to cheek, abdomen to abdomen. Furthermore, Nancy was enjoying it . . . "Moonlight Serenade," "Elmer's Tune," "Black Moonlight". . . They drew away from one another, took a long look into each other's eyes, laughed, and sailed away to the far end of the deck.

It was pretty much the older crowd that turned on to the music of the Big Bands, and you couldn't say the deck

was jammed. The noise would start at midnight with the
arrival of a rock group. Jan thought of another drink,
which she didn't need but wanted. She didn't even want
it. What in hell did she want? Fred and Dick were probably shooting pool in the basement. Billiards: a fine distinction. She did not like Eddie Dorfman. Or did she?
Maybe that was the trouble. Baby blue eyes and black
hair with a streak of gray, a whispery lower lip. The
women kept asking Jan who he was, as though she was
Nancy's keeper. It wasn't hard to guess the speculation.
Maiden's End (named after a family called Maiden) was
by no means famous for marital stability. Jan thought of
the switched couples at the party—the Eckstroms and the
Bellows. What a mix-up for the kids. And there were at
least three grass widows, as her mother called them.
She'd have been willing to bet that Liz Tooney would
make a play for Eddie Dorfman before the night was
over. She emptied her glass and thought of shifting to
champagne rather than having to go back to the bar again
alone.

Tom Winthrop came up and took the glass from her
hand and dropped it over the deck. "Come on, Jan.
They're playing our song."

Our song indeed. Neither in nor out of step, he took
her with him on a cruise of his guests, wanting to know if
everyone was happy and assuming she was, just to be in
on the trip. Not a word did he say to her, or she to him,
for that matter. When they came alongside Nancy and
Dorfman, Jan broke away from Tom and said, "May we
cut in?" You could almost say she plucked Eddie out of
Nancy's arms.

"What fun!" Dorfman cried, though he cast Nancy a
wistful glance. After that he gave Jan his complete attention. He even hummed "Sentimental Journey" in her
ear. She had never felt lighter on her feet. He was a good
dancer.

"I wonder," she said breathlessly between tunes, "if
they have 'Flatfoot Floogie with the Floy Floy.' "

"If they do, I hope it's not contagious."

She laughed too loudly and explained, "My mother used to play all her old records for me on a rainy day and we'd dance up in the attic."

"What fun," he said again. "No wonder you dance so well."

"I do with the right partner." She tossed her head and sang, a bit off tune, but urgently, " 'He danced divinely and I loved him so , but there I go . . .' That was another of my mother's favorites."

The music started again, another set of records. "Glenn Miller," Jan said, "oh, boy."

" 'I saw those harbor lights,' " he crooned, and held her close. He said after a few bars, "I'll be in London this time tomorrow."

"Will you? I wish I were."

He drew back and looked at her.

"I mean just that I love to travel."

He held her close again. "Perhaps we'll meet in some exotic port some day," he said. His cheek, soft, freshly shaven, was scented with lavender. A tango then. They dipped and glided a backward dip for Jan, something she had never risked before in her life, and then a waltz that dissolved into a seductive whine.

"Salomé," her partner said.

"I forgot my veils," Jan said; she tried to repress the impulse to lead.

"Let's pretend." He disengaged himself and with provocative little gestures coaxed her into letting go. Jan shed veil after imaginary veil, clownish at first, but with a growing feeling that she was actually graceful. Eddie posed as a macho Herod; he demanded more and more letting go. For a few seconds Jan danced with utter abandon, every pound of her a quiver.

"Help!" she cried finally, and collapsed in self-conscious laughter, sinking to the floor.

Eddie mimed the removal of his own head and brought it to her in cupped hands, which rather thoroughly distorted the story line, to say nothing of de-sanctifying John the Baptist.

Everyone, having given Jan space, now applauded, laughed, and slipped away into the next dance.

She blushed and got to her feet. "I need a drink," she said.

"I'll get it for you."

"I'll go with you," she said and caught his hand. Then: "I'll meet you at the bar. I've got to make some repairs first."

Nancy was waiting for her when she came out of the bathroom, a look of pure disgust on her face.

"Hey," Jan said, "What's the matter?"

"It wasn't funny, kiddo."

"I thought it was fun."

"It was pretty undignified, if you want the truth."

If it was the truth, it was the last thing she wanted. "That wasn't exactly a minuet the two of you were dancing when I pulled you apart," she said. "You wouldn't be jealous, would you?"

"Jan, I care about you and I don't like to see you make a fool of yourself."

"Okay. I get the message." The worst of it was that deep down it hadn't been fun; the make-believe that she had almost bought herself now fell apart.

"Don't sulk over it. For heaven's sake, you're not a little girl anymore."

"I never was a *little* girl."

"Just don't drink so much."

"It's none of your damned business how much I drink. Okay, keep your Don Juan. I'm going to find Fred."

She did not look for Fred right away. She went out to the garden to cool off, to sort out anger from hurt, as though they were divisible at the moment. She took a glass of champagne with her, drank it too fast, and then took another from the tray one of the teenaged helpers was passing as though his night's wage depended on the score in champagne corks. The feeling of humiliation began to set in, a replay of the exhibition she had made of herself. She did not know whom she disliked more, Nancy, Dorfman, or herself. Herself.

She almost went directly home then, but Fred was always accusing her of disappearing at parties. She spent a lot of time in bathrooms, especially if there was a children's bathroom where the ducks and frogs and floating pigs gave her surcease from the social tensions. Fred was not in the billard room. No one was. She wandered through the gun room, and wondered vaguely if any of the blunderbusses in the glass cases were loaded. She looked up at the moosehead over tne fireplace, its glassy eyes frozen in sadness. "You and me, baby."

THE DOUBLE ENTENDRE: the sign hung above the door. That's me, she thought. I'm a double entendre. She wandered with fascinated distaste from one to another of Tom Winthrop's pornographic objets d'art. He always set out a half-dozen or so for the titillation of his guests. For anyone who appreciated the sampling enough to tell him so, he would come down and show the really important things in the collection. Fred said he'd never seen anything like it. Fred, the connoisseur. It was a strange place to be alone, a strange place to be discovered if anyone came. That was all she needed. She remembered her mother opening the closet door on her, a precocious ten-year old with a flashlight looking at the illustrations in an anatomy book she had stolen from the locked bookcase. "Wicked girl." There were no locked bookcases in Fred's and her house. No anatomy books either.

She picked up a picture—in what medium she could not tell—of a unicorn. No larger than three by four inches, in a silver frame, it was exquisite, and she could not imagine what was pornographic about it. Then, when she went to set it down, she saw the trick: a shutter effect where beauty in a different angle of light turned into obscenity. She set it down and turned to flee the room. Dorfman was standing in the doorway.

"Here you are—in the naughty room. What fun!"

She stopped herself from saying that she was looking for her husband. She pushed by him. "Please tell Nancy—if Fred's looking for me, I've gone home."

"Don't leave on my account."

"I'm not," she said.

She found Fred herself. He was in the library where he and Dick and Phil Eckstrom were deep in conversation. Local politics, she gathered. Eckstrom was on the town board. She did not interrupt. The bar wasn't crowded, and she decided on one for the road. The bartender, who worked most parties at Maiden's End, didn't even ask her what she wanted. He knew: Scotch with a spalsh. Nancy, she observed, was dancing again. With Phil Eckstrom, senior.

Jan finished her drink and went out by way of the garden. From there she cut down along the ravine path that crossed the creek and meandered up near the Adams house, beyond which lay her own. There was a three-quarter moon, but she knew the path from her own childhood. What did Nancy see in him, she wondered. Something. Or she would not have left her poems at his bedside. He certainly wasn't going to understand them if Jan didn't. She often wondered if Dick did, all that symbolism. Not that Nancy cared: It isn't what they say, it's what they show. Simply fireworks? Jan had to believe they were deeper than that. She often imagined Nancy making them up, quite removed, while Dick was telling one of the stories in which he was the hero. It wasn't easy to be a hero in advertising, not and continue to make as much money as Dick did. Pure fantasy. To which all Nancy had to say, in effect, was "Yes, dear." She'd been flying in a holding pattern for years. But then, who hadn't? After the first child, Jan didn't say, "Yes, dear," to Fred. In Fred's stories he was always the victim; most people found that funny. The trouble was, Fred's stories were true. Nancy ought not to have spoken to her the way she had. She ought to have understood. Maybe she did. And that was worse, even more humiliating. The hall lights were on in the Adams house, upstairs and down. An unfamiliar car, which had to be Eddie's, sat alongside Nancy's battered V.W. in the driveway. They had taken Dick's Buick. Jan always felt that hall lights made a house look more empty than, say, a light in the living room or an upstairs bedroom. She went round to the kitchen window and got the key from the bird feeder. She returned it after opening the door. There was something she had to know—if there was anything to know: She wanted to see how Nancy had inscribed the book for Eddie Dorfman. In Jan's copy she had written, "Love, toujours."

The stairs creaked beneath her step. It was an old house with a curving banister that many a child's behind had polished over the years. She did not hesitate in turning on the bedside lamp. Somehow it seemed her right to be there. She saw at once that the book had been removed. Dorfman's one large piece of luggage was on the stand, the flap closed but not entirely zipped. So far as she could see, he had not unpacked at all: no hairbrushes or shaving kit, nothing on the dresser. She looked into the bathroom. Not even a toothbrush. And he had been freshly shaved. He reeked of after-shave cologne. The bathroom was still scented with it. It was as though, after dressing, he had repacked.

She went to the suitcase and ran the zipper far enough to lift the flap. Tucked into the corner was *Refraction*, the poems of Nancy Eldridge Adams. There was no inscription. Which brought the shame thundering in her ears. It was more difficult to fit the book back than it had been to take it out and in doing so she disturbed the bathrobe and partially uncovered something in chamois.

Now, Jan had given Nancy a chamois bag of several compartments two Christmases before. Nancy used it, when traveling, to carry such of her jewelry as she took along. She had several nice antique pieces and a valuable pearl necklace. Ordinarily they were kept in an ivory jewel box on Nancy's dressing table. Jan lost no time in discovering that the bag was the same and contained the pearls, a diamond brooch and earrings, and the lovely jade pendant, the only piece of jewelry Jan had ever coveted. Nancy had promised to give it to her some day.

The thought that Dorfman was a thief delighted her after the shock of discovery wore off. The question, however, was what to do about it without placing herself in even deeper disgrace. Her mind grew muddled with the sickening thought of how to explain the discovery: she also wondered then just when the theft had occurred. She had not met him until the party was well on. He could have stayed at the house on some pretext and come along later on his own. But surely he had to expect that Nancy would discover the theft when they came home? Jan understood then why the suitcase was packed: He expected to leave tonight, long before the Winthrop party was over. A rented car. London tomorrow . . .

However humiliating it might be, Jan resolved to bare the truth to Nancy. Replacing everything, she drew the zipper. And changed her resolution even as she put out the light. What was a handful of jewels in comparison to her own pride? She would let the matter run its course and never let on she anticipated the story when Nancy told her of the theft. It did not occur to Jan to wonder why Eddie Dorfman had not put the suitcase in the car before he left for the party. Her main concern was to get out of the house quickly.

But Dorfman was coming up the stairs when she reached the hallway. He quickened his step when he saw her and came round the banister smiling with that nasty lower lip. "I had a feeling we'd meet again before I took off," he said. "Something told me."

Jan gave a little moan of chagrin. She thought of accusing him outright. She had no subtlety, and she was able to defend herself only by striking out in anger. But at the moment she had no anger. Nor could she run: Dorfman stood between her and the stairs, one hand on the railing, the other on the wall.

"Let me guess: You've brought me something. A flower? Something that blooms in the night? Come on, let's have a look." He nodded toward the door. "You're not afraid of me, are you? I'm completely harmless unless stepped on."

Jan made a noise in her throat. No words came.

"I thought that would amuse you," he said. "Light the light and let's see where we are."

Jan turned back into the room and lit the lamp. She would run when the chance came. Simply run.

He leaned in the doorway, seeming to fill it, and looked all around the room before letting his eyes rest on her. "Nothing? Did you put something in my suitcase?"

Jan shook her head.

"I know: Nancy told you I was leaving and you wanted a few minutes alone with me first. If only I had more time . . ."

"You're making fun of me," she said.

"I don't make fun of women, Salomé." he said. He came in and closed the door. He drew the bolt across. There was no key.

"Don't! Leave the door open," Jan said.

He turned, smiling. "Then you shouldn't flirt with a man of my reputation. Didn't Nancy tell you?"

"Just let me go," she pleaded.

"Go." He stepped aside.

But as she tried to pass him, he caught her, pulled her around and kissed her, forcing her back to the closed door.

Jan yielded, as though that might gain her time, or some position of advantage, but with the thrust of his tongue between her lips, its probe of her clenched teeth, she broke away.

A few feet apart, they stood and stared at each other. He took his cigarette case from his pocket, opened it, and closed it again. He put it away without taking a cigarette. "Do you mind telling me what you were doing in my room?"

"I was looking for a book."

He began to laugh, as though at the ridiculousness of the excuse. He stopped. "Nancy's book? Why? Am I not allowed to have it?" Slowly his whole expression changed; he understood. "Salomé, you're jealous! You weren't flirting with *me*. It was an act. And me thinking all the time I was the object of your affections . . . Eddie, my boy, you're slipping. You should have caught that—no vibes, no sparks . . ."

Jan went to the door with as good grace as she could manage. Her main feeling was relief, and at the heart's core, something almost pleasurable. At the sound of the suitcase zipper she glanced back.

"Look here, Salomé. I'm left-handed. You've put the book back in the wrong corner." He plunged his hand into the case and brought out the chamois bag. "Ha! I've found the surprise." He weighed the bag in his hand, opened a compartment, and closed it again after a quick, pretended glimpse at what was in it. "Nancy's jewelry? Surely not." Slowly then in mock wonderment: "By God, I'd never have believed such mischief in a grown woman. You *are* a Salomé. You wanted my head."

Jan felt faint. Her whole body was perspiring. She pulled at the bolt and skinned her knuckles when it gave.

"Wait," he said as she stepped out of the room. "Listen to me for a minute."

Jan paused.

"Why don't you put these back—wherever they came from—and neither of us needs ever say a word." He brought her the bag.

Jan took it from him and went into the master bedroom where she put the jewelry, piece by piece, back in the ivory box on Nancy's dressing table. She tucked the chamois bag into the side drawer where Nancy kept it.

He was waiting at the stairs, smiling. He offered her his left hand, as to a child, the suitcase in his right. "No hard feelings. Come on now, give me your hand and no hard feelings."

Jan gave it to him as though it were a bribe.

"I'll bet Nancy doesn't even know," he said. "What fun."

A bribe for what?

With a crack-of-the-whip wrench she whirled him from his feet. He let go of her hand, trying to save himself, but while she fell backward, he hurtled down the stairs, the suitcase clattering after him. She listened for a few seconds and then picked herself up. All she could hear was the pounding of her own heart. The suitcase was lodged between his sprawled legs at the turn in the stairs, the rest of him out of sight from where she stood.

Jan went down carefully. When she stooped and looked into his face Dorfman's lashes fluttered like a wounded butterfly, but the baby blue eyes only stared. His cigarette case had flown out of his pocket, and a lighter. Jan was stepping round them when she blacked out.

Her first awareness was of rock music, the shattering beat of it breaking through what had seemed a silvery stillness. She was walking across the bridge on the ravine path, the moonlight more vivid than seemed natural. Her mind was crystal clear except that she could not understand why she was going in that direction when she had intended to go home. Then everything came back up to the moment of the blackout. She sat down on the bridge and said what she knew to be a futile prayer, that it was all a dream.

She got up after a few minutes and returned to the party going in the way she had come out, through the French doors onto the garden. Fred was standing just indoors, his pipe in hand, watching the disco dancing.

"No," Fred said when she approached.

"No, what?"

"I won't dance."

"Who asked you?" He had not even missed her.

Nancy and Dick were dancing together, very athletic,

the best-looking couple among a lot of very chic and handsome people. The Big Band crowd had all gone home.

"Come on," Fred said. "You're pouting. Let's get into the action." He knocked out his pipe and put it in his pocket.

"I don't think so," Jan said after a tremendous effort inside herself. "Why don't you ask Liz Toomey?"

"Why do you always try to make me dance with somebody else?"

"I don't always," Jan said.

"I don't suppose you want to go home yet?"

"Soon," she said.

It was after three when Dick and Nancy Adams drove home. They were surprised to see Dorfman's rented car still in the driveway. He had told them at the party he'd been able to get on a delayed flight taking off from Kennedy at two.

By the time the police came, Dick was fairly sure of what had happened, that Eddie had banged his suitcase into the railing and then lost his balance when it caromed into his legs at the top of the stairs. He did not touch anything, of course. When the police arrived he went into the study with Nancy.

"Poor, poor man," Nancy kept saying. "Poor restless man. Why couldn't he have waited until morning the way he'd planned?"

Dick sat with his head in his hands.

The police officer in charge came in presently and closed the door behind him. He asked more questions than seemed necessary to Nancy. He did not seem satisfied that Dorfman had left the party alone. She assured him that she had walked to the end of the Winthrop driveway with him.

He turned to Dick and asked him if he could identify the little silver-framed picture which, to all appearances, like the cigarette case and the lighter, had been jarred out of Dorfman's pocket in the fall.

"Yes, I can," Dick said heavily. "It's trick pornography and it belongs to Tom Winthrop."

"Are you saying the deceased stole it, Mr. Adams?"

"I'm not, but I think it's possible."

"Is it valuable? Was it valuable?" the police officer corrected himself.

"Yes."

"And did you notice it when you discovered the body?"

"Yes, sir, I noticed it."

"It looks like somebody ground a heel into it, doesn't it?"

"I only noticed that it was smashed," Dick said.

"A woman's heel, I'd say, but we can't be sure until we get some measurements and pictures." He turned back to Nancy. "I'd like to have the shoes you're wearing, Mrs. Adams, if you don't mind."

"Mine?" Nancy said.

"Well, ma'am, we've got to start somewhere."

1980

The Devil and His Due

Thomas MacIntosh Gordon III was learning a great deal about the devil, especially for someone about to turn fifteen. He had chosen as his subject for a Religious Studies term paper, "The Devil and All His Works." The reason he chose the devil—as opposed to such possibilities as St. Francis of Assisi (at least four of his classmates chose St. Francis), the Augustinian Hermits, the Spanish Inquisition, Savonarola, or John Knox, was the premonition of boredom as he pondered them. His religious instructor sanctioned his choice for the same reason: there was no more disruptive influence at St. Christopher's Preparatory School in east Manhattan than Thomas MacIntosh Gordon III when he was bored.

Thomas had to have special letters from both the school and his parents in order to gain access to the rare books he wished to see at the New York Public Library and the Morgan Library. The permissions having been granted at the top, the staffs extended him the privileges of a scholar. He accepted gravely and concentrated with all his might. But sometimes, to ease the feeling of gravity, he would stop off at one or another of the Fifth Avenue bookstores to search out more modern literature giving the devil his due. Most of it couldn't hold a candle to the ancients, but one day, at Glasgow's, he discovered something that quite enchanted him—an exquisitely illustrated new edition of Flaubert's *The Temptation of St. Anthony.*

* * *

There remained until this time, which was not so very long ago, a cozy, old-world atmosphere to Glasgow's. Customers and non-customers alike browsed undisturbed by the sales personnel. A few were disconcerted now and then by the cold eye of Frank O'Reilly, the store detective. He retired last year and uniformed security guards took over, putting an end to an era as well as to a man's career.

Frank was not popular on the floor. To him every browser was a potential thief, and according to Miss Murray, whose seniority equaled Frank's, he had scared off more buyers over the years than thieves. His eyes glowing, his breath a mixture of whiskey and cloves, he pushed among the customers like a pouter pigeon, bumping them out of his way rather than lose sight of a subject under surveillance. Many an order was abandoned on the way to the cash register because of Frank, and the story is told of the time Miss Murray turned on him after one such abortion and flung every book in the order at his head. Frank stood his ground stoutly, merely removing his bowler hat to protect it under his arm.

There were not many customers in the store when Frank first noticed Thomas. The boy caught his attention by glancing slyly around to see if anyone was watching him. Frank dropped his eyes before Thomas' reached them. When Thomas went back to the book, Frank sized him up: a well-dressed, sassy-looking lad, small for his age, no doubt, given to reading in corners when he should have been on the football field; cunning too, Frank decided; he wore a private-school blazer and a cap. He'd have money in his pocket which would only reinforce his larcenous impulses. He put Frank in mind of the youngsters old Mr. Glasgow had used to hire when he was running the store; he required only that they came of good family and had passed their sixteenth birthday, and he wouldn't have cared about that except for the law. The union shop put an end to the practice.

Frank sidled down the aisle and surreptitiously glimpsed the book the youngster was into—drawings of nude women and the horny heads of animals among them. For a respectable bookstore Glasgow's had some of the damnedest things right out where any school child could feast his greedy little eyes on them. There'd be a hot time in the locker room if he popped something like that out of his duffelbag, and if he could boast of having snitched it—what an example that to his chums! It would be far better for the boy in the long run to be caught in the theft of it. And not bad for Frank O'Reilly to whom a little thief was better than none. He retreated to the Sports and Wildlife section and took up his vigil, rather like a hunter in the blind.

Bradford Pope observed the scene from the balcony where he was waiting for old Mr. Glasgow to come with the key. Pope had the look of the diplomatic service about him—a European cut to his clothes, a school tie you felt you ought to recognize, and shoes polished to a gloss. He wore his graying hair in a crest to camouflage a barren stretch of scalp. His hand dangled languorously over the railing, and his dark eyes, while quick, were limpid.

When the boy looked up at him he smiled, meaning to convey a knowing sympathy. What he wanted was the boy to stay where he was and to continue to hold the security man's attention, something the boy seemed quite unaware of. The youngster blushed guiltily and averted his eyes. Pope was delighted; he had been about the boy's age himself when he stole his first book.

Mr. Glasgow came along in that brisk, gingerly step of the aging wherein they resemble tightrope walkers which, indeed, they are. He no longer owned any part of Glasgow's, but he had been allowed to stay on and write his memoirs while presiding over what was left of the once-famous Old and Rare Department. He knew very well that he and Old and Rare would go out of Glasgow's together.

"I knew you'd be back, Mr. Bishop," he said. "Matter of fact, I had my secretary make out the authentication when you left me Friday."

"Pope, Bradford Pope, Mr. Glasgow."

"Yes, of course, as in Alexander." Mr. Glasgow selected his key from a ring chained to his belt. "I don't suppose you'd be interested in an 1866 copy of *Satires and Epistles?*"

Pope shook his head regretfully.

"Pity." The old man proceeded to one of the finely crafted glass-doored cases with which the balcony was lined at the turn of the century when Glasgow's moved uptown from lower Broadway.

Pope hung back until the case was opened. "Mr. Glasgow?" He beckoned him to the balcony rail and pointed out Thomas MacIntosh Gordon. "I may be wrong, but I suspect that lad is about to steal a book."

Mr. Glasgow leaned over the rail and scouted the floor until he spotted Frank O'Reilly. "Hadn't better," he said. Then, with an appraising look at Thomas: "Bright-looking chap, isn't he? In my day we put this sort to work. Didn't stop their thieving, but we got something in return."

Pope had thought he'd have more time. He regretted the banality of the next ploy and delayed it by a second or two, saying, "But isn't it reassuring in these times that someone his age cares enough about a book to want to steal it?"

Mr. Glasgow gave a dry grunt of assent.

"Excuse me, sir, but your shoelace is untied." Pope dropped to one knee at the old man's feet and pulled the lace loose before Mr. Glasgow realized what he was about. "Get up from there! I'm not so feeble that I can't tie my own laces."

Pope retreated toward the open case. "No offense, Mr. Glasgow," he said almost obsequiously.

"None taken." But the old face, still handsome despite the sagging, quivering jowls, was flushed. He lifted his foot, straining to conceal the effort, and planted it on the rail. He tied a double knot while he was about it.

Pope, knowing exactly where the book he wanted was, deftly plucked it from the shelf and slipped it into a pouch at his waist. It was a slender volume containing Richard Hooker's life of Izaak Walton, an extraordinary find, published within fifty years of Hooker's own lifetime. It would bring him thousands if he waited a bit. Or took sufficient care in making up a provenance. He leaped forward and caught the old gentleman's elbow when he teetered, off balance. Mr. Glasgow shrugged off his assistance, returned to the bookcase, and got out the Leyden edition of an Eighteenth Century medical handbook; it was the item they had discussed and bargained over on Pope's last visit.

"I've often wondered," Pope said the while, "why the pilgrims pulled out of Leyden when they did. It's a mystery that's never been satisfactorily solved, you know."

"Won't find out here." The old man chortled and waved the medical handbook.

The moment Pope had smiled at him, Thomas knew the man was up to no good. He half expected to be sneakily beckoned up the stairs and hustled into some secret passage behind the bookshelves. Which was why he had looked away so quickly. He had been thoroughly instructed in how to repulse such an overture. But when the old man also came to the railing and Thomas felt himself the object of both their attentions, he wondered if Pope might not be a truant officer. People were always asking Thomas why he wasn't in school. He had composed several answers: "Don't you know it's St. Crispin's Day?" Or "Madam, I've been expelled for promiscuity." None of which he had ever used.

He returned to paging *The Temptation of St. Anthony.*

The fact was, he was having trouble with his project: the devil had too many works. It occurred to Thomas he might more easily contain his subject if he approached the devil from the viewpoint of St. Anthony.

Miss Murray wandered down the aisle and rearranged a stack of books across the table from Thomas. She had in mind to discourage this youngster if he intended mischief which, plainly, Frank O'Reilly anticipated. Frank shook his fist at her when she threw him a hypocritical smile. A customer, waiting at the cash register, asked if someone in the store wouldn't mind taking his money. Miss Murray hastened back to her station.

Thomas opened the briefcase at his feet and took out pen and notebook. He carefully wrote down the title and the author of the book that he might add it to his references. He also noted dates of publication and copyright, the text dated 1910. That set him to wondering just how Flaubert came to know what happened to St. Anthony, who had lived in the fourth century. Flaubert had made it up, of course, which set Thomas to further thought on whether it might not be a sin to make up such things about a saint. He'd thought before about the viewpoint of St. Anthony. Flaubert, he decided, was a hypocrite, pretending to write about St. Anthony, when what he really wanted to write about was the devil. Thomas jumped when the phone rang on the post behind him.

The woman clerk came and identified herself as Miss Murray. "Yes, Mr. Glasgow," she said. "I'll be waiting for him."

Thomas followed her eyes to the top of the balcony stairs. There stood the man he had suspected of flirting with him. Very shortly he was joined by the old gentleman.

Mr. Glasgow had brought the Leyden book and its authentication along with the bill of sale which Miss Murray would process when Pope got downstairs. The two men shook hands. Pope had with him a certified check for $1512; it had all but cleaned him out. He ran down the steps, paused there and saluted the old gentleman watching at the top. As soon as Miss Murray took over, Mr. Glasgow retreated to his nook among the executive offices.

Pope, to expand his air of casualness, pretended, in passing, an interest in the book which so absorbed Thomas. Thomas looked up at him icily. "Why aren't you in school?" Pope asked.

"Because I have the mumps," Thomas said.

Pope pulled in his neck, as it were.

Miss Murray, seeing the figure of Pope's purchase which, no matter how Bookkeeping dealt with it eventually, would appear with her initials on that day's register tape, began to hum to conceal her excitement. She made a mistake in punching the first digit and had to correct it.

"Miss Murray," Pope said, "hold on a moment, will you?"

Miss Murray remained crouched over the electronic keys, her fingers poised.

Pope moistened his lips. He was about to violate one of his basic rules: Don't get greedy. But the setup was irresistible. The youngster was putting something in his briefcase and the security officer, unnoticed by the boy, was so intent on him that he was actually on tiptoe, ready to take off after the youngster when he headed for the exit.

"I'm frightfully sorry if it's an inconvenience," Pope said, affecting a British accent which usually ingratiated him with elderly salesladies, "but you know, I'd like another day to consider. I'm sure Mr. Glasgow will understand."

"I'm sure he will," Miss Murray said, shooting her teeth at him. The following day was her day off. She cleared the register, then locked it, tucked the invoice and the documentation within the book's cover, and left the floor to take the book back to Mr. Glasgow.

Thomas hadn't missed a step. He had already decided

to follow the man out of the store on the chance of his committing himself to something not yet defined in Thomas's imagination. Thomas only knew that the man was wicked, a conviction best accounted for by his recent studies.

Pope waited until Miss Murray was almost up the stairs, then ambled into the Sculpture Department. It was a direct line from there to the Fifth Avenue exit. He gradually accelerated his pace.

Thomas grabbed his briefcase and ran after him, at which point every customer in the store, most of them in the Fifth Avenue wing, became aware that something was happening.

Frank O'Reilly was momentarily off balance, shocked at Miss Murray's leaving the floor without a word or a sign to him. He was sure that it was pure cantankerousness, her trying to prove that, left on his honor, the little savage would turn noble. The little savage, having dropped something into his briefcase, was galloping through Sculpture with it. Frank took a short cut behind the stairs. Up front, a woman screamed, "Stop thief!"

There was one in every crowd, Frank thought, someone doing his work for him. He could not make an arrest until the suspect got beyond the store premises.

As soon as Thomas heard the cry, "Stop thief!" he put things together approximately right, dead right in the conclusion that the man was on his way out of the store with a book he had stolen from the Old and Rare Department. Thomas paused long enough to call out to a clerk, "Call a cop, a policeman!"

"The store detective's right behind you, sonny."

"Thanks," O'Reilly said bitterly. There wasn't a clerk in the store who wasn't his enemy.

Thomas sprinted ahead. He caught up with Pope in the revolving door, hitting the door with enough force to send the unready thief reeling past the exit. O'Reilly, in the compartment behind Thomas, held the door back at that point, hoping to flush the boy outdoors: all he had to do was go, he was in the open. But Thomas had no intention of letting the thief get out of his sight. Pope was hung up like a bird in a glass cage.

Finally Pope braced himself, his back to the panel next to Thomas, and pushed. O'Reilly, surmising what he had in mind, yielded and the door slipped back a few inches; Pope was able to slither outdoors. He immediately collared Thomas and pulled him into the street where he delivered him into the detective's arms. He then intended to lose himself in the crowd that was gathering as though drawn by a magnet.

Thomas was not to be held. He wheeled his briefcase over his head and brought it up full force into O'Reilly's midriff. Frank let go of him and Thomas threw a flying tackle at Pope. He got him by the knees and brought him down. He hung on until Frank plucked him off and gave him over to the temporary custody of two willing bystanders. Frank helped Pope to his feet. Pope was swearing he would sue Glasgow's for the youngster's assault.

"You're as fine as new," Frank said heartily and brushed the dust of the street from Pope's suit. Thus did his hand come in contact with something that was unmistakably a book and in a place no man would ordinarily abide anything foreign to his person. Frank knew instantly he had caught a thief in spite of himself. When he saw Mr. Glasgow and Miss Murray conveying one another through the revolving door he caught onto the fact that the book must belong to Old and Rare. He clapped his hand on Pope's shoulder and pronounced a solemn arrest.

"Well done, Frank!" Mr. Glasgow cried. He had discovered the Richard Hooker missing when he returned the medical handbook to the shelf.

Pope surrendered the book. His one consolation was that he still had the certified check—at least he could post bail.

Mr. Glasgow noticed Thomas and remembered Pope's

using him as a cunning decoy. "And the little ruffian— you got him too!"

"Me?" Thomas said, a squeak.

His captors took a tighter hold.

Pope, knowing to whom he owed his captivity, said in his best Cockney, " 'Is name is Oliver," and bared his teeth at Thomas in a sardonic grin.

"My name is Thomas MacIntosh Gordon, Third," Thomas declared loudly so that several people in the crowd whistled mockingly.

"Best let the boy go," Frank whispered to the man he still considered his employer. "We don't have much on him."

"I knew his grandfather," Mr. Glasgow said. "Or was it his great-grandfather? Shipbuilders. Started in the Clipper days, the *Mary Ellen*, if I'm not mistaken."

At a sign from O'Reilly, Thomas' captors set him free. He gathered his briefcase and his cap and said with haughty scorn, "You will hear from my lawyers."

Thomas never doubted that the devil had had a hand in what happened to him that day at Glasgow's. He was therefore the more determined to get on with his term paper, and certainly not to yield to the all but overwhelming temptation to switch subjects. He considered it a moral victory the day he turned the paper in. But that term Thomas, to whom straight A's were a commonplace, got the first C-minus of his academic career. In Religious Studies.

1981

Natural Causes

When Clara McCracken got out of state prison I was waiting to bring her home. We shook hands at the prison gate when she came through, and the first thing I was struck with was how her eyes had gone from china-blue to a gunmetal-grey. In fifteen years she'd come to look a lot like her late sister, Maud.

There'd been twenty years' difference in the ages of the McCracken sisters, and they were all that was left of a family that had come west before the American Revolution and settled in the Ragapoo Hills, most of them around Webbtown, a place that's no bigger now than it was then. Maudie ran the Red Lantern Inn, as McCrackens had before her, and she raised her younger sister by herself. She did her best to get Clara married to a decent man. It would have been better for everybody if she'd let her go wild the way Clara wanted and married or not married, as her own fancy took her.

Maudie was killed by accident, but there was no way I could prove young Reuben White fell into Maudie's well by accident. Not with Clara saying she'd pushed him into it and then taking the jury up there to show them how. She got more time than I thought fair, and for a while I blamed myself, a backwoods lawyer, for taking her defense even though she wouldn't have anybody else. Looking back, I came to see that in Ragapoo County then, just after giving so many of our young men to a second World War, Reuben White was probably better

235

thought of than he ought to have been. But that's another story and the page was turned on it when Clara went to prison. Another page was turned with her coming out.

She stood on the comfortable side of the prison gate and looked at my old Chevrolet as though she recognized it. She could have. It wasn't even new when she got sent up, as they used to say in those Big House movies. The farthest I've ever driven that car on a single journey was the twice I visited her, and this time to bring her home. Then she did something gentle, a characteristic no one I knew would've given to Clara—she put out her hand and patted the fender as though it was a horse's rump.

I opened the door for her and she climbed in head first and sorted herself out while I put her canvas suitcase in the back. There were greys in her bush of tawny hair and her face was the color of cheap toilet paper. Squint lines took off from around her eyes. I didn't think laughing had much to do with them. She sat tall and bony in her loose-hung purple dress and looked straight ahead most of the drive home.

About the first thing she said to me was, "Hank, anybody in Webbtown selling television sets?"

"Prouty's got a couple he calls demonstrators." Then I added, "Keeps them in the hardware shop."

Clara made a noise I guess you could call a laugh. Prouty also runs the only mortuary in the town.

"You'd be better sending away to Sears Roebuck," I said. "You pay them extra and they provide the aerial and put it up. I wouldn't trust old Prouty on a ladder these days. I wouldn't trust myself on one."

I could feel her looking at me, but I wasn't taking my eyes off the road. "Still playing the fiddle, Hank?" she asked.

"Some. Most folks'd rather watch the television than hear me hoeing down. But I fiddle for myself. It's about what I can do for pleasure lately. They dried up the trout stream when they put the highway through. Now they're drilling for oil in the hills. That's something new. I thought coal maybe someday, or even natural gas. But it's oil and they got those di̦sy-doodles going night and day.''

"Making everybody rich as Indians," Clara said, and she sounded just like Maudie. That was something Maudie would have said in the same deadpan way.

What I came out with then was something I'd been afraid of all along. "Maudie," I said, "you're going to see a lot of changes."

"Clara," she corrected me.

"I'm sorry, Clara. I was thinking of your sister."

"No harm done. You'd have to say there was a family resemblance among the McCrackens."

"A mighty strong one."

"Only trouble, there's a terrible shortage of McCrackens." And with that she exploded such a blast of laughter I rolled down the window to let some of it out.

I felt sorry for Clara when we drove up to the Red Lantern. It was still boarded up and there was writing on the steps that made me think of that Lizzie Borden jingle, "Lizzie Borden took an axe . . ." Having power of attorney, I'd asked Clara if I should have the place cleaned out and a room fixed up for her to come home to, but she said no. It wasn't as though there wasn't any money in the bank. The state bought a chunk of McCracken land when they put through the highway.

While I was trying the keys in the front door, Clara stood by the veranda railing and looked up at the Interstate, maybe a half mile away. You can't get on or off it from Webbtown. The nearest interchange is three miles. But one good thing that happened in the building of the road, they bulldozed Maudie's well and the old brewhouse clear out of existence. Clara'd have been thinking of that while I diddled with the lock. I got the door open and she picked up her suitcase before I could do it for her.

The spider webs were thick as lace curtains and you could almost touch the smell in the place, mold and mice and the drain-deep runoff of maybe a million draws of beer. You couldn't see much with the windows boarded up, but when you got used to the twilight you could see enough to move around. A row of keys still hung under numbers one to eight behind the desk. As though any one of them wouldn't open any door in the house. But a key feels good when you're away from home, it's a safe companion.

The stairs went up to a landing and then turned out of sight. Past them on the ground floor was the way to the kitchen and across from that the dining room. To the right where the sliding doors were closed was the lounge. To the left was the barroom where, for over a hundred and fifty years, McCrackens had drawn their own brew. I knew the revenue agent who used to come through during Prohibition. He certified the beer as three point two percent alcohol, what we used to call near-beer. The McCracken foam had more kick than three point two.

Clara set her suitcase at the foot of the stairs and went into the barroom. From where I stood I could see her back and then her shape in the backbar mirror and a shadow behind her that kind of scared me until I realized it was myself.

"Hank?" she said.

"I'm here."

She pointed at the moosehead on the wall above the mirror. "That moose has got to go," she said. "That's where I plan to put the television."

I took that in and said, "You got to have a license, Clara, unless you're going to serve soda pop, and I don't think you can get one after being where you were."

I could see her eyes shining in the dark. "You can, Hank, and I'm appointing you my partner."

Clara had done a lot of planning in fifteen years. She'd learned carpentry in prison and enough about plumbing and electric wiring to get things working. I asked her how she'd managed it, being a woman, and she said that was how she'd managed it. Her first days home I brought her necessities up to her from the town. The only person I'd told about her coming out was Prouty and he's close-mouthed. You couldn't say that for Mrs. Prouty . . . It's funny how you call most people by their Christian names after you get to know them, and then there's some you wouldn't dare even when you've known them all your life. Even Prouty calls her Mrs. Prouty.

Anyway, she's our one female elder at the Community Church and she was probably the person who put Reverend Barnes onto the sermon he preached the Sunday after Clara's return—all about the scribes and the Pharisees and how no man among them was able to throw the first stone at the woman taken in adultery. Adultery wasn't the problem of either of the McCracken sisters. It was something on the opposite side of human nature, trying to keep upright as the church steeple. But Reverend Barnes is one of those old-time Calvinists who believe heaven is heaven and hell is hell and whichever one you're going to was decided long ago, so the name of the sin don't matter much.

I was hanging a clothesline out back for Clara Monday morning when maybe a dozen women came up the hill to the Red Lantern bearing gifts. I stayed out of sight but I saw afterwards they were things they'd given thought to—symbolic things like canned fish and flour, bread and grape juice, what you might call biblical things. When Clara first saw them coming she went out on the veranda. She crossed her arms and spread her feet and took up a defensive stand in front of the door. The women did a queer thing: they set down what they were carrying, one after the other, and started to applaud. I guess it was the only way they could think of on the spot to show her they meant no ill.

Clara relaxed and gave them a roundhouse wave to come on up. They filed into the inn and before the morning was over they'd decided among themselves who was going to make curtains, who knew how to get mildew out

of the bed linens, who'd be best at patching moth holes,
things like that. Anne Pendergast went home and got the
twins. They were about fourteen, two hellions. She made
them scrub out every word that was written on the steps.

During the week I went over to the county seat with Clara
to see if she could get a driver's license. I let her drive the
Chevy, though I nearly died of a heart attack. She had it
kicking like an army mule, but we did get there, and she
could say that she'd driven a car lately. I watched with a
sick feeling while the clerk made out a temporary permit
she could use until her license came. Then, without bat-
ting an eye at me, she asked the fellow if he could tell us
who to see about applying for a liquor license. He came
out into the hall and pointed to the office. Yes, sir. Clara
had done a lot of planning in fifteen years.

It was on the way back to Webbtown that she said to
me, "Somebody's stolen Pa's shotgun, Hank."

"I got it up at my place, Clara. You sure you want it
back?" It was that gun going off that killed Maudie and I
guess this is as good a time as any to tell you what happened back then.

Clara was a wild and pretty thing and Maudie was en-
couraging this middle-aged gent, a paint salesman by the
name of Matt Sawyer, to propose to her. This day she
took him out in the hills with the shotgun, aiming to have
him scare off Reuben White, who was a lot more forward
in his courting of Clara. It was Maudie flushed the young
ones out of the sheepcote and then shouted at Matt to
shoot. She kept shouting it and so upset him that he
slammed the gun down. It went off and blew half of
Maudie's head away.

I don't think I'm ever going to forget Matt coming into
town dragging that gun along the ground and telling us
what happened. And I'm absolutely not going to forget
going up the hill with Matt and Constable Luke Weber—
and Prouty with his wicker basket. Clara came flying to
meet us, her gold hair streaming out in the wind like a

visiting angel. She just plain threw herself at Matt, saying how she loved him. I told her she ought to behave herself and she told me to hush or I couldn't play fiddle at their wedding. Luke Weber kept asking her where Reuben was and all she'd say in that airy way of hers was, "Gone."

I couldn't look at Maudie without getting sick, so I went to the well and tried to draw water. The bucket kept getting stuck, which was how we came to discover Reuben, head down, feet up, in the well. When the constable asked Clara about it, she admitted right off that she'd pushed him.

"Why? Luke wanted to know.

At that point she turned deep serious, those big eyes of hers like blue saucers. "Mr. Weber, you wouldn't believe me if I told you what Reuben White wanted me to do with him in the sheepcote this afternoon. And I just know Matt won't ever want me to do a thing like that." I pleaded her temporarily insane. I might have tried to get her off for defending her virtue—there was some in town who saw it that way—but by the time we came to trial I didn't think it would work with a ten-out-of-twelve male jury.

But to get back to what I was saying about Clara wanting the shotgun back, I advised her not to put it where it used to hang over the fireplace in the bar.

"Don't intend to. I got no place else for the moose-head."

I took the gun up to her the next day and it wasn't long after that I learned from Prouty she'd bought a box of shells and some cleaning oil. Prouty wanted to know if there wasn't some law against her having a gun. I said I thought so and we both let it go at that. Clara bought her television from him. The first I heard of her using the gun—only in a manner of speaking—was after she'd bought a used car from a lot on the County Road. It was a Studebaker, a beauty on the outside, and the dealer convinced her it had a heart of gold. The battery fell out first, and after that it was the transmission. She wanted me to go up and talk to him. I did and he told me to read the warranty, which I also did. I told Clara she was stuck with a bad bargain.

"Think so, Hank?"

The next thing I heard, she got Anne Pendergast and the twins to tow the Studebaker and her back to the used-car lot. The two women sent the boys home and then sat in Clara's car until the dealer finally came out to them. "Like I told your lawyer, lady, it's too bad, but . . ." He said something like that, according to Anne, and Clara stopped him right there. "I got me another lawyer," she said and jerked her thumb toward the back seat, where the old shotgun lay shining like it had just come off the hunters' rack in Prouty's. Anne asked him if he'd ever heard of Clara McCracken.

Seemed like he had, for when Clara drove up to where I was painting the Red Lantern sign she was behind the wheel of a red Chevy roadster with a motor that ran like a tomcat's purr.

"How much?" I wanted to know. Her funds were going down fast.

She opened the rumble seat and took out the shotgun. "One round of shot," she said. "That's about fifteen cents."

I didn't say anything in the town about the partnership I'd drawn up so that Clara could reopen the bar in the Red Lantern. For one thing, I wasn't sure when we'd get the license if we got it, even though Clara was moving full steam ahead. For another thing, I had to stop dropping in at Tuttle's Tavern. I just couldn't face Jesse Tuttle after setting up in competition, even though it was a mighty limited partnership I had with Clara. I didn't want to be an innkeeper and it riled that McCracken pride of hers to have to go outside the family after a hundred and fifty years. We wound up agreeing I was to be a silent partner. I was to have all the beer I could drink free. That wasn't going to cost her much. Even in the days of Maudie's Own Brew, I never drank more than a couple of steins in one night's sitting.

The license came through midsummer along with instructions that it was to be prominently displayed on the premises at all times. Clara framed it and hung it where you'd have needed a pair of binoculars to see what it was. By then the rooms upstairs had been aired out, the curtains hung, and all the mattresses and pillows treated to a week in the sun. Downstairs, the lounge was open to anybody willing to share it with a horde of insects. Prouty had ordered her some of those fly-catching dangles you string up on the lightbulbs, but they hadn't come yet. What came with miraculous speed was a pretty fair order of whiskeys and a half dozen kegs of beer with all the tapping equipment. I asked Clara how she decided on which brewery she was going to patronize.

She said the girls advised her.

And, sure enough, when I spoke to Prouty about it later he said, "So that's why Mrs. Prouty was asking what my favorite beer was. Didn't make sense till now. We ain't had a bottle of beer in the house since she got on the board of elders."

"Didn't you ask her what she wanted to know for?"

"Nope. I wanted to be surprised when the time came."

I suppose it was along about then I began to get a little niggling tinkle in my head about how friendly Clara and the women were. Most of those girls she spoke of were women ranging from thirty to eighty-five years old.

Going across the street and up the stairs to my office over Kincaid's Drugstore, I counted on my fingers this one and that of them I'd seen up there since Clara came home. I ran out of fingers and I'd have run out of toes as well if I'd included them.

Jesse Tuttle was sitting in my office waiting for me, his chair tilted back against the wall. I don't lock up in the daytime and the day I have to I'll take down my shingle. I felt funny, seeing Tuttle and feeling the way I did about competing with him, so as soon as we shook hands I brought things right out into the open. "I hope you don't take it personal, Jesse, that I'm helping Clara McCracken get a fresh start."

Jesse's a big, good-natured man with a belly that keeps him away from the bar, if you know what I mean. It don't seem to keep him away from Suzie. They got nine kids and a couple more on the hillside. "I know it's not personal, Hank, but it's not what you'd call friendly, either. I was wondering for a while if there was something personal between you and her, but the fellas talked me out of that idea."

I don't laugh out loud much, but I did then. "Jesse, I'm an old rooster," I said, "and I haven't noticed if a hen laid an egg in God knows how long."

"That's what we decided, but there's one thing you learn in my business: don't take anything a man says about himself for gospel. Even if he's telling the truth, it might as well be a lie, for all you know listening to him. Same thing in your business, ain't that so?"

"Wouldn't need witnesses if it wasn't," I said.

I settled my backside on the edge of the desk and he straightened up the chair. I'd been waiting for it to collapse, all the weight on its hind legs. He folded his arms. "What's going on up there, Hank?"

"Well, from what she said the last time we talked, she plans to open officially when the threshing combine comes through." We do as much farming in Ragapoo County as anything else, just enough to get by on. But we grow our own grain, and the harvest is a pretty big occasion.

"She figures on putting the crew up, does she?"

"She's got those eight rooms all made up and waiting. She got to put somebody in them. I can't see her getting the cross-country traffic to drop off the Interstate."

Tuttle looked at me with a queer expression on his

face. "You don't think she'd be figuring to run a house up there?"

"A bawdy house?"

Tuttle nodded.

I shook my head. "No, sir. I think that's the last thing Clara'd have in mind."

"I mean playing a joke on us, paying us back for her having to go to prison."

"I just don't see it, Jesse. Besides, look at all your womenfolk flocking up there to give her a hand."

"That's what I am looking at," he said.

Every step creaked as he lumbered down the stairs. I listened to how quiet it was with him gone. I couldn't believe Jesse was a mean man. He wouldn't start a rumor if he didn't think there was something to back it up with. Not just for business. We don't do things like that in Webbtown, I told myself. We're too close to one another for any such shenanigans. And I had to admit I wouldn't put it past a McCracken to play the town dirty if she thought the town had done it to her first. I certainly wouldn't have put it past Maudie. There was something that kind of bothered me about what was taking place in my own head: I kept mixing up the sisters. It was like Maudie was the one who had come back.

Clara drove eighty miles across two counties to intercept the threshing combine—ten men and some mighty fancy equipment that crisscross the state this time every year. She took Anne Pendergast and Mary Toomey with her. Mary's a first cousin of Prouty's. And on the other side of the family she was related to Reuben White, something Prouty called my attention to. Reuben's folks moved away after the trial . . . It wasn't so much grief as shame. I didn't like doing it, but it's a lawyer's job, and I painted the boy as pretty much a dang fool to have got himself killed that way.

The women came home late afternoon. I saw them driving along Main Street after collecting all the

Pendergast kids into the rumble seat. Anne had farmed them out for the day. I headed for the Red Lantern to see what happened. Clara was pleased as jubilee: the combine crew had agreed to route themselves so as to spend Saturday night in Webbtown.

"And they'll check into the Red Lantern?" I said. Ordinarily they split up among the farmers they serviced and knocked off five percent for their keep.

"Every last man. Barbecue Saturday night, Hank."

"What if it rains?"

"I got Mrs. Prouty and Faith Barnes working on it—the minsiter's wife?"

"I know who Faith Barnes is," I said, sour as pickle brine. The only reassuring thing I felt about the whole situation was that Mrs. Prouty was still Mrs. Prouty.

I came around. The whole town did. Almost had to, the women taking the lead right off. Clara invited everybody, at two dollars a head for adults, fifty cents for kids under twelve. All you could eat and free beer, but you paid for hard liquor. I recruited young Tommy Kincaid and a couple of his chums to dig the barbecue pits with me. Prouty supervised. Mrs. Prouty supervised the loan and transfer of tables and benches from the parish house. They used the Number One Hook and Ladder to move them, and I never before knew a truck to go out of the firehouse on private business except at Christmastime when they take Jesse Tuttle up and down Main Street in his Santa Claus getup.

Saturday came as clear a day as when there were eagles in the Ragapoo Hills. Right after lunch the town youngsters hiked up to the first lookout on the County Road. It reminded me of when I was a kid myself and a genuine circus would come round that bend and down through the town. I'd expected trouble from the teenage crowd, by the way, with Clara coming home. You know the way they like to scare themselves half out of their wits with stories of murder and haunted houses. The Red Lantern seemed like fair game for sure. Maybe the Pendergast twins took the curse off the place when they scrubbed the steps, I thought, and then I knew right off: it was their mothers who set down the law on how they'd behave toward Clara. In any case, it would have taken a lot of superstition to keep them from enjoying the harvest holiday.

Along about four o'clock the cry came echoing down the valley, "They're coming! They're coming!" And sure enough, like some prefabricated monster, the combine hove into view. Tractors and wagons followed, stopping to let the kids climb aboard. Behind them were the farmers' pleasure cars, women and children and some of the menfolk, dressed, you'd have thought, for the Fourth of July. The only ones left behind came as soon as the cows were let out after milking.

There was a new register on the desk and one man after another of the harvesters signed his name, picked up the key, and took his duffle bag upstairs. They came down to shower in the basement, and for a while there you couldn't get more than a trickle out of any other tap in the house. By the time they were washed up, half the town had arrived. I never saw our women looking prettier, and I kept saying to myself, gosh darn Tuttle for putting mischief in my mind. Even Clara, with color now in her cheeks, looked less like Maudie and more like the Clara I used to know.

The corn was roasting and the smell of barbecued chickens and ribs had the kids with their paper plates dancing in and out of line. There were mounds of Molly Kincaid's potato salad and crocks full of home-baked beans, great platters of sliced beefsteak tomatoes, fresh bread, and a five-pound jar of sweet butter Clara ordered from the Justin farm, delivered by Nellie Justin. Clara sent her to me to be paid her three dollars, but Nellie said to let it take care of her and Joe and the kids for the barbecue. Neither one of us was good at arithmetic. Peach and apple pies which any woman in town might have baked were aplenty and you can't believe what a peach pie's like baked with peaches so ripe you catch them dropping off the trees.

It was along about twilight with the men stretched out on the grass and the women sitting round on benches or on the veranda, dangling their feet over the side, when I tuned up my fiddle and sawed a few notes in front of the microphone. I never was amplified before and I don't expect to be again, but Dick Moran who teaches history, English, and music at the high school set up a system he'd been tinkering with all summer and brought along his own guitar. We made a lot of music, with everybody clapping and joining in. Real old-fashioned country. You might say people danced by the light of the moon—it was up there—but we had lantern light as well. I'd called round that morning and asked the farmers for the loan of the lanterns they use going out to chores on winter mornings. And when it finally came time for these same farmers to go home, they took their lanterns with them. One by one, the lights disappeared like fireflies, fading away until the only outdoor light was over the hotel entrance, and it was entertaining a crowd of moths and June bugs, gnats and mosquitoes.

Most people who lived in town weren't set on going home yet. Tuttle had closed up for the evening, not being a man to miss a good meal, but he said he thought he'd go down now and open up the tavern. Tuttle's Tavern never was a place the womenfolk liked to go, but now they said so right out loud.

Without even consulting me, Clara announced I'd fiddle in the lounge for a while. The women took to the idea straight off and set about arrangements. The old folks, who'd had about enough, gathered the kids and took them home. The teenagers went someplace with their amplifying history teacher and his guitar. The men, after hemming and hawing and beginning to feel out of joint, straggled down to Tuttle's. By this time the harvesters, with their bright-colored shirts and fancy boots, were drinking boilermakers in the bar. I didn't like it, but they were the only ones Clara was making money on, and she kept pouring. Prouty hung around for a while, helping move furniture. I asked him to stay, but he must have sneaked away while I was tuning up.

It gave me a funny feeling to see those women dancing all by themselves. I don't know why exactly. Kind of a waste, I suppose. But they sure didn't mind, flying and whirling one another and laughing in that high musical trill you don't often hear from women taught to hold themselves in. A funny feeling, I say, and yet something woke up in me that had been a long time sleeping.

Clara came across the hall from the taproom now and then, hauling one of the harvesters by the arm and kind of pitched him into the dance. His buddies would come to the door and whoop and holler and maybe get pulled in themselves. I kept thinking of my chums, sulking down at Tuttle's. I also thought Clara was wasting a lot of the good will she'd won with the barbecue. Man and wife were going to have to crawl into bed alongside each other sometime during the night.

Along about midnight Clara announced that it was closing time. Everybody gave a big cheer for Hank. It was going to take more than a big cheer to buoy me up by then. I could've wrung out my shirt and washed myself in my own sweat.

I couldn't swear that nothing bawdy happened the whole night. Those harvesters had been a long time from home and some of our women were feeling mighty free. But I just don't think it did, and I'll tell you why: Clara, when she pronounced it was closing time, was carrying a long birch switch, the kind that whistles when you slice the air with it, and the very kind Maudie had taken to Reuben White one night when he danced too intimate with Clara.

I was shivering when I went down to bed. I thought of

stopping by Tuttle's, but the truth was I didn't even want to know if he was still open. I'd kept hoping some of the men would come back up to the Red Lantern, but nobody did. I did a lot of tossing and turning, and I couldn't have been long asleep when the fire siren sounded. I hadn't run with the engines for a long time, but I was out of the house and heading for the Red Lantern before the machines left the firehouse. I just knew if there was trouble that's where it was.

I didn't see any smoke or fire when I got to the drive, but Luke Weber, our same constable, waved me off the road. I parked and started hiking through the grass. The fire trucks were coming. I started to run. When I got almost to where we'd dug the barbecue pits, something caught my ankle and I fell flat to the ground. Somebody crawled up alongside me.

"It's Bill Pendergast, Hank. Just shut up and lie low."

I couldn't have laid much lower.

The fire trucks screamed up the drive, their searchlights playing over the building, where, by now, lights were going on in all the upstairs rooms.

Pendergast said, "Let's go," and switched on his flashlight.

A couple of minutes later I saw maybe a half dozen other flashes playing over the back and side doors to the inn. By the time I got around front, Clara was standing on the veranda with the fire chief. She was wearing a negligee you could've seen daylight through if there'd been daylight. The harvesters were coming downstairs in their underwear. A couple of the volunteer firemen rushed up the stairs, brandishing their hatchets and their torches.

By then I'd figured out what was happening and it made me sick, no matter what Tuttle and them others thought they were going to flush out with the false alarm. Not a woman came down those stairs or any other stairs or out any window. They did come trooping down the County Road, about a dozen of them. Instead of going home when Clara closed, they'd climbed to where they could see the whole valley in the moonlight. The fire chief apologized for the invasion as though it had been his fault.

"I hope you come that fast," Clara said, "when there's more fire than smoke."

I was up at the Red Lantern again on Sunday afternoon when the harvesters moved on, heading for their next setup in the morning. Clara bought them a drink for the road. One of them, a strapping fellow I might have thrown a punch at otherwise, patted Clara's behind when she went to the door with them. She jumped and then stretched her mouth in something like a smile. I listened to them say how they'd be back this way in hunting season. They all laughed at that and I felt I was missing something. When one of them tried to give me five bucks for the fiddling, I just walked away. But I watched to see if any extra money passed between them and Clara. That negligee was hanging in my mind.

A few nights later I stopped by Tuttle's. I figured that since I'd laid low with the fellows I might as well stand at the bar with them, at least for half my drinking time. I walked in on a huddle at the round table where there's a floating card game going on most times. But they weren't playing cards and they looked at me as though I'd come to collect the mortgage. I turned and started to go out again.

"Hey, Hank, come on back here," Pendergast called. "Only you got to take your oath along with the rest of us never to let on what we're talking about here tonight."

"What's the general subject?" I asked.

"You know as well as we do," Jesse Tuttle said.

"I reckon." I stuck my right hand in the air as though the Bible was in my left.

"We were going to draw straws," Pendergast said, "but Billy Baldwin here just volunteered."

I pulled up a chair, making the ninth or tenth man, and waited to hear what Baldwin had volunteered to do. I haven't mentioned him before because there wasn't reason, even though Nancy Baldwin was one of the women that came whooping down the road after the fire alarm. Billy wasn't the most popular man in town—kind of a braggart and boring as a magpie. Whenever anybody had an idea, Billy had a better one, and he hardly ever stopped talking. The bus route he was driving at the time ran up-county, starting from the Courthouse steps, so he had to take his own car to and from his job at different times of day and night. By now you've probably guessed what he'd volunteered for.

I made it a point to stay away from the Red Lantern the night he planned to stop there. I got to admit, though, I was as curious as the rest of the bunch to learn how he'd make out with Clara, so I hung around Tuttle's with them. The funny thing was, I was the last man in the place. Long before closing time, Pendergast, then Prouty, then Kincaid, all of them dropped out and went home to their own beds. Tuttle locked up behind me.

The next day Baldwin stopped by the tavern on the way to work and told Jesse that nothing happened, that he'd just sat at the bar with Clara, talking and working up to things. "The big shot's getting chicken," Pendergast said when Tuttle passed the word.

None of us said much. Counting chickens. I know I was.

Well, it was a week before Billy Baldwin came in with his verdict. As far as he could tell, Clara McCracken might still be a virgin, he said. He'd finally come right out and slipped a twenty-dollar bill on the bar the last night and asked her to wear the negligee she'd had on the night of the false alarm. At that point, Clara reached for the birch stick behind the bar and he took off, leaving the money where it was.

"You're lucky she didn't reach for the shotgun," Prouty said.

We all chipped in to make up the twenty dollars.

Things quieted down after that and I continued to split

my drinking time between Tuttle's and the Red Lantern.
Clara would get the occasional oiler coming through to
check the pumps, and the duck and deer-hunting seasons
were good business, but she never did get much of the
town custom, and the rumors about her and that negligee
hung on. It wasn't the sort of gear you sent away to Sears
Roebuck for, but the post office in Webbtown was run by
a woman then and I don't think any of us ever did find out
where that particular garment came from. Maybe she'd
sent away for it while she was still in prison. Like I said
early on, Clara had done a lot of planning in fifteen
years.

Now I just said things quieted down. To tell the truth,
it was like the quiet before a twister comes through. I
know I kept waiting and watching Clara, and Clara
watched me watching her. One day she asked me what
they were saying about her in the town.

I tried to make a joke of it. "Nothing much. They're
getting kind of used to you, Clara."

She looked at me with a cold eye. "You in on that
Billy Baldwin trick?"

I thought about the oath I was supposed to have sworn.
"What trick?" I asked.

"Hank," she said, "for a lawyer you ain't much of a
liar."

"I ain't much of a lawyer, either," I said. Then, looking her straight in the face, sure as fate straighter than I
looked at myself, I said, "Clara, how'd you like to marry
me?"

She set back on her heels and smiled in that odd way of
having to work at it. "Thank you kindly." She cast her
eyes up toward the license, which I'd just about forgotten. "We got one partnership going and I think that ought
to do us—but I do thank you, old Hank."

I've often wondered what I'd have done it she'd said
yes.

But I've come around since to holding with the Rever-

end Barnes. Everything was set in its course long before
it happened—including Clara's planning.

September passed, October, and it came the full, cold
moon of November. You could hear wolves in the
Ragapoo Hills and the loons—and which is lonesomer-
sounding I wouldn't say. I've mentioned before how
light a sleeper I am. I woke up this night to a kind of
whispering sound, a sort of swish, a pause, and then
aother swish, a pause, and then another. When I realized
it was outside my window, I got up and looked down on
the street.

There, passing in the silvery moonlight—a few feet between them (I think now to keep from speaking to one
another)—the women of the town were moving toward
the Red Lantern. By the time I got within sight of them
up there, they'd formed a half circle around the front of
the inn which was in total darkness. One of the women
climbed the steps and went inside. I knew the door had
not been locked since I unlocked it when I brought Clara
home.

I kept out of sight and edged round back to where I had
been the night of the false alarm. I saw the car parked
there and knew it belonged to Billy Baldwin. If I could
have found a way in time, I'd have turned in a false alarm
myself, but I was frozen in slow motion. I heard the
scream and the clatter in the building, and the front door
banging open. Billy Baldwin came running out stark naked. He had some of his clothes with him, but he hadn't
waited to put them on. Behind him was his wife Nancy,
sobbing and crying and beating at him until one of the
women came up and took her away down toward the
town.

Billy had stopped in his tracks, seeing the circle of
women. He was pathetic, trying to hide himself first and
then trying to put his pants on, and the moonlight throwing crazy shadows on the women. Then I saw Clara
come out of the door on my side of the building. She was

wearing the negligee and sort of drifted like a specter around the veranda to the front.

The women began to move forward.

Billy, seeing them come, fell on his knees and held out his hands, begging. I started to pray myself. I saw that every woman was carrying a stone. They kept getting closer, but not a one raised her arm until Clara went down and picked up a stone from her own drive which she flung at Billy.

He was still on his knees after that, but he fell amost at once beneath the barrage that followed. One of those stones killed him dead, though I didn't know it at the time.

Clara went back up the steps and picked her way through the stones. She kicked at what was left of poor, lying, cheating Billy as hard as she could. The women found more stones then and threw them at her until she fled into the inn and closed the door.

Nobody's been arrested for Billy's murder. I don't think anyone ever will be. It ought to be Clara, if anyone, but I'd have to bear witness that the man was still alive after she'd thrown the stone. She's never forgiven the women for turning on her. She kept telling me how glad she was when they came to take Billy in adultery. And I wore myself out asking her what the heck she thought she was doing.

Along toward summer a baby boy was born to Clara. She had him christened Jeremiah McCracken after his grandfather. At the christening she said to me, "See, Hank. That's what I was doing." I'm going to tell you, I'm glad that when Jeremiah McCracken comes old enough to get a tavern license, I'll be in my grave by then. I hope of natural causes.

1983

CHARLOTTE MACLEOD
America's Reigning Whodunit Queen
PRESENTS

"Murder among the Eccentrics of Boston's Upper Crust"* with

**Art Investigator Max Bittersohn
and Sarah Kelling**

THE FAMILY VAULT	49080-3/$2.95 US/$3.75 Can
THE PALACE GUARD	59857-4/$2.95 US/$3.50 Can
THE WITHDRAWING ROOM	56473-4/$2.95 US/$3.75 Can
THE BILBAO LOOKING GLASS	67454-8/$2.95 US/$3.50 Can
THE CONVIVIAL CODFISH	69865-x/$2.95 US/$3.75 Can

AND

"Mystery with Wit and Style and a Thoroughly Engaging Amateur Sleuth"**

Professor Peter Shandy

REST YOU MERRY	47530-8/$2.95 US/$3.95 Can
THE LUCK RUNS OUT	54171-8/$2.95 US/$3.50 Can
WRACK AND RUNE	61911-3/$2.95 US/$3.50 Can
SOMETHING THE CAT DRAGGED IN	69096-9/$3.95 US

and coming soon

THE CURSE OF THE GIANT HOGWEED	
	70051-4/$2.95 US/$3.75 Can

*Mystery magazine
**The Washington Post